"In this book, James Gardner takes you on a thrill- ride through so many terrifying places and events in darkest Africa, you have to pull the covers over your head to finish it.

Hell of a trip for us adventure readers!"

—**Dan Jenkins,** Novelist & Journalist

"Sara and I were blown out of our chairs by the power of your presentation, and we wish you a whole lot of luck with 'The Lion Killer'!"

**—Barry Farber**

National talk radio host

———————————

"'The Lion Killer' is an excellent read on an extraordinary mission. For those that consider the future of Africa, it may very well change their perspective."

**—Douglas Harrington**

Hamptons.com

———————————

"Gardner's storytelling approach follows in the path of Dashiell Hammett. "Life is disposable; the Land is beautiful, and the search is fatal."

**—James Edstrom**

Times Square Gossip

# THE

# CONGO AFFAIR

## THE DARK CONTINENT SERIES Book V

# James Gardner

**PENNINGTON PUBLISHERS**

ISBN: 978-1-63649276-6
Trade Paperback
© Copyright 2020 James
Gardner All Rights Reserved

Requests for information should be addressed to:
Pennington Publishers, Inc.
PO Box 718
Decatur, GA  30031

Pennington Publishers and the Pennington
logo are imprints of Pennington Publishers, Inc.

Cover design: Donald Brennan / YakRider Media
Interior design: Donald Brennan / YakRider Media

Artwork and illustrations by Larry Norton and used
by permission.

Printed in the U.S.A.

# ACKNOWLEDGEMENTS

For William Flaherty, Robert Halmi, Robert Barrett, Lynn Denney, and John Jolley. Steadfast friends who have supported my writing.

We are grateful for the illustrations by Larry Norton.

—DB

# About the Author

James Gardner's first African safari was in 1968. Subsequently, he's made twenty trips to Africa. He has written numerous magazine and newspaper articles about modern Africa, its culture, its people, and the difficulties they face. He is the author of *The Dark Continent Chronicles*, a series of political thrillers that includes *The Lion Killer*, *The Zambezi Vendetta*, *The Honeyguide,* and *The Last Rhino*. He is also an award-winning screenplay writer. He is an avid animal wildlife conservationist.

## About the Artist

Born in Zimbabwe in 1963, Larry Norton grew up on a game farm in Zimbabwe. He started drawing as a boy and, in 1988, he began a professional career specializing in African wildlife. Larry is one of Africa's most celebrated artists.

www.larrynorton.co.za
E-mail:- info@larrynorton.co.za
P.O. Box CT 534
Victoria Falls, Zimbabwe

**Joseph Conrad on the colonization of Africa:**

"The vilest scramble for loot that ever disfigured the history of the human conscience."

## The Characters

**Rigby Croxford:**  A decorated war hero in the Rhodesian Bush War. He is an anachronistic white African struggling to come to grips with the new black Africa. After his farm is confiscated by the government and his wife is murdered, economic adversity forces him into the only profession he knows, soldiering.  As a mercenary, he's exposed to Africa's darkest secrets. When his friend, Jesse Spooner, asks for his help rescuing thirty schoolgirls abducted in central Africa, he's all in. The only law is the business end of an AK-47. Good and evil men come and go on the Dark Continent. Rigby Croxford is as enduring as the land.

**Jesse Spooner:** The black American is Croxford's closest friend. Jesse's a rugged maverick all men want to emulate. The ex-marine has collaborated with Rigby Croxford on other hazardous ventures in Africa. This time, Spooner and Croxford are walking into the belly of the beast. They have faced death before, but this is different.

**Otto Bern:**  A retired soldier of fortune with nine lives. He lost his right leg to a landmine and three fingers to a Gaboon viper. Africa was whittling on Otto like termites eating a *Mopani* stump.  He resides with a vervet monkey on the Zambezi River. Rigby and Jesse seek Otto's guidance about their upcoming venture into central Africa. He tells them he only thinks of Congo when he defecates.  Congo has brutal weather, incurable diseases, and the most inhospitable natives in Africa. His warnings are ignored.

**James Cheatham:** A loner employed by the same overseas security company that hires Jesse Spooner. His life is turned upside down when he finds his fiancé in bed with another man. As he waits on death row, he plots revenge on the man responsible for his sister's suicide.

**Reverend Ray Carson:** An unscrupulous Bible-thumping televangelist with an insatiable appetite for underage women. He travels to central Africa, seeking a fortune. He does not find redemption.

**Nickolas Pieter:** A Belgian born captain of a tramp-steamer on the Congo River. He interrogated prisoners during the Great Congo War. None of the prisoners survived. He's a drunken sadist who married twenty native women, including one pygmy. He is described as a man who would crawl across his dying mother to fornicate with his dead sister. Pieter is the epitome of evil.

**Mohamed bin Sali:** A vicious ex-*Hutu* commander who played a role in the Rwandan genocidal massacre. His *Boko Haram* militia rapes and pillages a bloody swath on the Congo River. Besides the meager spoils of war, illicit drugs, and fear, the glue that cements his gang is a constant supply of sex-slaves.

**Winnie Obo:** A teenage schoolgirl abducted by *Boko Haram* terrorists. Winnie is the bravest of the brave. She endures unspeakable depravities. After her escape, she sets off on a harrowing search to find her family.

**Rose:** Nickolas Pieter's battered African wife. When men are fearful, Rose is as bold as a lion.

**Father Sebastian.** A black priest and a medical doctor. His flock is lepers. Sebastian is a puritanical purveyor of man's best qualities.

**Nigel Birtwistle:** An Oxford-educated ex-patriot. The former British subject finds Africa more receptive to his unconventional lifestyle. A bush pilot with a penchant for flying into warzones.

# CHAPTER ONE

## Zimbabwe

**Rigby Croxford** turned off onto a washboard road. He stopped at the lopsided cattle gate guarding the entrance to what had been the Croxford farm. Desperate for rain, the land appeared lifeless. Against his better judgment, he consented to his daughter's request to visit her mother's gravesite on the anniversary of her passing. Two years ago, the Croxfords were forced off their farm. There were rumors of vandalism. They hoped for closure. Little did they know.

Rigby snubbed out his cigarette. "Are you up for this?"

"Quite," Christine answered, paddling the smoke.

Her father sighed. "In my opinion, this is a dreadful mistake."

"Wallowing in self-pity isn't healthy."

"So, this is about me, is it? I guess you mean to lecture me about moving on with my life."

"Now that you mention it," she said.

"I can't help how I feel, Christine."

"You can't go on like this. Not for the rest of your life."

"You're a medical doctor, not bloody Sigmund Freud. It's my life, and I intend to live it on my terms."

"I just want what's best for you," she said, attempting a ceasefire. Remembering her mother triggered tears.

Rigby downshifted his geriatric Land Rover into first gear. The spinning tires produced orange Kalahari dust. He started uphill to the spot where their farmhouse once stood.

"The rains will be late," he said, glancing at his daughter. She's the spitting image of Helen, he thought. "Tough exterior and a compassionate underbelly."

"What happened to the fences?" she asked.

The fence posts had been consumed by cooking fires. The barbwire retooled into poaching snares. Only the stumps of the blue-flowering jacaranda trees that lined the driveway remained. Once golden wheat fields lay fallow and invaded by *Mopani* scrub. Maize fields had capitulated to wild grasses. Livestock barns and the cattle-pens had been destroyed by looters who butchered the dairy cows. Rusting irrigation pumps stood idle. Without water, the fruit orchards had withered. Arsons burned the farmhouse to its foundation. It was as if the black perpetrators needed to erase any evidence of white-rule. If it meant murdering their futures, so be it. Rigby and his daughter weren't prepared for the devastation.

Two years before, the Croxford farm was confiscated by Robert Mugabe's government. Ten-thousand acres homesteaded over one-hundred years ago by Rigby

Croxford's grandfather. The Croxfords transformed a rock-strewn wasteland into one of the most productive farms in what was then Rhodesia and is now Zimbabwe. His grandparents, his parents, and his wife were all buried here, as were the black farm-workers who died defending the Croxford farm.

"I told you this was a mistake."

Time had not healed Rigby's lesions of guilt. Witnessing the destruction triggered hidden memories. An unsympathetic Africa killed my wife, and I was an accessory, he thought. He shied away from the painful memory and concentrated on avoiding the potholes.

His daughter controlled her emotions until she saw the granite chimney silhouetted like a memorial to her former life. Nothing was as it had been. She brushed away tears.

"In one of your blue moods, are we?" he suggested. "Not that I blame you."

"How could they?" she whispered.

He patted her shoulder, tenderly. "Such a bloody waste."

Her voice was choked by grief. "What did our ancestors do to make them hate us?"

"Rubbish. We led them out of the darkness. Fed them when they were starving. Put clothes on their naked backsides. And last but not least, cured their hideous diseases. Your mother gave her life for these people. And this is how they repaid her. Ungrateful munts."

"You know I hate that word," she said. "Our ancestors brought nothing but misery to Africa. Slavery was a big part of it."

"Slavery existed for a thousand years before the first European explorer set foot in Africa."

Unhearing, she said, "How many generations will come and go before they forgive us?" He handed her his handkerchief, which she used to daub her nose. "People use chaos as proof of the black man's inferiority. A hundred years is a nanosecond in African history. We need more time."

He also spoke as if he hadn't heard her. "This country doesn't have a future, at least not in my lifetime. But then again, I've got more yesterdays than tomorrows."

"Daddy dearest, always the pessimist," she said. "Mom was an optimist."

He swerved, missing a pothole. "I'm a pragmatist, always have been. We have ninety-percent unemployment, and the banks have closed. I've said it before, and I'll say it again, I killed your mother by keeping her in Africa. I'll carry that to my grave."

"Mom loved Africa. She would never have agreed to leave Zimbabwe. Stop blaming yourself."

"I'm the one who deserved to die, not her."

"The only thing my mother loved more than Africa was you. You carry that to your grave." Her words defused their disagreement. They sat a while without arguing.

Finally, he said, "I reminded a few of your black commie friends that our late prime minister, Ian Smith, was quoted as saying that it would take the blacks a thousand years to rule this country properly. I added that they only had nine hundred and fifty years to prove him wrong because the last fifty has certainly been a cock-up."

"What did they say?" she asked.

"They laughed. Hysterically, I might add."

"Things might improve if we can get the farms up and

running," Christine stated.

"Just like that, is it? Get the farms up and running, you say. The farmers are never coming back. Who can blame them or me, for that matter?"

They didn't speak for a few long seconds. Finally, Rigby opened her door. "Come, let's sort out the family plot."

Christine said, "I always find it shocking when you quote Ian Smith, the man who presided over the demise of your dearly beloved Rhodesia."

"Ian Smith was a man of his time. That's the only proper way to judge him. Must I remind you that Smith was a decorated Spitfire pilot in the Second World War?"

"You're a decorated war hero, and look what it got you. I didn't mean that," she added quickly.

"Different war, different time," he said. "And anyway, who said life is fair?"

They walked up the stepping stones to a scorched-black foundation. The intense heat had crumbled the walls. Rigby picked up a charred brick and tossed it aside.

His daughter's voice sounded strained. "Why destroy everything? It doesn't make sense."

Unable to answer, he shook his head.

The Croxford burial plots were on a small rise. They trudged up the hill, occasionally stopping to catch their breath. Skeletal teak trees framed the graveyard. Dappling sunlight shining through the boney limbs made dancing shadows on the ground. Curiously, the grounds were spotless. Someone had even pruned the hedges— wildflowers decorated each gravesite. The headstones were straight and legible. Leaning against a tree, Rigby lit a cigarette. His daughter sat on the ground in front of her mother's grave. They were so overcome; they did not speak for several minutes.

An ancient African and a young boy stepped out from behind a tree. Both were diminished from malnutrition. Folds of leathery skin covered the exposed parts of the older man's body. Deep wrinkles etched his face. He looked like a living corpse. The boy was also pitifully thin. Both had clean-shaven heads. They were dressed in rags.

The old, old African flashed an affectionate smile. "*Baba*, do you not remember me?"

Rigby showed no emotion. But in his heart, he smiled. "I see you, Joseph. I thought you were...." Emotions throttled his response. "Seeing you makes my heart sing."

The African grabbed the boy's hand. "We are the only ones still alive. The slow-puncture has taken them to a better place." Africans refer to AIDS as the slow-puncture because the victims wither and shrink like a deflating tire. "If God wills it, I think we shall all die."

"Seeing what's happened to my farm makes me want to die," Rigby said.

The man gazed wistfully at his surroundings. "I tried to stop them. They laughed. Said I was a foolish old man. Said, this is the new Africa. Said, there is no place for the white man in Zimbabwe. Now, they are starving. They are no longer laughing," Joseph said.

"His Excellency, Robert Mugabe and his cronies aren't starving."

"What you say is true." Joseph clasped his hands together and thought for a long moment. "Do you think our country has a future?"

"Not in my lifetime."

"This is what I told my grandson."

"You've done a wonderful job caring for the cemetery. We're both very grateful," Christine said, interrupting the depressing topic.

Joseph said, "Dr. Croxford was a great woman. I was blessed to call her my friend. I knew you would follow in her footsteps. He pushed the boy forward. "This is my grandson, Michael. He is a clever boy." The boy stared at the ground. Rigby greeted Michael in English but switched to Shona when he got no response.

Without hesitating, Rigby said, "Joseph, you and your grandson must leave this place. There's nothing left for you here. Come live with us. Let us take care of you."

Nodding at Helen Croxford's grave, Joseph said, "I could never leave her. My departed wives have spoken to me. I know my life will end soon." He bowed his head. "I look forward to joining them. My only wish is to be buried here."

Rigby knew arguing was futile. "Very well, but what about your grandson?" he said, placing his hands on the boy's boney shoulders. "He needs to be in school." Michael escaped Rigby's grasp and threw his arms around his grandfather's legs. He refused eye contact, preferring to hide behind his grandfather.

Joseph said, "This man will look after you better than I can." Michael burst into tears. "I'll have none of that." Joseph forged a frown. "You shame me, boy."

Rigby squatted down to eye level. "What if we visit your grandfather each month? Bring him food and medicine. How does that sound?"

The boy hiked his shoulders. After glancing at his grandfather, Michael nodded halfheartedly.

***

After reminiscing with Joseph about better times, Rigby, Christine, and Michael left the remnants of the Croxford farm. In due course, Michael's sobbing subsided. As they drove home to the medical clinic on the outskirts of Victoria Falls, Christine's spirits were improved, but the change was short-lived.

Rigby stopped, allowing a small herd of female elephants to cross the road. The matriarch acting as a rearguard trumpeted a warning and shook her massive ears like a dog shaking off water. Using her trunk, she gently pushed her calf. Satisfied her family was safe, she shuffled off, disappearing into the dusty underbrush.

"What's so amusing?" Rigby asked, watching the elephants.

"You are," she answered.

"How so?"

"You make the most God-awful racist remarks, and then you adopt him without batting an eye," she said, nodding at the boy in the backseat. "Not to mention, your best friend, Jesse Spooner, is black. I think you enjoy torturing me."

"It's been one of my greatest pleasures. Now that you're in a better frame, there's something I need to tell you. Before you go, ballistic, hear me out. Funny, you should mention Jesse. I've got a business opportunity up north with him." He steeled himself for her fury.

A flash of rage pinkened her cheeks. Her voice became testy. "Where up north?"

"Congo."

"Bloody hell. Didn't I just read about five United Nations peacekeepers murdered in the northern Congo? Their smoked body parts were sold in native food markets. What kind of work?"

"Christine, if I lie, you do know I can do it with great dexterity. The truth is, I don't know. Jesse arrives here in two weeks. Thought we'd spend a few days with Otto Bern. Otto knows everything about the Congo Basin."

"Why haven't you mentioned this before?" she asked.

"Because I knew you'd pitch a fit."

"Am I supposed to approve of you getting yourself killed?" She paused, daring him to argue.

"Living is hard," he said. "I reckon dying will be easy. I've lived longer than I deserve to. Every soldier has his name on a bullet. Soldiering is what I do. Let me rephrase that it's the only thing I know how to do. And besides, we start dying from the day we're born."

"Spare me the fatalism. You can't put a good face on this. Soldiering for money is despicable."

"I'm guessing that was a criticism? I've never hidden from the truth. I've killed everything that works or crawls on this continent, including Africans, I'm embarrassed to admit."

Her tears reappeared. "Do you know how many nights I lay awake, not knowing if I would ever see you again?"

"What's one more sin to a sinner? Hey, how's the view from your lofty perch. Our bank accounts are running on empty. And yes, mercenaries can be immoral in this imperfect world. Sometimes, not always, we get paid for defending the defenseless. As the wise-man once said, soldiers-of-fortune are both indefensible and indispensable."

"Damn you, and damn Jesse Spooner."

He raised a white flag. "Christine, no father has ever loved his daughter as much as I love you."

Their quarrel ended. Christine put her head on his

shoulder. A spark of mutual understanding passed between them. They drove home regarding each other in silence.

***

# CHAPTER TWO

## Congo

### Two thousand kilometers north

### Six months earlier

**A crowing rooster** signaled the crack of dawn. Grudgingly, the details of the jungle took form as the morning mist lifted. The air was soggy. A blood-orange sun peeked above the tallest mahogany trees. Yellowed-billed hornbills cocked their heads, listening for grubs on the twisted limbs of red-cedar trees. Insect-eating bats speckled the flamingo-colored sky. Hunting marsh harriers divebombed the bats. Tropical birds sang seductively to prospective nest-mates. The ear-piercing howl of a hunting chimpanzee silenced a gibbering colobus monkey. Diamond-shaped spider webs, bejeweled by morning dew, connected the papyrus reeds framing the river. Hippos played hide-and-seek between floating lily-pad islands. Basking crocodiles waited for the life-giving sun on sandbars.

Loci Obo heard his father carry on a rambling monologue with the river. Stanley was asking the river-god, Bumba, to be generous. The father and son seldom spoke. There was an undeclared understanding between them. Ten years ago, during a civil uprising, Stanley witnessed his wife's rape and her execution. Stanley's left hand was amputated. For months, his son would stare at their hut's doorway, hoping his mother might reappear.

Stanley's shame made him incapable of comforting his son.

The day before, they set their grass-woven fish-traps in a quiet pool beneath a cascading waterfall. If the fish-traps were left unmolested by the cormorants, it should be a good catch. Fishing was always better during the start of the rains. Loci edged his way down the slippery rocks to the pool. Using a long bamboo pole attached to a fish-trap, he lifted it to his father, waiting on the cliff above him. Stanley dumped the contents and shouted in Swahili, 'Pifa Mungu,' Praise God. Two catfish and four slimy cichlids wiggled at his feet. The other traps were equally successful.

They paddled back to their village. Muddy paths from the palm-thatched huts crisscrossed to the river's edge. Drying fishing nets hung draped over bushes. Turned-over dugouts in various conditions of disrepair dotted the shoreline. The centerpiece of *Ugigi* was an abandoned Catholic mission.

Loci removed the viscera and wrapped their catch in bananas leaves. Fresh fish brought higher prices. Two hollow-bellied dogs squabbled over the fish guts. Mostly women gathered to inspect the catch. Years of warring had reduced the men.

An ancient woman, handicapped by a clubfoot, approached Loci. Her right eye was milky. Villagers believed she possessed mystical powers. Some people thought she was a sorceress. "You must not leave the village today," she warned, leaning on her homemade crutch. "If you do, you shall never return."

"How do you know this?" Loci asked her.

She cocked her head, allowing her working eye to focus. "Last night, my ancestors spoke to me in a dream."

Loci handed her a stringer of small catfish. "Take this offering and go. Go, before my father hears you."

When Stanley asked his son what she said, Loci shrugged it off, saying, "What difference does it make. Everyone knows she's crazy." Loci couldn't allow anything to get in the way of their trip.

The plan was to paddle their wooden pirogue down the *Ubangi* and enter the Congo River, where they hoped to tie-off to the regularly scheduled ferryboat stopping at *Mongala*. Selling the excess fish would provide them with enough francs to buy palm oil, salt, and cornmeal. Loci's mouth watered when he thought about the orange soda he could buy. His father was especially excited about this trip. He hadn't seen his daughter in six months. Winnie Obo was a student at the Catholic Girls Academy.

Stanley and his son waved goodbye to the villagers. It was prudent to steer clear of the shallows where hippos slipped beneath the surface, leaving only their periscopic nostrils and beady eyes. A bull hippo was prone to charge any boat invading his territory. Crocodiles, hoping to reap the benefits of a capsized canoe, exploded off the riverbanks. The scaly monsters' filmy- eyes followed the longboat as Stanley circumnavigated around floating vegetation islands and paddled past natives setting drift-nets. Pairs of Egyptian geese and flocks of white pelicans sailed overhead in arrowhead formations. Blue-crested kingfishers hovered over the shallows, searching for minnows. Bullfrogs plopped into the water. Sunning turtles slithered off flat rocks. The shoreline was spiky ferns and elephant grass whitewashed by bird droppings. White-faced monkeys studied them from overhanging banyan trees. The coffee-hued river exuded an earthy aroma.

Stanley shaded his eyes, checking the angle of the sun. Loci got the message; he increased his paddling. Two hours before sunset, they entered the Congo River. One hour later, they spotted black smoke on the horizon. Soon, that smudge became a tentacle attached to a riverboat. A frayed

Congolese flag snapped from the vessel's masthead. The wind carried the ship's sulfurous stench. It was difficult for Stanley to paddle with one hand, but they managed to intercept the riverboat.

Nicolas Pieter, the Belgian-born captain, throttled back, allowing them to tie-off to the other gumwood dugouts moored to his steamer. Stanley glided alongside and hooked on neatly.

The *Esperance*'s rusting hull showed streaks from human excrements and black scars from dockings. The ship's heads were holes cut in planks hung out over her gunnels. Her cargo holds contained burlap bags of yams, *cassava*, mangos, sacks of cornmeal, stalks of green bananas, and blackened chimpanzees with their eyes sealed shut and their mouths locked open like they had been cooked alive. The meat attracted swarms of green-headed blowflies. Wood-slatted crates contained clucking chickens. Straw-baskets imprisoned river turtles gasping for air.

A bamboo cage occupied the bow. The enclosure imprisoned two female chimpanzees and their suckling infants. The mothers and babies looked emaciated. Both had festering sores. The apes' eyes appeared lifeless. Pieter bought female chimps from native hunters and resold them to the illegal wildlife dealers in Kinshasa. In Congo, male apes were coveted as bush-meat.

How Captain Pieter survived Congo's violent history was a mystery. Natives proclaimed him indestructible. Pieter was almost a giant, weighing on the backside of one-hundred and thirty kilograms. Pieter's face was scorched red from the unrelenting equatorial sun. His longevity, where life expectancy is only forty-two years, spoke volumes. A surplus of chins cushioned his jaw; the lowest one resembled a hairy scrotum. Like his bulbous nose, a short black cigar was one of the regular features of his face. His fingernails were blackened deep into the quicks. Pieter's salt-and-pepper eyebrows looked like porcupine quills. The natives called him *Nahodha Nungu,* meaning "Captain

Porcupine" in Swahili. One could summarize his description by comparing him to an enlarged gargoyle. Locals said Pieter had dined on human flesh with *Bangala* cannibals in the *Ituri forest*. He had wedded twenty native women, including one pygmy. To say Nicolas Pieter had gone native was an understatement.

Native fishermen sold their catches to Pieter, who resold the fish in villages on the river. The fishermen knew Pieter cheated them, but traveling on the river was dangerous. Bandits were thicker than the mosquitoes. The *Bangala* and *Ngombe* tribes controlled most of the river. Smaller boats passing their villages were forced to pay tributes.

Pieter bellowed at Stanley Obo to hold up a fish. Stanley felt a familiar loathing as he acknowledged the captain. He started small and worked his way up to larger fish but kept the biggest ones hidden from view. The captain shouted over the thumping Lister engine, "Stanley Obo, I'll make you a special rate today. Roundtrip to *Mongala* will cost you only one catfish. Not that one, one of the fat ones you're hiding." His laughter merged into a rattling cough. He spat a gob of yellow phlegm overboard and wiped his chin.

Stanley Obo paid the captain with a medium-sized catfish. Pieter handed it to a massive black woman. Her pendulous breasts acquiescing to gravity struggled against the confines of a tee-shirt decorated with a portrait of Bob Marley. A look of dissatisfaction said she was his current wife.

Pieter said, "So, my good friend, you and your son are visiting your beautiful daughter in *Mongala*. I understand she studies to be a Catholic nun. Such a waste. She should marry me. Tell her I asked about her, will you?" He took a long swig of Primus beer and belched. "I would treat your daughter like a queen. For that, you can rest assured." The captain's expression screwed up in pain and then softened as he released a screeching gas discharge.

The father and son moved upwind out of harm's way. Ignoring his proposal, Stanley asked, "What rumors have you heard about the fighting? Is the end near?"

Pieter hiked his disobedient eyebrows. He relit his stogie. "End? This is Congo. One war ends–another war begins. They say the rebels are closing in on *Mongala*. Another reason you should put your daughter under my protection." He walked to the railing, covered one nostril with his thumb, and blew with an incredible force loud enough to startle the goats tethered to the guard railing. He wiped the results on his greasy overalls.

Pieter redirected the conversation back to Obo's daughter. "Of course, there's a healthy 'Mahari,' dowry. As you know, I'm a rich man. You think about that, my friend." He shot Stanley a pleasant grin and slapped him on the back. The blow partially buckled Stanley's legs.

Loci asked, "Don't you already have a wife?"

Pieter studied his dirty fingernails meditatively. "If your father would agree to my proposal, I could sell her to the *Bangala* cannibals." He laughed and, ignoring his obesity, joked, "A woman her size should fetch a hefty price. And anyway, important men should have at least two wives. Don't you agree?" His face went inscrutably blank.

Sensing his father's anger, Loci changed the subject. "How long will it take us to reach *Mongala*?"

Pieter spoke using his upper lip to conceal a rotting tooth.

"Maybe five hours, no more than six. The current is favorable this time of year." He rolled the cigar from one corner of his mouth to the other.

"*Merci beaucoup,*" Loci said, walking away.

Stanley followed his son, stepping over sleeping soldiers. A woman stirred a pot of *cassava* porridge over a petrol drum fired by charcoal. Bare-breasted *Lingala* women gossiped. Children spoke French. Men with shaved heads argued politics. A mother breastfed her baby. Two men played dominoes. Most passengers dozed. A prostitute solicited.

Loci looked at his father, whispering scornfully, "Someday, I will cut Captain Pieter's throat for robbing us."

Stanley said, "Many have tried. All have failed."

"I won't fail. For that, you can rest assured, my friend," countered his son. He spat over the railing complimenting his imitation of Pieter. His father suppressed a grin.

The sun hovered momentarily over the jungle's crest, and then it dropped below the horizon like a golden cannonball. The sky erupted into a green and crimson explosion. A waxing moon and Venus decorated the artist-easel sunset. It was getting darker. Soon, the night sky would be star glutted.

Pieter used moonshine to navigate the river until night-fog blotted out the light. When the ferryboat plunged into darkness, he located the rock-snags with a powerful searchlight.

Later that night, Stanley and Loci sat together watching the shadowy riverbanks pass by. Occasionally, cooking fires from villages winked. A drumbeat sounded from one village and then from another. Once more, an uncomfortable silence descended on them as neither dealt easily with words. To the north, in the Mountains of the Moon, a storm was brewing. Zigzag bolts of white lightning painted the heavens, followed by rumbling thunder.

"If it rains tonight, you must remember to bailout our boat," Stanley reminded his son. "A fisherman without a boat is like a farmer without a hoe."

"Father, tell me about my mother."

Stanley always protected his son from the details of his mother's death. "Your mother was a gift from God. That's all you need to know. She brought the sun into my heart. Go to sleep, my son. We have a busy day ahead of us." He pulled the canvas tarp over his head and pretended to fall asleep.

When Loci closed his eyes, he envisioned his mother's face. He shied away from the painful memory and concentrated on makebelieve sex.

Stanley found sleep elusive. Suffering from the old man's curse, he urinated over the side several times during the night. It rained so hard the throbbing engine was muffled. Rather than wake his son, he bailed out their dugout.

Stanley crossed himself, watching the ferryboat's white-foamy wake disappear into the night. During the day, the river was the angel of life. But the nights were ruled by diabolical ghouls. It was the resting place for those sluiced away by violence. He dozed off, revisiting the night that changed his life. It started like it always did with a vision of his wife's face as she was violated. It ended with her execution. And then the reruns began.

***

Just before daybreak, Pieter anchored in the middle of the river two miles upriver from *Mongala*. The sound of the rattling anchor chain stirred Stanley and his son.

The sleepy-eyed captain barked orders in Swahili punctuated by French. His voice croaked. "My friends, I'm afraid I have bad news. *Mongala* has come under siege."

The ship's radio squawked. Pieter freed himself from the grasp of the helmsman chair and sprang to answer it. After he finished the call, he looked even more concerned.

The passengers groaned.

"Is it *al-Shabab*?" a passenger asked.

Pieter ignored the question. He hacked overboard, clearing his throat. "It's far too dangerous for me to dock at *Mongala*. Those of you who wish to take your chances in the pirogues. You have five minutes to disembark. This ship is turning around." He rubbed his bloodshot eyes and apologized. "I am sorry, but it is out of my control." Pieter continued speaking, but disappointment had deafened his listeners.

Passengers hissed Swahili expletives.

Stanley and Loci scrambled over the side, into their bobbing dugout. The ferryboat idled ahead, retrieving the anchor.

Captain Pieter yelled to Stanley, "If you find your daughter, remember to tell her about me."

Stanley nodded, cursing Pieter under his breath.

They rowed, their paddles dipping and pulling hard for a marshy inlet two-hundred meters upriver from *Mongala*'s commercial jetty. The throaty pops of intermittent gunshots interrupted the silence. The air, usually perfumed by night-blooming jasmine, reeked of death. Fighting the swirling current fatigued them. They landed in a thick stand of river reeds and rested on their paddles. Stanley pointed. "Her school is in that direction." His voice cracked. "Go well, my son, find your little sister. God be with you." He brushed his son's cheek.

Loci grabbed his father's hand and held it to his face. For them, showing affection was an unknown emotion, but they both sensed this goodbye could be their last. Anguish warped Stanley's face.

Loci waded ashore using a machete to hack a pathway through the reeds. The riverbank was sloppy with ripening sewage, the stench revolting. Loci ducked behind a smoldering truck.

*Mongala* was unrecognizable. Nothing of value remained. Loci headed down the dirt road to the school. Animal carcasses littered the ground. As creepy as undertakers, hunch-backed vultures waited in the denuded trees for sunrise to resume their feeding. Two skinny dogs fought a tug-of-war over a section of bluish intestines. Loci picked up a stone and hurled it. The dogs cowered, but they wouldn't surrender their prize. He pulled his shirt up over his nose and kept walking.

The sign read: *Ecole Catholique Filles.*

Congolese rap music blared from the administration building. Loci ducked behind the brick wall surrounding a soccer field. The iron-gate was ajar, but using it made him an easy target. Sunrise was minutes away. He vaulted the fence and landed on something squishy. He lost his balance and came face to face with a corpse.

As Loci ran across the playground, he tripped on another body; the tiny girl's hands were missing. The loud music muted his shriek. He hid under an open window. Fear-sweat blurred his vision. He tried unsuccessfully to slow down his breathing. The light was greying. He heard blood-curdling screams.

What Loci witnessed looking through a window was so hellish; he couldn't believe his eyes. Please, God, let me find her alive, he pleaded. Bile filled his throat. A large man was plunging into a tiny girl bent over a desk. Two men fondled themselves, waiting for their turns. Naked bodies packed the room. One woman was only recognizable as a nun by her bloodied habit.

Panic-stricken; Loci burst through the front door. The floor was a minefield of fecal curlicues. He scanned, searching for his sister. The rapist didn't see the machete in Loci's hand, nor did he anticipate the powerful chop that partially severed his neck. The man's eyes widened. He dropped to his knees. What had been erect was now limp. His gurgling death-bellow sounded more animal than human. Loci never saw the man standing behind him.

When Loci Obo regained consciousness, the sun was at its zenith. The room was as hot as Lucifer's breath, the smell revolting. He felt dizzy and tasted blood. He struggled against his bindings and tried to focus on the girl lying next to him. His sister stared back at him with sad, defeated eyes. At that moment, Loci knew he was going to die. He prayed his death would be painless. His prayers were unanswered.

***

Mohamed bin Sali commanded the ragtag militia that carried out the raid on *Mongala*. Sali claimed affiliation with *Boko Haram*, a Muslim terrorist group wreaking havoc across central Africa. The self-appointed commander wore a necklace of human teeth centered by a petrified penis. He sported mirrored sunglasses and crisscrossing ammunition bandoliers. Sali was an ex-military *Hutu* commander who took part in the genocidal massacre in Rwanda. His private army came primarily from the *Ngombe* tribe. They were best known for thievery.

Sali's criminals and their captives disappeared into a wasteland infested by diseases, venomous snakes, and bloodsucking leeches. Besides the meager spoils of war, illicit drugs, and fear, the glue that cemented his gang was a constant supply of sex-slaves. The raid on *Mongala* had been a success. They'd kidnapped thirty schoolgirls, some of them not yet teenagers. By the time the Congolese army patrol responded to the attack on *Mongala*, Sali had a ten-day head-start. He knew the patrol wouldn't pursue him. A soldier's pay wasn't worth the risk.

The next three months were brutal. The jungle took a toll, as did the constant marching. The sexual demands of the kidnappers occupied the nights. Beatings from hippo-whips were frequent. The younger ones died first. Some had been so traumatized; they would just give up and stop living. They were left to die, their existence erased by carrion eaters.

Winnie Obo thought her morning sickness came from the contaminated water collected from stagnated pools. Winnie didn't know she carried a rapist's seed in her belly.

# CHAPTER THREE
## Dallas

**The term** 'Laying on of hands' has a faith-healing connotation, but for Reverend Bowden Ray Carson, the idiom had a different meaning. The reverend looked straight into the television camera with all the artificial tears he could muster.

He wore a virginal white suit and matching necktie. Tearfully, he said, "Brothers and sisters, I ask you to remember the words of our Lord and Savior, Jesus Christ. 'If you want to be perfect, go, sell your possessions and give to the poor. You will have treasure in heaven. Then come, follow me.'"

Carson wiped the tears from his cheeks and outstretched his arms, palms up. "Just last week, I received an anonymous donation from a generous viewer who asked me to help those lost African girls in the news. Thirty young Christian schoolgirls kidnapped by wicked savages. Raped and beaten by Godless devils. I ask you in His name, to give so I can save these poor wretched souls. Mail your tax-deductible donations, no matter how small, to this ministry at the address provided on your screen. I will say a special prayer for you. With His help and yours, I'll see you next Sunday. Praise the Lord."

He laced his hands together in prayer, looked up, and announced, "May God bless you all." The image of Reverend Carson faded away. Gospel music accompanied the credits on the television monitor.

***

Reverent Carson looked into the dressing room mirror at the man standing behind him. The man said, "RC, don't shoot the messenger. I'm your lawyer. We've known each other for what, twenty years? I'm telling you as a friend. You fucked up this time. Pardon my English. I've bailed you out before, but this time it's as serious as cancer."

An attractive young woman carrying a clipboard entered the room without knocking. "Do you want the pledge total, Reverend?" She asked.

"Sweetheart, what's your name again?" Carson asked, visually undressing the teenager. He involuntarily licked his lips as he envisioned her naked.

"Kitty," she said, her cheeks turning rosy.

"Councilor, Kitty's our new intern. She's got a great future in television. I'm going to make damn sure she gets her shot." His hand lingered on her arm a little too long. The lawyer shook his head. Kitty smiled. She excused herself and left the dressing room. Carson's eyes stayed glued on Kitty's ass until the door closed. He sighed.

Without turning around, Carson asked, "So, how much?"

"At this point, I'm not sure," the lawyer replied.

"Don't give me that shit. How much will it take?" Carson pressed.

"I'm afraid it's not that simple," stated the lawyer raising a doubtful eyebrow.

Carson clasped his hands together and thought for a moment. "What about an abortion?" Still deeper in contemplation, he drew heavily on a cigarette. He brushed cigarette ashes from his white lapels.

"Not in the cards. Let me rephrase that, not a chance in hell unless there's a settlement."

Carson shook another Marlboro from its pack. After taking a long lazy drag, he spoke through a smoke ring. "Everyone has a price, councilor. Like it says in the Good Book, 'Dishonest money dwindles. But whoever gathers money little-by-little makes it grow.'"

The lawyer scratched his head, trying to decipher the relevancy. Finally, he said, "It's not her. It's her mother. You knocked-up her daughter. She knows she's got you by the short hairs, plain and simple. You're her ticket out of government housing."

Ray wiped the last vestiges of makeup from his face. He grimaced, checking his teeth and drummed his fingers on the dressing table. His upper lip was grooved from being puckered around too many cigarettes.

"Offer her twenty-five thousand. That ought to do it."

"God damn, RC, I already offered her fifty."

Carson stubbed out his cigarette. "And?"

"She said, and I quote, 'You tell that phony Bible-thumping child molester, Ray Carson, fifty thousand isn't even a down payment. He'll pay me, or I'll blow the whistle. He can say adios to his shitty TV show.'"

The lawyer's remark merged Carson's smirk into a

concerned frown. "Look, I gotta run. I'm driving to Huntsville."

"What's in Huntsville?"

"The state prison. A condemned prisoner wants me to hear his confession. I'm guessing he saw me on television. An execution like this one is bound to make the headlines, which is great publicity for my ministry. Remember what the Bible teaches us. 'He has delivered us from the domain of darkness and transferred us to the kingdom of his beloved Son, in whom we have redemption, the forgiveness of our sins.' That's Colossians 1:13."

"RC, I need you to stay focused. Hey, are you listening to me?"

Deep in thought, Carson didn't respond for several long moments as the clock on his dressing table ticked the seconds away. "I hear you. Like I said before, start earning what I pay you." He applied more hair spray to his white-streaked bouffant. Most of his hair was a shade too dark to be natural. He looked like he was wearing a dead skunk for a hat.

The lawyer raised a placating hand. "What can I say to make you understand? Statutory rape includes sexual penetration and sexual contact between an adult and a child. No doubt about what happened, her being knocked-up. The penalty for this first-degree felony is at least five years in prison. That's Texas penal code 1:13," the lawyer recited, making light of his client's Bible quotes. He added, "The court can demand a DNA sample. This is serious, RC."

Carson's memory drifted back to the last motel rendezvous. The velvety smoothness of her skin. The soapy smell of her hair made his member move. "Tell you what—I'll marry the little tramp. That'll damn sure solve the problem."

"Are you seriously suggesting? Sweet Jesus, RC, you're insane. She's just a kid.

"Oh yeah, what about Woody, what's-his-name?"

"The last time I looked, Manhattan wasn't in Texas. Everyone knows New Yorkers are immoral democrats. You're an ordained minister in Texas, for Christ's sake. The evangelicals will tar and feather you, and then they'll hang you from the nearest oak tree."

Carson thought for a second. "I need breathing room. Tell those trailer-trash bitches–they're fixin' to cook the goose that lays golden eggs. I'll ring you on my way back from Huntsville."

"Let me see what I can work out," said the lawyer.

"You do that, councilor. Anything else?"

The lawyer's cell phone played Dixie; he put the call on hold and answered. "Stay the hell away from her and her mother. No telephone calls and certainly no contact. Nada. Are we clear on that?"

"Crystal."

***

As Carson drove his white Coupe Deville down interstate 45 to Huntsville, he considered his predicament. He was flat busted. A teenage girl from his last congregation in Houston was blackmailing him. He was six months behind in his child support payments. And his ex-wife was threatening to take him back to court. The donations couldn't offset those fixed expenses and his lifestyle. He contemplated skipping town and starting up a new ministry, but his television exposure made that choice a long-shot. He reached under the front seat and retrieved a quart bottle of Wild Turkey. He took a long swig and sighed. "Oh, Lord, show me the path." He started humming 'What a friend we have in Jesus' and kept on driving.

Huntsville is known as the death-penalty capital of the

world. A laidback southern city with a main street sprinkled with antique shops and cozy cafes. The town has as many churches as bars. The swampy Trinity River dissects the city. A sixty-foot statue of Sam Houston is a landmark. The prison museum is the town's major tourist attraction. The redbrick penitentiary in Huntsville stands out like an angry pimple on a beautiful woman's nose. Opened in 1849, Huntsville State Prison was initially constructed for white inmates only. The more expedient sentences available for black criminals were whippings and hangings. During the Civil War, inmates manufactured tents and uniforms for the Confederacy. In 1878, the legendary Kiowa chief, White Bear, refusing to complete a life sentence, committed suicide by jumping out of a window. Since 1982, 537 prisoners have been executed at Huntsville. Today, 290 inmates await their fates on death row.

A carnival atmosphere prevailed at Huntsville. Lights from the guard towers illuminated the night. Without the homemade signs, it looked like a college football tailgating party. An enterprising vendor hawked tee-shirts, asserting opposing views on capital punishment. One shirt read, 'Thou Shalt Not Kill.' Another one advertised, 'Protect Victims' Rights.'

The demonstrators descended on Carson's Cadillac as he pulled into the prison's parking lot. An objector yelled, "Capital punishment killed Jesus, you fucking creep." Opponents spit on his windshield. When Carson rolled down his window, a woman screamed, "How does it feel giving comfort to a murderer?"

Two Texas state troopers escorted Reverend Carson through the prison's maximum-security entrance.

A correctional officer scrutinized his credentials. "Reverend Carson, everything seems to be in order. Guess there's no need for patting you down. Hell, I'm just kidding." His prison humor did not lighten the mood. The only item he was allowed to keep was his Bible. The rest of his belongings were locked in a metal box.

"Follow me, reverend." The barred door opened.

The correctional officer gave him a guided tour of the execution chamber. The chlorine-odorized room had turquoise painted walls and a white tiled floor. The execution gurney was visible from three glass-windowed adjoining rooms. One observation area was reserved for the victim's family. The other room was for the family of the condemned inmate. The third room was the operational area containing the pump that would intravenously inject a lethal dose of potassium chloride into prisoner number 475209.

\*\*\*

# CHAPTER FOUR

## Two years earlier

**James Cheatham** came from a bump-in-the-road-town in rural west Texas. He was raised by a single mother who had a fondness for married men and wasn't bashful about bringing them home. Cheatham never knew his father. He was a below-average student but an exceptional fullback on his high school football team. After college scouts overlooked him, he joined the Marine Corps. James thrived in the military. Clean sheets, new clothes, and three squares a day was a dream come true. He reenlisted after four years and had every intention of making a life in the military. He did two combat tours in Afghanistan, followed by one in Iraq. James Cheatham was awarded two Purple Hearts. He attained the E-7 rank of gunnery sergeant.

During the early years of his military service, Cheatham controlled a binge-drinking problem, which he inherited from his mother. For the most part, he put aside the war and the things he'd done and seen others do. Occasionally, in his sleep, he saw the faces of the men he'd killed. Those nightmares left him wide awake. His mother's death took a toll on him, or he used her death as an excuse. Whatever the reason, his weekends entailed heavy drinking. Beating a lieutenant to a pulp in a drunken barroom brawl got him busted back to corporal. That confrontation landed him in Camp Pendleton's brig for six months. Knocking an abusive MP's front teeth out ended his hopes for a military career.

Cheatham drifted back to his hometown in West Texas. He found day-work cutting calves for a local rancher. His next job was as a scaffolding rigger in the Midland Basin oil fields. He yearned for the camaraderie of the military. Most of all, he missed the everyday direction of having someone telling him what to do. After six months of boredom, it was time to move on. He'd packed on thirty pounds of bulk during his stint in the Marines. Heavily tattooed arms and a shaved head made Chatham look like a man best avoided.

Cheatham found work as a bouncer in a Dallas honky-tonk bar whose patrons had more tattoos than teeth. When an ex-marine friend offered him a job driving trucks in the Middle East, he jumped at the opportunity. The trucking company was under contract to a private security contractor. The subsidiary specialized in transporting freight in and out of warzones. The work was nerve-wracking, but the pay was great. More importantly, he regained his identity. It was a perfect fit. His military experience made him a valuable asset. He was promoted from truck driver to personal driver to special operations in one year. His work took him to Indonesia, the Middle East, and Africa. Protecting an oil company executive, guarding an arms dealer, or escorting politicians were all in a day's pay. James Cheatham was in heaven, and he was making a fortune.

Between his overseas assignments, he met Angela, an exotic dancer at an upscale Dallas strip club. He had cash to burn. The strippers fought for his attention, but he only had eyes for Angela. She had the face of an angel, raven black hair, and a perfect body. Angela radiated sexuality like a yellow rose exudes fragrance. But like most strippers, she carried personal baggage in spades. They began dating. He showered her with expensive gifts, including a Corvette. At his insistence, Angela quit her job and moved in with him. He helped her tame her drug addiction, or so it seemed. On the surface, they looked like a perfect couple. For the first time in James Cheatham's troubled life, he was head-over-heels in love.

Following six months of abstinence, Angela yielded to the drug demons. Her relapses coincided with his overseas business assignments. The beginning-of-the-end happened while he was working in central Africa. His job was to provide security for an electronics firm making a multimillion-dollar black market purchase of Colton, a rare earth mineral. Cheatham found himself in the middle of a robbery. He survived, but everyone else died. Neither the money nor the minerals were recovered. If James Cheatham had not been wounded, he would have faced an uncertain future.

After recuperating in a South African hospital for two months, he booked a flight home to Dallas with a stopover in Atlanta. He called Angela from the Cape Town Airport. They talked for an hour before he got around to proposing marriage. She accepted without hesitating. Angela was enchanted. They planned a Mexican honeymoon.

"When can I expect you?" she asked with joy creeping into her voice.

"Another week." He smiled, knowing he would land in Dallas in forty-eight hours. The idea of surprising his fiancé made him smile. The deception would be life-changing.

"Angie, decide where you want to live. Our ship has come in. I'm retired, or I will be."

"We've got some catchin' up to do, cowboy. I'm gettin' wet just thinkin' about you," she purred. "I love you, darlin'. Goodbye."

"I love you too," he said, hanging up. Jim was giddy. He

couldn't wait to get home.

He bought her a diamond-studded Rolex at the airport's dutyfree shop.

***

The mind-numbing transatlantic flight and the excitement of reuniting with Angela overwhelmed him. He washed down two Ambient with vodka. One drink won't kill me, he reasoned. He closed his eyes, revisiting the shootout and the subsequent interrogation. His conscience was conflicted. Have I thought of everything? Have I covered the bases? They said they believed me. No reason not to. Damn it, I almost died. To hell with third world-shitholes and fleabag flophouses. But I've never stolen anything in my life. A few candy bars don't make me a thief. What changed me? It was Angela's expensive tastes. He reprimanded himself thinking, don't blame her. This is your doing. He looked at his reflection in the cocktail glass. I'm rich if everything falls into place. At least now, I can keep an eye on my angel.

He signaled the stewardess for a refill. Mental images flashed before his mind's eye. He remembered meeting the client's private jet at the Kinshasa Airport. He was short, rat-like, bespectacled with a hook nose and beady eyes. He appeared nervous. His shirt was sweat-soaked. Why wouldn't he be worried? He was carrying a fortune in the most lawless city in the world.

Cheatham dozed off. Every so often, his snoring startled him awake, but he lapsed back into dream-laden sleep. He dreamt about the helicopter ride and the three-day boat ride up the Congo River.

The trucks unloaded the minerals. The seller was Belgian. The buyer was French. His bodyguards looked like undisciplined gangsters. My men were also criminals, but they had been Congolese soldiers.

The buyer and the seller exchanged small talk. My client

tested the purity of the minerals. The seller counted the money. The barge was loaded. The transaction was running smoothly.

And then, without warning, the mood turned ugly. It started as a minor disagreement but quickly escalated into a heated argument. I saw it coming and moved to protect my client. Weapons were drawn. Safeties unlocked. I don't remember who fired the first shot, but bullets ricocheted. The gunsmoke was thick. Both the buyer and seller went down. Instinctively, I jumped over the side, but not before I got hit. The first shot grazed my neck. The second bullet entering my left shoulder must have been partially deflected by my bullet-proof vest. My motto saved the day. When in doubt, wear Kevlar.

I surfaced without my weapon. The firing had stopped. I dog-paddled to the shoreline, trying to get my head around what had gone down. There was fear, the kind of fear that makes a man lose control of his bowels. I climbed back on board. Everyone was down. The deck awash in blood smelled metallic. One soldier was groaning. I knew his gut-shot was a death sentence. I took his sidearm. Another soldier, feigning death, jumped up. He pointed his weapon at me, but I fired first. My bullet made a meaty thump.

I checked my client's pulse. The bullet entering his right eye had shattered his sunglasses. The seller had also suffered a fatal head-shot. He had blood trickling from his ears. My left arm was stiffening, but I'd seen enough gunshot wounds to know my injury was superficial. And then, everything came into focus. This was the luckiest day of my life.

He woke up with a start. "Stewardess, another vodka and tonic. Better yet, make that a double."

\*\*\*

By the time James Cheatham landed in Atlanta, he was dead drunk. When he arrived at the Dallas Fort Worth Airport four hours later, he was too loaded to find his car, let alone drive home. He hired a taxicab.

"Where you coming from?" the black cabby asked.

"From South Africa," Cheatham slurred.

"No, shit. Always wanted to visit Africa. What brings you to Dallas?"

"I live here." Cheatham added proudly, "I'm getting married tomorrow."

"Good for you. I been single now on thirty years. Ain't nothin' like marriage, if you find the right woman that is. I got a theory about marriage. I think hookers make the best wives. They're damn good in the sack and they ain't gonna cheat on you cause they already had a million dicks. Mostly, they're so surprised someone would be willin' to marry them, they treat you right. No, sir, I would never marry a woman unless she was a whore. What did you say your gal does for a livin'?"

Cheatham prevaricated, "Schoolteacher."

"Hmm. I don't know nothin' about teachers. Good Luck."

"Thanks, man."

Their chit-chatting ended. Jetlag got the best of Cheatham. He closed his eyes and fell asleep.

Thirty minutes later, the taxicab stopped in front of his house. "Hey, man, we made it." The cab driver shook him awake. "You need help?"

"I can manage." He handed the cabby a fistful of money. He yawned. "Thanks, pal. Keep the change. Go, Cowboys."

"Right on, bro." The cabby gave him a high-five.

The second the taxicab disappeared into the night, he felt a cold shiver run down the back of his neck. Why was a Ford pickup parked behind Angela's Corvette? And why was the house so dark? He dismissed his concerns as he slipped around the back of his house and entered through a sliding glass door. A muted television provided soft lighting. The Johnny Cash song, "I walk the line," boomed from a radio.

He had a clear view of the living room. Angela and her lover hadn't bothered to use a bedroom. They were locked in a writhing tangle on the floor. Drug paraphernalia littered a coffee table. Cheatham stood there, too stunned to move. He prayed it was all a bad dream.

James Cheatham crossed the thin line between love and hate. Love gave way to a crushing betrayal, which succumbed to demoralizing humiliation. It ended in pure hatred. An out-of-body trance gripped him. The ringing in his ears grew louder. Time slowed down to a dreamlike unreality. As an observer, he watched himself walk from the living room into his den. He retrieved the .38-Smith and Wesson from a desk drawer and reentered the living room.

Without hesitating, he traced the man's backbone with the pistol's red laser dot, stopping at a spot just above his bobbing testicles. The rhythmic thrusting into Angela ended when the bullet entered the man's anus, severing his spinal cord. Angela screamed, pushing the limp body off with a heave. Cheatham calmly delivered a coup de grace shot to the back of the man's head. The quivering stopped.

He turned off the radio. Except for Angela's sobs, it was deadly quiet. Cheatham turned his attention to her. He stood frozen, looking down at her. He felt nauseous, but it passed in a long moment. She looked up at him, her bloodshot eyes filling with terror.

"Don't hurt me, Jimmy."

He slurred, "Why, Angela? We were getting married." His face tightened into misery.

She tried to speak, but fear strangled her words. "I, I don't know why. " Her blubbering produced a spit-bubble.

He drew his forearm across his mouth. Misreading him, Angela breathed a sigh of relief. Fear receded from her face. He won't hurt me, she said to herself. She smiled but was too close to panic to hold it. Angela raised her arms, inviting him to hold her.

"My God, you're so beautiful." His mind flashed like a camera taking snapshots of his childhood. Nauseating visions reappeared. He remembered his mother and her lovers and the night-sounds they made. "You're just like her," he whispered. The sly smile on his lips faded. He pressed the pistol against his temple.

"Don't," she screamed.

He placed the barrel between Angela's eyes and pulled the trigger.

Cheatham blacked-out. Then he snapped out of his trance. He fell onto a sofa and dialed 911. "There's been a double shooting at 740 Rodeo Drive. No, there's no need to send an ambulance. They're both dead. Yes, I'm sure. I'm the shooter." He dropped the receiver and passed out.

# CHAPTER FIVE
## Huntsville Prison

### Death Row

### Back to the present

**The maximum-security** guard fanned the pages of Reverend Carson's Bible. Satisfied, he returned it. "Reverend, we've provided a chair for you in front of Mr. Cheatham's holding cell. And we cleared the cells around him for privacy. You are not to pass anything to the prisoner. Do you understand the rules?"

"I do." Vigorous nodding accompanied Carson's acknowledgment.

"Oh, there's one more thing. Don't even touch the bars. A few years back, a condemned prisoner grabbed a preacher's arm, pulled it through the bars, and secured it with a bedsheet. By the time we responded, the inmate had amputated the preacher's arm with a razor blade. It was a mess to clean up, as you can imagine. Any questions?"

Carson shook his head. "Well, maybe one. Just out of curiosity, what did the prisoner order for his last meal?" Unconsciously, Carson rubbed his arm.

The guard ejected a brown squirt of tobacco juice into a Dixie cup. "We stopped doin' last meal requests. The State figured given the condemned special treatment didn't make sense. And besides, it was a damn waste. They all puke when their time comes. It's hard not feelin' some sympathy. But then again, the ones I get done terrible crimes."

"Tell me about Mr. Cheatham?" Carson inquired.

"Jimmy? He's different. Cheatham's a good-old-boy from west Texas, same as me. We're both Marines. Hoorah. We did basic at Paris, at different times, mind you, but we had the same drill instructor." The guard looked dejected. "They warned us about fraternizin' with the inmates. I wish to hell I'd listened. I took a likin' to Jimmy right off. I gotta admit, I'm damn sure gonna miss him. He won't raise a ruckus when his time comes. No, sir, he'll go like a man, not like the fuckin' crybabies I see. They all shit themselves. He won't. You can take that to the bank."

"What about a pardon?"

"Ain't you heard? Jimmy denied his lawyer's request to appeal. Said he's guilty as hell, and he's ready to pay for what he done. Truth be known, he more or less demanded the death penalty."

"Ever think about his victims?" Carson asked the guard, scrutinizing him with searching eyes.

"Sometimes, I do. But, hell, I can't say I blame Jimmy none. A man comes home drunk and finds his fiancé gettin' plowed. Shit happens. Know what I mean? I'm surprised he asked to see you, you being a preacher and all. Never knew Jimmy was religious."

Carson bowed his head. "Jesus said, 'I am the resurrection and the life. The one who believes in me will live, even though they die, and whoever lives by believing in me will never die.'"

The guard said, "Better save the psalm-singin' for Jimmy. I'll walk you down to his cell. Will you be a witness?"

"If he asks me, I'll stay. I understand he doesn't have a family."

"His mother liked the bottle. She drank herself under the ground, according to Jimmy. He had a sister. Committed suicide three years back. Lived in Houston, I believe he said. By his account, the only two people he ever loved was that sister and the gal he killed. It's a cryin' shame if you ask me. Reverend, a word to the wise. The only thing worse than witnessing an execution is being executed."

"I'll keep that in mind."

"Alrighty then. Follow me." The prison-guard led the way to the holding cell. Carson received catcalls from other condemned convicts. He avoided making eye contact. The guard had a how-do-like-my-world look on his face.

"Reverend Carson, James Cheatham." Both men nodded. "I'll leave you two alone." The prison-guard had grief showing at the corners of his mouth.

Cheatham looked between the bars at Carson. His eyes felt scratchy from not having slept. He went red in the face. It upset him to reveal himself. He had to be careful not to overplay his hand.

Cheatham's incarceration had reduced him to ordinary, except for a spade-shaped goatee and his pale color. His face was haggard with deep parentheses framing his mouth. Carson assessed him for a few tense moments, and then he dropped his gaze to the floor. "There's something very familiar about you, Mr. Cheatham. Have we met before?" His eyes narrowed as he racked his brain.

Cheatham stared back at him. "Oh, I doubt that's possible. Hey, thanks for coming."

Carson nodded, asking, "So, how's it going?" He looked embarrassed by the absurdity of his dim-witted question.

"Well, considering, not too well."

"Sorry. Would you like me to read to you from the Bible?" An idiot's grin painted Carson's face.

Cheatham laced his hands behind his head and leaned back in the chair. "That's not why I asked to see you. I'm guessing you received my $25,000 check by now. Ring a bell?"

"That was you?" Carson's eyes narrowed as he wondered where this was going. "God bless you."

Cheatham waved off the blessing. "The twenty-five was to get your attention. I've got a story to tell and not much time to tell it. They've scheduled a medical exam for me to make sure I'm healthy enough to kill. The people running this nuthouse are crazier than the inmates. Reverend, I aim to make you rich. If you play your cards right, you stand to make millions, or rather your ministry will. One thing's for sure. You'll be able to help those African girls. The ones you spoke about on television." He watched Carson's reaction and knew he had touched the right nerve. It was almost invisible, but it was there. The reverend was his for the taking.

Carson raised a skeptical eyebrow, not fully believing he was having this conversation. "And you're doing this because?"

"Well, let's just say, I'm hoping the Man upstairs will go easy on me."

"Praise the Lord," Carson gushed. "With God, it's never too late. Remember His words. 'In Him, we have redemption. Through his blood and the forgiveness....'"

Cheatham interrupted him. "What I did was wrong. I

knew it then, and I know it now. I'm ready to pay for my sins." He could feel Carson's greed radiating through the bars. "Let me start at the beginning." He opened the door; stepping through it was crucial.

Carson squirmed until he was sitting on the edge of his chair. He was spellbound–his unblinking eyes fixed on Cheatham.

Cheatham summarized his life, fast-forwarding to the shootout on the Congo River. "What was I supposed to do? Shit, I'm bleedin' like a stuck pig. Everyone's dead. There's ten million in cash plus another ten in minerals just sitting there. Okay, let's say I went to the cops. That wasn't my first rodeo in central Africa, you know. Why, hell, they would've locked me up and thrown away the key. I've worked with them bastards before. I'm talking about the Congolese police. They're all as crooked as a pig's dick." The recollection gave him pause.

"So, what did you do with the money?" Carson asked, filling in the gap. His mouth had gone dry. He licked his lips.

Cheatham spoke softly. "Buried the money in a fresh grave next to a Catholic mission." He flashbacked to the robbery, hiding the money, and then running the boat back upriver. "Reverend, I can't say I didn't plan to go back and keep it for myself. But, well, my life kinda got hijacked. Not that I don't deserve this." He spread his arms, indicating his confinement. "I figured, put in the right hands, that money could do some good."

Cheatham glanced wistfully at the barred window. He addressed Carson asking, "Are we on the same page?"

Carson nodded vigorously. "Absolutely. So, what happens now?"

"That one's easy enough. There's ten million over there with your name on it. I'd forget about the minerals. But, look, if you have second thoughts, I'll understand. I mean, it is blood money."

Carson showed no qualms. "But how can I...?"

Cheatham held up his hand. He looked through the bars checking right and then left for eavesdroppers. Satisfied, he handed Carson an envelope. "This spells out everything you'll need to know, including the GPS coordinates pinpointing the exact location of the money. There are two men you'll need to contact. The first is Jesse Spooner. He knows the ropes in Africa like I know west Texas, and he's got great contacts. The second is my lawyer. He's got a check for you. If my girlfriend hadn't pissed away a fortune on drugs, there would be more, but there's enough. Police bribes and Spooner won't come cheap. Your biggest expense will be the reward money. Just remember, everyone will be looking to rip you a new one."

When Carson started to tear open the envelope, Cheatham stopped him. "Not here, for Christ's sake."

Carson slipped the letter into his Bible. "Can I trust this man, Spooner?" he asked, and holding up the Bible, added, "A greedy man can stir up strife."

The irony made Cheatham smile inwardly. He shared his history with Jesse Spooner in the Marines and later in the security business. Truth be known, Jesse had become a very close friend. Noting Carson's apprehension, he said, "Getting you into Congo isn't a big deal. Getting you out with the money is the hard part. You can't do this without Spooner. Besides, he doesn't know about the money. As far as he's concerned, your purpose is rescuing the schoolgirls. Are you in or out? Before you answer, don't think for a minute your collar will protect you. There's bad blood between missionaries and Africans."

Carson nodded his approval. "I understand."

"Good. As a man of the cloth, I know I can trust you. If you save those schoolgirls, I can rest in my grave knowin' I did one decent thing in my life." Cheatham allowed himself a skeletal grin, trying hard not to appear triumphant.

Carson thought for a moment, and then he raised his right hand. "I swear before God. I'll do everything in my power."

"That's good enough for me, reverend."

Impatient, Carson fidgeted. "May He give you comfort, Mr. Cheatham." He stood up to leave. It was quiet enough to hear his stomach gurgle.

"Before you go, there's something else," Cheatham said.

"And that is?" Carson asked, attempting another grin that failed. Please don't ask me to be a witness, he thought.

"Jesse Spooner operates a charter boat in Key West, Florida. You'll need to contact him in person. He's expecting you. You can't miss him. He's the only black charter boat captain in the Keys, maybe in the world."

"God bless you, sir," Carson said.

Cheatham said, "I know you plan to share some of the money with those girls."

"But, of course," assured Carson, thinking, not a penny.

They said goodbye. Carson vanished down the walkway separating the cell blocks. The sound of his footsteps faded until there was only a chilling stillness.

*** 

The guard escorted the prison doctor to Cheatham's cell. It was time for his medical evaluation. "Is there anything I can get you, Jimmy?" the guard asked, examining an errant piece of chewing tobacco he extracted from the gap between his front teeth.

"A blond nymphomaniac would be nice."

The guard ignored him, asking, "So, how'd it go with the holy-roller?"

"Good." Cheatham smiled. "Vengeance is mine, sayeth the Lord." *God be with him, and I don't envy God.*

### Two Hours Later

At 11:30 PM, the warden at the Huntsville State Prison received a telephone call from the Governor's office telling him that the execution of James Cheatham should proceed. The warden, accompanied by a chaplain and four guards, escorted Cheatham to the death chamber. Leg-irons caused him to shuffle in baby-steps, but he stood erect and didn't falter. The chaplain attending the prisoner offered to give Cheatham spiritual absolution, which he declined. The warden asked the prisoner if he wished to address the victim's witnesses. A microphone dropped from the ceiling. Cheatham shook his head. The warden then asked him if he had any questions about the execution process. Again, he answered *no.*

A guard removed Cheatham's ankle shackles. He was strapped down to the table, face up with his arms fully extended, and secured on supports. The witnessing parties were escorted by guards to their respective observation rooms. Intravenous needles were inserted into Cheatham's arms. A saline drip was started. The guards exited the chamber. The warden positioned himself behind the prisoner. The chaplain stood at Cheatham's feet with his hand on the prisoner's ankle.

The warden leaned forward, whispering, "Mr. Cheatham, would you care to make a final statement?"

"You mean like begging for mercy? Sorry, that ain't my nature. Let's get this show on the road. If you're locked and loaded, I say, let her rip."

# THE CONGO AFFAIR

"May God Almighty grant you eternal peace," said the warden. He glanced at his watch, stepped back, motioning to a hooded man in the adjoining room.

The executioner turned a valve, releasing the dose of pentobarbital that would render Cheatham unconscious followed by the potassium chloride that would stop his heart.

James Cheatham saw himself riding a painted stallion galloping across an open meadow. The wind swayed golden tipped grasses. The air smelled sweet. The setting sun warmed his face. Above him, a red-tailed hawk soared under puffy clouds cast against a cerulean sky. He saw vivid bursts of red and white lights. Suddenly, he tasted something foul, and he felt cold. He stared at the ceiling, the life fading from his eyes. His last vision was of Reverend Carson. He smiled.

*** 

As Ray Carson drove back to Dallas, his mind went into overdrive. He believed his good luck was by divine intervention. He was dead-tired deep into his bones, but the thought of all that money made his heart race. Carson dialed his cell. "How's my darlin'? Did you miss me?"

"Momma says I shouldn't talk to you. Says you took advantage of me. You did me wrong, Ray."

"Ah, c'mon, Maria, don't be like that."

"You told me not to worry. Said you didn't need a rubber. You said you were fixed. I was gonna be a beautician. Now, look at me. What am I supposed to do?" She sniffled.

"That's why I'm calling, baby-doll. Will you marry me?"

"Ray Carson, you're lying." Despair mutated into jubilation.

"Would I lie to the only woman I ever loved? 'The Lord detests lying lips, but he delights in those who are trustworthy.' That's from Proverbs."

Maria gushed, "I told momma you wouldn't run out on me."

"How about I pick you up at eight? Pack some clothes. I'm taking you to Florida. I wouldn't mention this to your mother. Let's make this our little secret."

"I love you to pieces, Ray Carson."

An aroused smile creased Cason's lips. "Me too, baby doll. See you soon."

He fixated on the highway and turned up the radio. George Strait's "All My Ex's Live in Texas" was interrupted by a special report from the Huntsville State Prison. James Cheatham was pronounced dead at 12:32 a.m. Carson switched channels until he found one playing country gospel music. The Hank Williams recording of "At the Cross" was playing. He turned up the volume and sang along at the top of his lungs.

***

# CHAPTER SIX

## Key West

**Jesse Spooner** was depressed. Watching tourists book the charter-boats moored on either side of his sport-fisherman was a downer. Jesse needed to stay in port. Where is this Reverend Carson, he asked himself for the hundredth time? Engine repairs and alimony were eating up his savings. His friends warned him, saying he could make a small fortune in the charter fishing business as long as he started with a large one.

He loved the rhythm of his Jimmy Buffet lifestyle. Jesse was struggling to stay afloat and never happier.

The news about his longtime friend, James Cheatham, was not surprising. Jesse believed rescuing the "Forgotten girls of Congo," as the press had dubbed them, was a long-shot at best. But the security assignment would pay his bills, and besides, he'd given his word to Cheatham. It had been two years since his last visit to Congo. Time to get up to speed, he thought. He opened his Apple and scanned the Congolese headlines. The following headings popped up:

United Nations to investigate Congo killings

New Ebola outbreak declared

Seventeen new mass graves found

Rape victims come forward

UN accuses rivals in Congo of fueling ethnic hatred

Rebel fighters kill 40 policemen

Congo militia attack kills dozens in the eastern region

Congo rebels are eating pygmies, UN says

Jesse shut-down his computer. Nice to know nothing's changed, he thought. He noticed a middle-aged man and a young woman strolling arm-in-arm down the dock. The man's lizard skin boots and Stetson hat looked out of place, even for Key West. He looks like a Texas redneck, he reasoned. The girl must be his daughter. The first adjective that sprang to mind was tacky.

"You Spooner?" the man asked, shading his eyes. His voice

modulated like a newscaster.

"I am, and I'm guessing you're Reverend Carson." They shook hands. Jesse glanced up at the young woman standing on the dock, waiting to be introduced. She wore a loose-fitting halter top. Short shorts outlined a perfect ass. Although Maria's pregnancy had been terminated, her enlarged breasts were still perky.

Jesse tried unsuccessfully to avoid giving her a visual frisk. "Watch your step," he said, taking her hand. Maria discreetly adjusted her shorts. She held his hand longer than necessary. Her perfume was nostril-clearing. After helping them to board, he ushered them into the salon. The girl clung to Carson's arm like a barnacle. When the boat moved, she trembled like they had been broadsided by a rogue wave.

Jesse and Reverend Carson discussed their associations with James Cheatham and the tragic circumstances surrounding his death.

"Booze was always Jimmy's Achilles' heel," Jesse said.

"The devil's blood has ruined many lives," Carson sermonized, neglecting his weakness. "Mr. Spooner, you look too young to be retired."

"I guess you could say my retirement from ATF was mutual, whatever that means. Ambition led me too close to the sun." Instead of elaborating, Jesse sidetracked the exchange. "This your first visit to Key West?"

Carson spoke before she could. "Our first and our last." He pursed his lips together as he'd sucked on a lemon. "Key West is far worse than Sodom or Gomorrah."

Jesse's eyes turned inward. "Mm, sounds like you folks aren't overly impressed."

"Impressed? We are revolted. I've never seen so many

queers. 'Wrongdoers shall not inherit God's kingdom. Neither the sexually immoral nor idolaters nor homo-erotic partners nor homosexuals shall enter heaven.' I'm quoting Corinthians."

Jesse scratched his head, trying to differentiate between a homo-erotic partner and a run-of-the-mill gay. Confused, he said, "Best fishing in the world, bar none. And as far as the gays go, well, my motto is live-and-let-live." This guy gives me the creeps. Don't blow this. You need the money. "So, I know why you're here. Before we get into the details, let's discuss my fee."

"The late Mr. Cheatham mentioned twenty-five thousand, plus another twenty-five if you rescue the girls," Carson stated.

"The twenty-five is in advance," Jesse said, and then he amended the demand, "Plus travel expenses."

Carson handed Jesse a thick manila envelope. "Your expenses are covered carte blanche, within reason. Can I ask you a question, Mr. Spooner?"

"Of course."

"What are the odds of saving those girls?"

Jesse scratched his head. "Unfortunately, I'd say someplace between slim and none. Bribes might loosen a few tongues. There's no telling how many false leads I'll have to track down."

Reverend Carson studied Jesse. The man's expression gave no access to his thoughts. Does he know about the money? Will he try to keep it for himself? He corrected himself. He has no way of knowing.

"We couldn't begin to do this without you, Mr. Spooner. I believe God has brought us together."

"Whatever you say, reverend. Now then, this won't be my first time in central Africa. How much do you know about that part of the world?"

"I'm afraid we're neophytes. But so were most missionaries sent to Africa."

Jesse raised a curious eyebrow. "I beg your pardon. Are you seriously suggesting? Don't tell me you think you're going with me?"

"God has chosen us to rescue those Christian girls. We aim to do His will. I'm sure He will look after us. Like it says in the Scriptures, 'The wicked flee when no man pursueth, but the righteous are as bold as a lion.'"

"Okay, let me give it to you straight. Congo is the most violent, the most backward, the most chaotic place on this planet and certainly unsuited for your daughter or you, for that matter. There hasn't been a functioning government since I don't know when. The only law is the business end of an AK-47."

"Maria is my wife, sir." Carson's tone registered indignation. When Maria giggled, Carson admonished her with a glance.

Jesse narrowed one eye and tried a softer approach. "Well, folks, I wouldn't recommend Congo for a honeymoon."

Carson's frown ended when his cellphone vibrated. He excused himself and stepped out into the cockpit.

Jesse attempted to fill the awkward void, "Mrs. Carson, can I offer you something to drink? You look a bit under the weather."

"No, thanks. I've never been on a boat before. I just got out of the hospital," she said, avoiding eye contact.

Sensing her distress, Jesse led their conversation into

calmer waters. "I live on this tub. It took me a year to get my sea-legs." He got no response. Jesse and Maria watched Carson in silence. Carson's hand gestures indicated a heated conversation.

"RC, please tell me Maria Lopez isn't with you?" his lawyer inquired.

"Uh-huh," Carson answered.

"What!" the lawyer exclaimed.

"Take it easy, councilor. Everything's under control. We're hitched."

The lawyer was wordless. He cleared his voice. "But I thought I told you... You don't get it, do you? Transporting a minor across state lines with the intent to engage in sexual activity is a crime.

It's called statutory rape."

"Hey, you forget who pays you."

The lawyer countered. "Let me refresh your memory. I'm the one who kept you out of jail for the last umpteen years."

Carson ignored the retort. "Councilor, I want you to call Maria's mother. Tell her I'm fixing to come into a pile of money. There'll be enough for everyone, including her. The Bible says..."

The lawyer cut him off. "I don't give a diddlysquat what the Bible says. Find yourself another lawyer. Oh, one piece of free legal advice. Stay the hell out of Texas." The lawyer hung up.

Carson pretended a friendlier farewell with a dead receiver. He closed his flip-phone and reentered the salon. "Sorry about that. You were saying, Mr. Spooner?"

"Reverend, maybe you should read this." Jesse reopened his laptop. He clicked on a news article describing Congolese atrocities. As Carson read, his eyes grew another rim around their sockets. His Adam's apple bobbed. Jesse watched him with cynical amusement. The salient points in the article were as follows:

Untold horrors are taking place in the *Ituri Forest*. Cannibalism is as prevalent as any time in Congo's history.

Many of the displaced refugees were reporting that rebel fighters are capturing and eating forest-dwelling pygmies. Some say their flesh confers magical powers. Sex organs are the preferred delicacy.

The summary reported additional accounts of unbridled cruelty, massacres, genocide, and reports of human beings being hunted down and eaten like farm animals.

Even though Jesse wasn't in a particularly good mood, he couldn't help smiling at the fear in Carson's eyes. "As I said, Congo isn't for the faint-hearted. The only difference is, now, the cannibals have Kalashnikovs."

"I had no idea. Why I could never expose my wife to such godless savages." Carson kissed his wife, long and hard. Maria swooned. Their display was so stomach-churning, Jesse turned his back. "We will do as you recommend, Mr. Spooner. But we are all in God's hands."

Heeding Jesse's warning, the Carsons agreed to forego their trip to Africa; at least that's what they told Jesse. Truth be known, Reverend Carson had no intention of letting anyone get between him and ten million dollars. They discussed logistics over the next two hours. Carson invited Jesse to join them for dinner, which he declined.

After they were gone, Jesse breathed a sigh of relief. He let the circumstances of the meeting move through his mind.

As he watched them walk down the pier, he felt the sudden urge to bathe. Beyond the obvious, there was something about Ray Carson that made him queasy. He felt like he was missing something right in front of him. Unconsciously, he wiped his hands on his shirt. Jesse Spooner fished the money out of his pocket and sniffed it.

*** 

As Jesse prepared to leave for Africa, two things happened that made him even more apprehensive about his involvement with Reverend Carson. This first incident was a letter he received from James Cheatham's lawyer. In the letter, the lawyer stated that in accordance with his client's final wishes, he had transferred funds to a bank account in the Advans Banque in *Kisangani*, Congo. Jesse was at liberty to withdraw the money, but only in person. The lawyer also revealed that a sealed letter addressed to Jesse Spooner from James Cheatham was at the bank. It was as if Cheatham had anticipated Jesse's hesitancy.

The second event was a late-night telephone conversation with a man who claimed affiliation with Global Security. The caller, Reed Cunningham, knew that Jesse had worked with Cheatham in central Africa. He asked Jesse if he was interested in rejoining Globa. Jesse told the caller that his charter business required his full-time attention. And besides, he hated international travel. The man laughed. When Jesse pressed him on his position, he became evasive.

Then Cunningham asked if he knew the circumstances surrounding James Cheatham's last Congo assignment. Jesse admitted knowing about the robbery. The caller claimed that millions in cash and the rare earth minerals were still missing. Jesse professed ignorance, which wasn't exactly true. In closing, Cunningham said something that Jesse found peculiar. The man stated that his company had posted a reward. And that Jesse should consider pursuing the reward money. Although Reed Cunningham didn't say that he knew Jesse was leaving for central Africa, Jesse sensed he knew. The question was how he knew. The call ended.

Fifteen minutes later, Mr. Cunningham called back. "Say, Mr. Spooner, would it be possible to charter your fishing boat tomorrow?"

"I don't see why not."

"What's her name, and where is she moored?"

Jesse thought about turning him down, but the call intrigued him. "The *Omo* is docked at the Oceanside Marina on Stock Island. Can you get here by seven?" Jesse asked, hoping the answer was no.

"See you then." The man hung up.

\*\*\*

The next morning as Jesse checked the engines' fluids, he felt the boat roll slightly and knew someone had stepped on board. He stuck his head out of the engine hatch, "I see you made it."

Cunningham spoke with disarming cordiality. "I wouldn't miss this for the world. It looks like we've got glorious weather." He tried to shake hands, but Jesse's hand was oily. They fist-bumped.

"We'll get underway as soon as my mate shows up if he shows up. It depends on how much he drank last night."

"Say, I was wondering where you got her name?"

"Omo is a soap powder made in England. During the war, English housewives having affairs with American servicemen used to put a box of Omo in their kitchen windows. It stood for old-man-out. It's a double entendre.

I'm an old man gone fishing."

"How original."

The mate showed up, notwithstanding a lethal hangover. They departed the Oceanside Marina. Jesse steered his Hatteras between the last set of channel markers and set a course for deeper water. He pushed the throttles forward, letting the Omo accelerate to 20-knots.

One hour later, the water changed from pea-green to dark-blue as they skirted the edge of the Gulfstream. Jesse climbed from the flying bridge up into the tuna tower. It was his refuge beyond the reach of customers. From this vantage point, he looked down at Cunningham with a twinge of irritation. The wire-rimmed glasses perched on the tip of a waspy nose. He carried himself with an air of superiority. You work for the State Department or the CIA. Another Ivy League asshole, Jesse, observed bitterly.

The ocean was glossy. But gradually, the tradewinds generated rolling swells. The bow-wake frightened flying fish; they scattered away on silver-tipped transparent wings, dipped their tails for propulsion gliding out of danger, and then plunged under tangles of orange seaweed. Seagulls hovered over the weed-lines. A man-of-war bird patrolled high above the gulls, hoping to steal their dinner.

Jesse was surprised when his customer managed to climb up into the tuna tower. "What a stunning view," he said, holding on for dear life.

Jesse said nothing. His mind was too active for speech. Finally, he said, "Mr. Cunningham, I'm guessing you're not interested in deep-sea fishing." He eased back the throttles allowing the Hatteras to slow down to trolling speed. He motioned to the mate to put out the baits. The mate let out a rigged ballyhoo on one side and a mullet on the other. He attached both fishing lines to the outriggers. The baits skipped on the surface.

"Something tells me you work for the government, Mr. Cunningham."

"Is it that obvious?"

"What branch?" Jesse asked, scanning the horizon with his binoculars.

"My employer's second commandment is uncertainty?" Cunningham said.

"What agency?" Jesse asked.

"I can't remember. That's their first commandment."

"If you're selling cloak-and-dagger, I'm not a buyer," Jesse said. "What do you want from me?"

"Okay. First of all, we know about your upcoming trip to central Africa."

"How did you find me?"

"How we found you isn't relevant."

"It is for me. I worked for ATF for eighteen years. We didn't part on friendly terms."

"Come hard-over, Captain Spooner, you're heading into dangerous waters.'"

When Jesse didn't respond, Cunningham knew he would have to tell him more. "At any rate, you worked for Global Security, for what, five years?"

"More like six."

"What makes you think we didn't invent Global? Sometimes we need separation, for the use of a better term. Companies like Global afford us barriers in delicate situations."

Jesse studied him thinking separation means fucking up people with impunity. "Why are we having this conversation? What do you want?"

"We, by we, I mean the United States government has a problem. Our strategic interests in Africa are threatened. China would like to minimize our influence. Congo is a smorgasbord of natural resources. The Chinese government is trying to prevent us from having a seat at that table. We need to know who inside the Congolese government is being paid by the Chinese Communist Party. It's a matter of national security. We'd like you to be our eyes and ears. And we're willing to pay you, handsomely, I might add."

"The last time I heard those words, I damned near got killed. My government sent me to Sudan. Directed by nameless people with a delicate situation, I might add," said Jesse sardonically.

Cunningham wiped the beads of sweat from his brow and yawned, both signs of seasickness. "Mr. Spooner, I appeal to you as a patriot. We need your help." He belched painfully.

"Not before you tell me how you got my name."

Cunningham appeared conflicted, but he knew he faced an impasse. "As a former government insider of sorts, I'm sure you know we enlist sophisticated listening techniques. We monitor international telephone conversations. Our software highlights catchwords or phrases. Are you following me so far?"

Jesse lied. "You lost me."

"Over the last few months, you've received several overseas telephone calls from a gentleman residing in Zimbabwe, Africa. If memory serves, the man's name is Croxford. In those conversations, you mentioned James Cheatham. Cheatham worked for us, albeit indirectly. I'm guessing the words, Cheatham, Congo, and Global Security in the same exchange triggered closer scrutiny by one of our analysts."

"Fool that I am. I thought snooping on my private conversations was a violation of my constitutional rights."

"Would you believe me if I told you we were monitoring Mr. Croxford's conversations?"

Jesse shook his head, doggedly. "Not a chance.

"Didn't think so."

"You must think I'm a fool." Listening techniques, my ass, Jesse thought.

"Look, here's the bottom line. America needs a reliable supply of a certain rare-earth mineral found exclusively in the Congo Basin. China is attempting to exclude us from that procurement. Our national security is at stake, or it will be. Those minerals are essential to the navigational systems of drones and smart bombs. We're talking about saving lives. Navy pilots, to be precise. Jesse, you were a marine."

Jesse frowned, trying to hide his interest. "So, the Congo robbery was more than thieves after ten million bucks."

Cunningham lowered his voice like he was sharing classified intelligence. "Everything points in that direction," he answered with a vagueness that was meant to discourage probing.

Jesse said, "If you want my help, I'll need to know everything. I'd be putting my life on the line. I'm not melodramatic. Congo's a snake-pit."

"First of all, it wasn't ten million. It was fifteen. There was another five million in uncut diamonds. Plus, the minerals, which I'm sure, have been salvaged by now. Look, we're not interested in the money or the minerals. It's all about pinpointing the informant if you get my drift. Did I mention there's a one-million-dollar reward?"

Jesse said, "You've got assets in central Africa who handle delicate situations. Why not use them."

"We have. The last two disappeared. You're going into the belly of the beast using the perfect cover story. No one will suspect you. And you know Congo's inherent risks. You'd be doing your country a great service."

"Patriotism doesn't feed my cat. What's my country willing to do for me?"

"I've been thinking about how we can compensate you. You ended your employment with the ATF two years short of retirement. How about we alter the records. Increase your tenure to twenty years. That way, you'll qualify for a pension." Cunningham scanned Jesse's aging Hatteras. "I'm guessing your vessel could use some TLC."

"Altering my employment records can't be easy."

"As easy as one phone call."

"I'll do this, providing you put the pension deal in writing. Not that I don't trust you."

"Done. One more question. Did James Cheatham ever mention the money?"

"I thought you said your people weren't interested in the money," Jesse said.

"Just curious," Cunningham answered. "Now that we have an agreement, I suggest we head back." Cunningham added, "I'm feeling queasy. Must be something I ate." A stink emanating from the bilge rose like noxious fumes from a sulfurous swamp. The rolling action added to Cunningham's nausea.

Jesse pointed. "See those seagulls. See the fish feeding underneath them. I'm guessing those are yellow-fin tunas. You're lucky. Not often, we catch yellow-fins. I hope you like sushi. Raw red tuna is like steak tartare."

"Mr. Spooner, I'm prepared to pay you for a full day's charter," he said, stifling a painful burp. Cunningham looked like he'd sucked on a rotten egg.

"Why, we've got a whole day ahead of us." Jesse's voice had taken on a torturing quality. "You just need something in your tummy. How does a tuna-fish salad sandwich sound?"

Cunningham barely made it to the cockpit. He fell to his knees and barfed over the gunwale.

Fucking Ivy Leaguer, Jesse reflected happily.

\*\*\*

# CHAPTER SEVEN

## Kisangani

### Thirty miles north of the equator

**Bantu villagers** rebuilt *Mongala* as they had done many times. Violent raids are not unusual in central Africa. After Stanley Obo buried his son, he decided not to return to his village on the *Ubangi* River. There was nothing left for him in *Ugigi*. Any connection to his daughter, Winnie, was in *Mongala*. Stanley's heart, full of hope, sustained him. He ventured into the *Ituri Forest*, searching for his daughter. The criminals who kidnapped her had vanished without a trace. The forest dwellers were so terrified of Mohamed bin Sali; they refused to help him.

In desperation, Stanley begged Captain Pieter for a job on his ferryboat. Motoring up and down the Congo River, he might uncover news about his daughter. Grudgingly, Pieter agreed to hire Stanley. Winnie's abduction had ended Pieter's fantasy of taking her as another wife. Inwardly, he blamed Stanley, and as a result, he mistreated him. Unloading cargo in the sweltering heat was back-breaking, especially for a man with one hand. At night, Stanley huddled under a leaky oilcloth that wasn't immune to the mosquitoes or the rain. Pieter slept with his barrel-shaped wife in a dry cabin. Stanley survived on boiled *cassava*. The captain and his wife gorged on bush-meat and sweet potatoes. If some unknown person had not left food for Stanley, he could have starved.

On this day, Captain Pieter refueled his ferryboat at *Kisangani*, a city half-starved from decades of violence. Here the Congo River is interrupted by Stanley Falls. No birds tweeted, or monkeys gibbered, or dogs barked as in most villages.

Stanley noticed three rail-thin *Bokongo* women standing on the shoreline next to their beached longboat. Two women balanced bundles of charcoal on their heads. The third woman carried an infant on her back. They waved, getting Stanley's attention.

He walked down the gangway and greeted them. Their skins were drawn taut from malnutrition. The mother handed him her glassy-eyed baby. The infant's eyes appeared too large for its shrunken skull. Malaria is as common in Congo as begging for the medicine to cure it. The women offered him charcoal in exchange for the malarial drug. When Stanley declined, the women offered him their bodies. Stanley told them only his captain had the malarial medicine and that he would speak to him.

Stanley approached Pieter. He scoffed, saying he would never waste medicine on a dying *Bokongo* baby. What's more, he didn't need charcoal, and skinny women were not to his liking. Stanley was appealing his captain's refusal when a loud bang from the foredeck distracted him. The crane operator had accidentally dropped a two-hundred-liter fuel drum. The ruptured drum spewed fuel into the scuppers, causing a rainbow-colored oil slick.

Pieter went ballistic. "Waste my bloody fuel, will you. You black ape." He grabbed his knobkerrie and ran from the wheelhouse to the foredeck. The crane operator, anticipating the captain's rage, jumped over the railing.

Pieter took a wild swing with the club and fell on top of the man. The laughing passengers scattered. No riverboat has ever disembarked its occupants as swiftly. Pieter emerged from the water cursing in three different languages.

Stanley used the distraction to slip into the wheelhouse unseen. He was rummaging through the captain's belongings when suddenly it became too dark to see. He spun around and found someone standing in the passageway large enough to eclipse the sunlight and block his escape.

"Thief!" Pieter's wife, Rose, screamed. She lunged at him swinging her balled-up fist like a battering ram. He bobbed right and then left, ducking underneath. She re-cocked her massive arm measuring him.

He shushed her. "Be quiet, woman. I am no thief. I need medicine for a dying baby."

Rose contemplated his remark for a few long seconds. Stanley could feel his heart pounding against his chest. She moved toward him; her fist still clenched. Stanley stepped back against the bulkhead. He held his breath and braced himself. Slowly, the woman's scowl amended into a warm smile. She closed the cabin door and placed her finger on her lips. Stanley exhaled.

After rifling through the ship's medical chest, she handed him some pills. "Give the baby one-half of a pill for three days. Go before he sees us. He will only beat me, but he will kill you. Walk in God's shoes. Go well, my friend." Stanley kissed her hand. She patted his head like a Catholic nun rewarding a well-behaved child. They both appeared puzzled by the unexpected flicker of attraction they felt for each other. Stanley grabbed his knapsack and ran down the starboard gangway. Pieter's wife used her hips to block the view of his escape.

The women on the shoreline heard the commotion and realized Stanley was making a run for it. They climbed into their longboat and made ready to cast off. Stanley vaulted over the transom and nearly capsized the boat. They paddled hard until the current swept them away. The sound of the captain's threats carried on the water until they disappeared behind an oxbow.

Pieter burst into the wheelhouse. Rose steeled herself. Brutalizing her always aroused him. "You let him steal my medicine, didn't you? I should have dumped you years ago." He jerked the leather belt from his pants and twisted it tightly around his fist. He came at her swinging like a madman.

She tucked her shirttail into her mouth to protect her teeth and closed her mind. This beating was more brutal than the others. She tried to cover her face, but a blow to her stomach was so powerful, she dropped her guard. A punch to her face jettisoned a compromised tooth. Fueled by sadistic pleasure, the beating escalated. She knew he meant to kill her.

It was either resist or die. Rose slammed her elbow into his temple. The blow staggered him giving her time to reach under the mattress and grab the stiletto hidden there. He saw the knife and gasped, "My compliments, bitch, you just made killing you legal." He came at her intending to strangle her with his belt, but she struck at him with the swiftness of a puff adder, driving the knife deep into his cheekbone. The blade lodged between two molars. He bumped off bulkheads, trying to extricate the knife, but she was on him in a flash, driving the knife deeper into his jawbone. The tables had turned. Pieter was fighting for his life. She blindsided him with a wind-milling knockout punch.

The crew watched her steal their captain's outboard-powered dinghy and did nothing to stop her. The engine coughed and sputtered a few times before coming to life. Rose turned downriver.

***

The shorelines were beginning to lose their clarity. Lightning flashed in silence; some flashes lasted longer than others. The river grew dark, and the sky darker. Stanley and the Bakongo women drifted downriver as the longboat's bow and stern gently traded places throughout the night. It rained nonstop after midnight. When the night sky cleared, it triggered a bullfrog cacophony of high-pitched squeaks and thunderous croaks. Those night-sounds were no match for the mosquitos' harmonic buzz. A sentinel baboon's alarm bark silenced a hooting bay owl. While Stanley and the women slept, their boat came to rest against a mangrove island.

The bulrushes draped motionless, foretelling a pale promise of dawn. Sunrise provided tortuous blood-sucking botflies and swarming gnats. Stanley and the women found relief in the middle of the river, but the wind and waves drove them back to the leeward shoreline.

The baby's fever broke. The fussy infant suckled greedily, but undernourishment had rendered its mother's breasts so stingy, the baby rejected her nipples.

Stanley's pressing issue was how to feed his new family. The only option was to return to *Ugigi*. As the women paddled downriver, Stanley set out a trolling line. Fishing was slow, but he managed to catch two small tiger-fish.

Around midmorning, they beached the dugout on a papyrus fringed island. One woman roasted the fish while the others built a lean-to. Stanley was scavenging the shoreline for turtle eggs when he heard shouting. A large woman in a boat was waving. As the launch drew closer, he recognized Captain Pieter's wife. The woman's face was so swollen; her eyes were reduced to reptilian slits. A missing tooth impaired her speech, but he understood enough to know she had suffered a beating by her husband. He guessed the reason was the missing medicine.

"Thank God, I found you, Mr. Obo." the woman yelled, throwing him the bowline. The women camouflaged the stolen launch under papyrus reeds.

"What shall we call you?" Stanley asked, handing her a dampened rag, which she used to daub her face. Intuitively, he was reluctant to call her Mrs. Pieter.

Her husband's mistreatment had sharpened Rose's tongue. "The *kinuka makundu* called me many names. Rose is my Christian name." Referring to Captain Pieter as a smelly asshole made the women giggle.

Stanley also laughed, slapping his thigh. Rose is a woman to be reckoned with, he ascertained.

When pressed on why she left her husband, she knuckled tears from her eyes. "He has beaten me many times, but this time I knew he wanted to kill me."

Stanley asked, "So, then what happened?" The women pressed forward.

"I cut him," said Rose, making a stabbing motion.

"Good for you," one woman said. The others murmured their approvals.

"Did you kill him?" another woman asked.

"No, but I tried."

"Too bad," Stanley said. The women nodded. "He won't rest until he gets his boat back. We need to find a safe way to return it."

"I paid for this old boat," Rose said, stroking the gunwale.

"How could you pay him?" Stanley asked skeptically.

"He took everything from me, even my *amour propre*."

She pointed at her face. "I would rather die than return it."

Stanley felt inadequate to be in Rose's presence. He found her stoutness eye-catching. One thing was certain: this woman would sweeten the remaining years of a man's life. The problem was feeding her. For the time being, the food shortage was alleviated. Rose had stolen enough food to counterbalance her weight in the longboat. There were enough *cassava*, bananas, and yams to feed an army.

"We are leaving for *Ugigi*. I think you should join us," Stanley said to Rose.

"That would please me," Rose said. And then, out of the blue, she whispered, "I have dreamt about you many times, Mr. Obo. I know you won't rest until you find your daughter. Sometimes, it takes more than one ant to bring down a scorpion. I'm the one who left the food for you."

Her admission shocked him. Stanley was a man of few words, always struggling hard with the difficulties of expressing himself. He hesitated for a second, like a man facing the gallows asking for mercy. When he realized she might misinterpret his feelings, he touched her face. She grabbed his hand and kissed it.

\*\*\*

# CHAPTER EIGHT
## Ituri Forest

The key to Mohamed bin Sali's survival was mobility. Extortion was his criminal niche. The victims included mining companies, isolated villages, and unlucky travelers. Sali stayed one step ahead of the Congolese police by escaping into Uganda or Rwanda. Stealth was equally important as his gang kidnapped, robbed, and raped a bloody swath through the Congo Basin. The extermination of babies born to the gang's sex slaves was a common practice. A crying baby could spoil an ambush or alert pursuing soldiers.

Winnie Obo, who was now sixteen, had been missing for eighteen months. Memories of her past life were so vague she sometimes wondered if they were real. Her existence was a living hell. She was passed between her abductors like a *ganja* pipe, never knowing who she was sleeping with, which sometimes included as many as five men in one night. Death would have been welcomed. After giving birth, she had a reason for living. One month after her baby was born, Winnie was distracted by a gang member demanding sex. When she returned to her tent, she found her baby was missing. Like a lioness protecting her cub from a marauding male lion, there was nothing Winnie could do. She knew her baby had been buried alive like the others. At that moment, Winnie Obo vowed to watch Mohamed bin Sali die.

Sali's band of thugs suffered a defeat at the hands of the Ugandan People's Defense Force. They were chased back across the border. Once again, their depleted ranks were overwhelmed by a Congolese military patrol. Desertions became endemic. In desperation, Sali conscripted young children, who he transformed into cold-blooded killers by forcing them to participate in the vilest atrocities imaginable.

Of the thirty schoolgirls abducted in the raid on the Catholic Academy, only twenty were still alive. Winnie gave up on being rescued. As far as she knew, her father had suffered the same fate as her brother. Her last chance at freedom was to enlist the help of one of her abductors. But as the months dwindled, that option also seemed hopeless.

The flickering light from the campfire leaked into Winnie's tent. She heard drunken laughter and wondered how many men she would have to satisfy before she could sleep. Sali burst into her tent. He pushed a small naked boy with pencil-thin arms and legs forward. She saw the boy's testicles hadn't dropped and guessed he was no more than eight.

Sali growled, "Tonight, I give you Sefu, a virgin. Tomorrow morning, I expect a warrior." He stepped outside and zipped the tent-flap shut. The older gang members shouted vulgar encouragements.

Winnie spoke softly. "Are your parents alive?" Sefu shook his head.

"Is your village near?" He hiked his frail shoulders and dropped his chin against his chest.

"Do you have any memory of your past?" Again, Sefu shook his head. Glistening tears streaked his cheeks. He shivered.

Poor child. What has Sali done to you? Winnie asked herself. She tried to take his hand, but he recoiled. When he yawned, she encouraged him to lie down. Within seconds, he was sleeping.

Over the following weeks, Sefu waited for Winnie to pleasure the older gang members before slipping into her tent to sleep. Little by little, he adopted Winnie as the mother he couldn't remember. Throughout the more difficult nights, she cuddled the orphaned boy ad-libbing cradle songs. If they didn't escape soon, she knew they would both die. At night she spoke to Sefu about running away, but the conversation was one-sided. The unthinkable acts had rendered the boy mute.

\*\*\*

It was the brightest night imaginable, only wispy clouded with a full moon. Moonshine could compromise their escape. But Sali had ordered an ambush on a Congolese military patrol the next day. Older children often used younger gang members as cannon fodder. Winnie was afraid Sefu might be wounded or even killed.

As soon as everyone slept, Winnie and the boy vanished into the night. Sefu, as stealthy as a leopard, ducked underneath the hanging vines and creepers. It seemed like he could see in the dark. Winnie tripped, forced herself up, and tripped again. Thorny plants slashed her legs. Prickly thistles burned her arms. Soon, her running slowed down to a quick trot and then to fast walking. She handed the single-barreled shotgun she'd stolen to Sefu, who slung it over his shoulder.

Both knew the jungle well, but like most Africans, they were superstitious. Venturing in the jungle at night was hair-raising. The light breeze moaned demonic warnings. Shadows turned trees into towering ghouls. Hooting owls spoke the language of the dead. They followed the animal trails, occasionally stopping to listen for danger. The night wore on.

They were startled by a loud pop. Sefu stopped dead in his tracks. Winnie bumped into him. After a few fearful seconds, Sefu recognized the sound as a foraging elephant. They were close enough to hear the animal's stomach grumble. They gave it a wide berth and moved on. The jungle sounds increased with sunrise. A leopard's guttural cough quieted a squawking grey parrot. Sefu found a hide in the pleated sinews of a giant strangler fig tree. After making leaf-beds, both succumbed to dreamless sleeping.

Sefu woke up staring at the copper-colored snake slithering over Winnie's foot. He recognized the boa constrictor as harmless and was too exhausted to move. He snuggled up to Winnie and closed his eyes.

Around midday, Winnie was awakened by what she feared was a baboon spider crawling on her face. Sunbeams dancing through the fig tree branches blinded her. She shaded her eyes and thought she was looking at Sefu, but she found him sleeping next to her. A Lilliputian sized native, shorter than Sefu, had been tickling her nose with a grass stem. Her scream startled his companion; he jumped forward, menacing her with a drawn arrow. The pygmies appeared agitated. They conversed in a high-pitched dialect. Winnie tried Swahili before switching to *Lingala* to calm them. Sharpened teeth made them look like miniature vampires. Decorative tattoos adorned their distended bellies. The pygmies wore only loin clothes fashioned from monkey skins. They were knobby-kneed, their feet calloused.

Sefu, who hadn't uttered a sound in months, became talkative. When he mentioned Mohamed bin Sali, the pygmy hunters appeared terrified. He handed them the stolen shotgun as a peace offering. They squatted like grasshoppers, clapping their hands and then opening them as a sign of gratitude. Sefu spit into their outstretched hands, one at a time. The pygmies wiped Sefu's saliva into their eyes. Not only did they recognize Sefu's tribe, they believed his clan possessed magical powers and that his spit was medicinal.

Winnie followed Sefu, who fell in behind the pygmies.

They marched for hours. The canopy thickened until almost no light shone through the treetops. Winnie fretted. Did pointy teeth mean they were cannibals? Are we to be eaten like bush-meat?

"Sefu, where are they taking us?" she asked, lowering her voice.

Sefu picked his nose thoughtfully, an African peculiarity of concentration. "They mean us no harm, mama."

They scaled higher into the base of clouds. The light was failing, and the vegetation changed. It grew bone-chilling cold. Watery mist moistened the ground, which made the footing slippery. Winnie struggled to breathe. She slipped and fell repeatedly. Frustrated by Winnie's progress, one pygmy offered her some crushed leaves, which Winnie chewed on. Within seconds she felt life returning to her legs. Her heart-rate slowed, and her breathing improved. Renewed, Winnie picked up her pace.

They were now just above a cloud layer. Suddenly, the lead pygmy stopped dead in his tracks. Both pygmies looked terrified. Something dark rustled in the underbrush. Winnie saw a large black shape darting in and out of the shadows. The ear-piercing thunderous thumping was followed by the sounds of tree limbs snapping. Whatever it was came at them in a blur. A mountain gorilla burst into the clearing, making deep resonating snorts. He stopped, leaned forward on his massive arms, and glared at them with red eyes. They had wandered into the silverback's territory. Without hesitating, they backtracked. The gorilla swaggered away. The silence returned, as did Winnie's breathing.

Just before nightfall, the mountain trail was interrupted by a deep ravine. The raging river below produced a rumbling roar. The pygmies scaled a felled-tree spanning the gorge. Sefu followed them over, but Winnie looked down and froze. A slip meant certain death. Sefu ran back across and took her hand, but she refused to move. Winnie sat on the ground, pulled her knees up under her chin, and closed her eyes. The pygmies had transported heavy objects over the gorge many times. They constructed a makeshift litter built from two bamboo poles interlaced with crisscrossing vines. Their homemade gurney was ready, but Winnie wanted no part of it. Sefu, acting as a guinea pig, allowed them to carry him across the deep expanse and then back again.

Winnie wasn't impressed. "Leave me alone," she mumbled shivering.

Sefu tried to encourage her. "You must, mama. They say Sali is following us."

"You are a great liar. That devil never leaves the safety of his campfire at night," she said.

The same pygmy who gave her the herbs offered her some seeds, which she swallowed. The grinning pygmy tugged on his chin whiskers. Instantly, her tongue felt thick and numb. Within a few minutes, she had no feeling in her legs, and her arms hung lifeless. Ignoring her threats, they rolled her onto the litter and ran across the slippery log like squirrels. Halfway over, one of them staggered, pretending to lose his balance. They found Winnie's shrieking hilarious.

On the other side, Winnie stood up wobbly. She was too relieved to scold them.

The pygmies' village was a short walk from the gorge. The sun disappeared, leaving no afterglow in the forest. Flickering light from a cooking fire illuminated curious faces. A smoke-blackened pot hung over glowing embers. Conical grass-huts centered the clearing. Pot-bellied children played with an emaciated monkey. When the children saw Winnie, they ran to their mothers for protection. Women with deflated breasts stared at Winnie and Sefu as if they were from another planet. Colorful beads ornamented the women's foreheads. The men, mesmerized by the shotgun, paid them little attention.

# THE CONGO AFFAIR

No humans have been as mistreated as pygmies. They are considered subhuman in the Congo Basin. The *Bantu* often keep pygmies as pets. Because their average life span is only twenty years, evolution has granted pygmies a rapid growth rate. Everyone in the village was the same size. Winnie was a head taller. Even Sefu was slightly larger.

The weeks passed slowly. Winnie's memories of her life at the Catholic mission were so distant they seemed like dreams. Gradually, Winnie established herself with the pygmies. She found them to be generous and caring. But she was a part of a bigger world and knew it was only a matter of time before she would leave their mountain refuge. Avenging her baby's death was never far from her thoughts.

The flirtations of the tribal leader became problematic. He was smitten over Winnie, smothering her with gifts of flowers and food. She worried about rejecting him. Marrying a pygmy was not her idea of marital bliss. And then one night, Winnie and Sefu disappeared. The rejected pygmy was heartbroken. His four wives were euphoric.

***

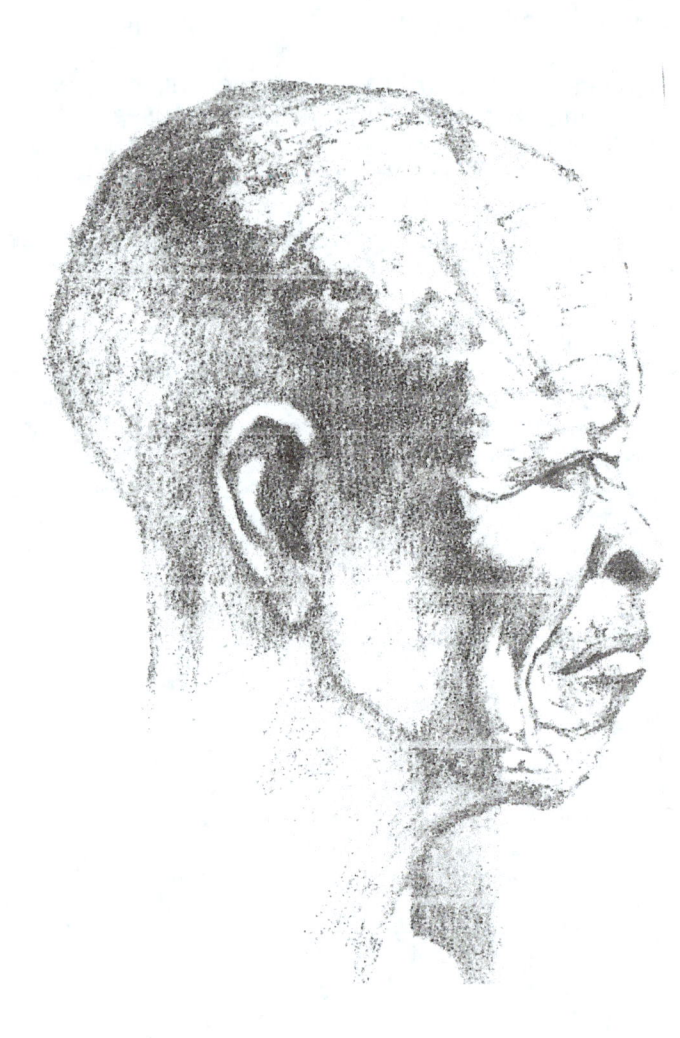

# CHAPTER NINE

## Zimbabwe

**Rigby met** Jesse Spooner's South African Airways flight at the Victoria Falls Airport. The plan was to drive to *Msuna Island*, where they could borrow a pontoon boat and travel downriver to his friend, Otto Bern's mountain retreat overlooking the Zambezi River. Otto had lived in Africa longer than anyone could remember. Bern's experience in central Africa was unparalleled. Picking his brain could prove helpful. More importantly, keeping Jesse and Christine separated was prudent, given her recent outburst. Rigby had promised that if Jesse's undertaking sounded too dangerous, he would pass. His daughter said she believed him, but deep-down, Christine knew that come hell or high water, her father was going to central Africa with Jesse.

As Rigby drove to *Msuna*, Jesse discussed his failed marriage and his new life in Key West. Rigby talked about his daughter, but he resisted mentioning his wife's passing. They recounted their past adventures together. Finally, Jesse outlined the Congo assignment and his relationship with James Cheatham.

As Rigby talked, Jesse studied him. His short hair was graying at the temples. He had uncompromised teeth and a bronzed tan. Decent teeth are a rarity for white Africans. Hard-earned muscles resisted his worn khaki safari jacket. The crow's feet have deepened, but overall, he hadn't aged one iota, Jesse thought.

"Croxford, you don't look a day older. What's your secret?

"Cheap whiskey and sexual abstinence."

"I'll pass on the last one," Jesse said. They both laughed.

When they ran out of things to say, Jesse said, "I want you to know how much I cared for Helen. She was special."

"Helen was very fond of you, Jesse. Always thought a wounded animal or a pissed off native would finish me. I've had every tropical disease known. Life expectancy for a mercenary is five years. I've been at it for ten. Rumors of my impending death persist, I reckon. Never imagined Helen would go first."

It was clear that Rigby didn't want to continue. Jesse changed the topic. "So, how're things in Zimbabwe?"

"Well, let me see. I'd say someplace between appalling and catastrophic."

"It can't be that bad."

"We have ninety percent of our population unemployed. Our currency has collapsed. In one year, we had an inflation rate of—get this, eighty-six billion percent. We have more Chinese living here than baboons. Without American charities, we would all starve to death. Beyond that, everything's rosy."

"My God, I had no idea. Maybe things will get better."

"Now, you sound like my daughter. Just remember,

Zimbabwe's a fucking mess, but   compared to Congo, it's bloody Switzerland."

Jesse changed the subject again. "So, how's Otto Bern? I remember him as a cantankerous old coot."

"You won't believe how little Otto's changed."

A few words about Otto Bern:  Otto was a mercenary slash bush-pilot with nine lives. He lost his left leg below the knee to a landmine and two fingers of his right hand to a venomous Gaboon viper. Friends said Africa was whittling on Otto like termites eating a *Mopani* stump. He had flown clandestine missions in and out of African war zones for sixty years. Otto once worked as Congolese President Laurent-Desire Kabila's helicopter pilot. He quit one month before Kabila was assassinated, which undoubtedly saved his life. Otto's flying resume was replete with many close calls. He lived alone with a vervet monkey. The last of his five wives left him because of what most people viewed as bizarre behavior. Visitors sometimes found him sunbathing in the nude, with the monkey happily picking dead skin from his private parts. Another motivating factor for divorcing Otto was his fondness for spirits.

\*\*\*

Their pontoon-boat kissed the shoreline jetty.   Otto Bern's houseboy, driving a dilapidated, roofless Land Rover, met them. Rigby waved up at Otto, who looked down at them from his hilltop retreat.

After negotiating hair-raising switchbacks, they found Otto with his pet monkey perched on his shoulder, standing in front of the bungalow. He wore repaired steel-rimmed spectacles, which gave his head a lopsided appearance. He was tall and thin. A once muscular physique had suffered from countless battles with malaria and overindulgence. His sapphire-colored eyes were still piercing.

"Afternoon, Otto.  You remember Jesse Spooner?"

"Indeed. Flew you out the Darfur, wasn't it?" Otto said. Liver spots covered his hands, but the grip was ironclad. "I know I played a minor role, but defeating those camel jockeys was brilliant. What a dazzling piece of soldiering. I felt like Lord Kitchener retaking Khartoum."

"What's his name?" Jesse said, referring to the monkey.

"He's a she, and her name's Scarlet. Better company than my two last wives. Not as talkative, and she doesn't cut the cheese as much. She's a jealous little bitch. An older woman shows up–Scarlet's fine with it. But if a young lady comes around, she attacks her straightaway. They're more human than you'd expect. Aren't you, sweetheart?" Otto said to Scarlet using baby-talk. The monkey hugged Otto's neck.

Rigby said, "Otto, we've got a business opportunity in central Africa. We were hoping you could lend us your expertise."

"Where in central Africa, may I ask?" Otto inquired, stroking Scarlet's tail.

"Congo," Jesse said.

Otto fell into a deep recollection. "I only think of Congo when I defecate. It has beastly weather, hideous diseases, and the most barbaric tribes in Africa. It's a shithole, to put it mildly." He tapped on his hollow artificial leg, saying, "Part of me is buried there."

"Landmine?" Jesse asked.

Otto nodded. "Whatever you're up to, I'd drop it straightaway."

"I'm afraid it's too late for that," Jesse said.

"Rigby, for God's sake, tell him I know of what I speak. You fought there twice if I'm not mistaken. Why I wouldn't go back for a million bucks." Otto raised his hands, making parenthesis marks with his fingers. "End of story."

"Jesse has worked in central Africa before. And he's committed," Rigby said.

"You ask for my advice, and then you ignore it. It's never simple with you, Croxford. Come, let's have our sundowners." Otto's tone exposed mild exasperation.

They followed him into a chalet constructed from roughhewn granite blocks. The high-beamed roof was grass-thatched. Animal horns and bookshelves decorated the walls. Black and white photographs showed Otto standing next to vintage military aircraft. The veranda overlooking the Zambezi River contained a swimming pool fed by a human-made waterfall. A large cage housed tweeting African love birds. Flowering, white and red bougainvillea framed the sunset. A servant took their drink orders.

Jesse gushed, "Otto, your home's magnificent."

"We like it." Otto indicated, including Scarlet. The monkey sipped Chardonnay from a dish. "Here's something that might interest you." He picked up what looked like a dark brown soup bowl from the fireplace mantel and handed it to Jesse. "This was sold to me as the *Mahdi's* skullcap presented to Kitchener as an inkwell. Retribution for killing General Gordon, I hazard. They say Kitchener was appalled. I find it quite lovely."

Spooner examined the skullcap, holding it up to the light. "Think it's authentic?"

"Found it in an antiquity shop in *Omdurman*. I'm sure it's a fake, but the story's amusing. Bloody towel-heads."

Otto marches to a different drummer, Jesse thought.

"Now then, let's discuss this Congo business," said Otto.

Jesse outlined his meeting with Reverend Carson and the missing Congolese schoolgirls. Otto listened intently, occasionally interrupting to ask questions. Finally, he said, "This wanker, Carson, sounds a bit dodgy to me. I'm skeptical about your entire undertaking. Things don't add up. Congo has become very dangerous. I haven't been there in five years, but I hear it's gone downhill if that's possible. You need to be very cautious. Anyway, you two know the ropes."

"Have you ever been to the *Ituri* region?" Jesse asked

"Many times. Dropped napalm on the rebels, the last time." Otto seemed oblivious to any guilt. "I hold the record for flight time. Seventeen-thousand hours."

Jesse said, "Seventeen thousand can't be a record."

"Sorry, I meant combat hours. Hell, anybody can fly an airplane. Flying with people shooting at you, now that's aviating, at its best."

Jesse said, "I read there are still cannibals in the *Ituri*."

Otto smiled. "All I can say is…, it didn't taste like chicken."

Jesse added, "Not even with fava beans and a nice Chianti?"

"A bit stringy, as I recall. Before you pass judgment, just remember starving is what Africans do best. There's a Congolese saying, he who lives by the river shall never starve, which is absolute rubbish. The explorer, Sir Henry Stanley, faced dreadful diseases and hostile natives, but what he feared most was starvation. There's simply nothing to eat. Another English explorer, John Speke, participated in a ceremonial dinner, which featured a roasted child as the main course. The natives eat chimps and monkeys. Humans aren't that much of a stretch. I partook on a dare. Enough said about that. Don't want to upset my sweet Scarlet. She's thin-skinned about eating monkeys."

Jesse swallowed hard when he realized Otto wasn't joking.

Rigby, who knew Otto was telling the truth, seemed tickled by Jesse's revulsion.

"Say, Croxford, I finished your book on Richard Burton–a marvelous life. Burton had none of the virtues I detest and all of the vices I admire, except his diddling into homosexuality. He despised Victorian society, which I find laudable."

Jesse looked perplexed. "Richard Burton was gay?"

Rigby elucidated. "Sir Richard Francis Burton, the English explorer. Not the drunken actor married to Elizabeth Taylor."

"I'm an idiot," said Jesse swallowing hard.

Otto continued. "Excluding Charles Darwin and Sir Isaac Newton, Burton might have been the smartest Englishman who ever lived. Spoke twenty-nine languages—translated the Kama Sutra and Arabian Nights. Burton authored dozens of books. He was with Speke when he discovered the source of the Nile. Down with malaria when Speke made the final push. Bloody shame, if you ask me. As far as I know, he was the only non-Muslim to visit Mecca and live to tell about it. Burton memorized the Quran and his Arabic so fluent–he corrected Bedouins' diction. A rather complex personality, to say the least."

Jesse held up his wine glass. "Peace be to Burton's ashes. And glory to his memory."

"Here, here," Otto added.

Rigby interrupted them, "Back on point. Let's assume we're going ahead. Who's your best contact?"

Otto remained silent as the name played hide-and-seek. "Damn it–the name is on the tip of my tongue." His face registered a flash of recognition as the name drifted into view. "Now, I remember. There's a Belgian national operating a tramp-steamer on the Congo River. He's the kind of man who would crawl over his dying sister to fornicate with his dead mother. Trusting him could get you killed. Get my drift?"

"Not a ringing endorsement," stated Rigby between sips of a gin and tonic.

"A nasty piece of work," Otto added.

"Any chance we can trust him?"

"Frankly, no. Nickolas Pieter interrogated prisoners during the last Congo war. They say he rather enjoyed his work. And that none of the prisoners survived. Anyway, having warned you, Captain Pieter is the best-connected intelligence source on that Godforsaken river. You just need to be cautious, that's all I'm saying. He'll rat you out for a few extra francs in a heartbeat."

The afternoon wind in Zimbabwe is unique. One minute it can blow hard enough to slam doors or spawn dust-devils, and then without warning, you can hear an insect buzzing. Jesse waited for some bamboo wind-chimes to stop clacking.

"Otto, what's the worst thing you ever witnessed in central Africa?"

Blood drained from Otto's face. His grouchiness was overlapped by sadness. "Well, I..." He was too overcome to speak. Sensing his distress, Scarlet began to groom Otto's thin goatee. He pushed her away. "Not now, sweetheart."

"I shouldn't have asked," Jesse said.

"You needn't apologize. I've never mentioned what I'm about to tell you to a living soul. I guess I was afraid of the consequences. That's the only good thing about growing old. You just don't give a shit." Otto drained his whiskey and shuddered when it struck bottom. He stared at nothing, but his eyes said he was reopening a troubled time in his life. He withdrew within himself for a few more tense moments.

"If it upsets you, don't go there," Jesse reiterated.

Otto popped out of his trance. "I recall flying a B-26 bomber for the Congolese government in the Great Congo War. After flying several sorties, I was being escorted back to my barracks by a bodyguard. A roadblock staffed by two soldiers waylaid us. Twelve children, accused of being related to rebel sympathizers, had been impaled on wooden stakes driven up their rectums. They were barely alive. One small child cried out for mercy. At that moment, I knew there was only one way to end their suffering. That's when I decided to play God. I grabbed my bodyguard's AK and shot each child, killing them one at a time. When the soldiers and my bodyguard complained, I killed them too."

Otto fell silent again. His mind was no longer there; he was reliving the incident. Finally, he said, "Told the authorities, we were ambushed. Reckon, that was the worst day of my life. I left Congo one week later. As I said, I've never talked about what happened. Embarrassed, I guess."

"In what way?" Rigby said, adding, "Given the circumstances, what else could you have done?"

"You know...," Otto said, "I've never thought about it in those terms."

"I would've handled it the same way," Rigby said.

"Croxford, you've been a mate of mine for more years than I can remember. We've been to hell and back together. Like I said, Congo's a fucking mess. Something tells me you've already made up your mind. When do you leave?"

"In two days. Our search starts in *Kisangani*," replied Rigby.

"If God wanted to give the world an enema, He would insert the nozzle in *Kisangani*. Good luck, you're damn sure going to need it. All this talk about cannibals has made me hungry. Dinner is served, gentlemen." Otto laughed. "You look somewhat piqued, Mr. Spooner. Not to worry. My cook has prepared sautéed Zambezi bream and sweet potatoes. Congolese food is vile. Just think, this could be your last decent meal until you return if you return."

They moved to the dining room. Otto moved as fast as his artificial leg allowed. He sat down and removed his prosthesis. Rubbing the stump radiated his pleasure. The table was candlelit. The houseboy poured a sampling of Sauvignon Blanc for Otto's approval, which he gave. He refilled Scarlet's wine dish.

"Otto, I must say, your optimism is most reassuring," said Rigby sarcastically.

"You both understand the need for caution. Vigilance is the key to surviving Africa, always has been. Pay close attention to your surroundings, gentlemen. I wouldn't trust the locals if I were you. They'll be out to rob you or kill you or eat you. Enough said. I'm rambling."

"They can't all be bad," Jesse interjected.

"Misplaced trust can get you killed, Mr. Spooner," said Otto. "You asked for my counsel. Now, you have it."

Rigby said, "Listen up, Jesse, to the intellectual droppings of the wisest man in Africa."

"Croxford, you're a dreadful exaggerator."

"Modesty is such a vastly overrated virtue, Otto. Bottoms up, gentlemen."

Otto raised his glass. "In victory, we desire it. In defeat, we need it. Here's to victory."

# THE CONGO AFFAIR

Jesse toasted, "Here's to the god of vices."

Otto said, "I'll certainly drink to that. Although unlike Mr. Burton, my vices these days are all nonsexual. Regretfully, that's a curse you two can look forward to."

They ended the evening by singing, 'God save the Queen' so out of tune, they terrified Scarlet. She sought refuge in her cage.

They laughed and clicked glasses.

# CHAPTER TEN

## Congo

### Kisangani

**A tattered** Congolese flag hung flaccidly from the terminal building. *Kisangani* Airport was grungy. Jesse and Rigby wore threadbare clothes in an attempt not to draw attention. Little had changed during Rigby's ten-year absence. The mayhem that greeted the disembarking passengers was a seething mob of self-appointed baggage handlers, pickpockets, counterfeit moneychangers, and water-sellers.

An ink-black dwarf approached Rigby as they stood in the Congolese immigration and customs queue. "You give me twenty U.S. dollars. I get you through this line in a jiffy. I know these guys," the dwarf whispered in broken English. Rigby shook his head.

When he attempted to grab Jesse's passport, Rigby seized his chubby hand, growling, "*kutomba mbali.*" The dwarf appeared shocked by Rigby telling him to 'fuck off' in Swahili. He repeated his sales-pitch to a better-dressed gentleman standing behind Jesse. Rigby warned the passenger. "Sir, I wouldn't give him your passport if I were you. These people have larceny in their veins." The black dwarf evil-eyed Rigby. Undeterred, he moved on and tried again with another unsuspecting passenger.

*Kisangani*, formerly Stanleyville, is a port city in decline. The outskirts have surrendered to the tropical rainforest. Before Congo gained independence from Belgium in 1960, *Kisangani* was reputed to have had more Rolls-Royces per capita than any city in the world. Continuous warring has atrophied *Kisangani*. It's a city of farting motor scooters, pedal-cabs, and overstuffed buses with suitcases and crates stacked on the roofs. Most structures need painting, which gives the city an overall grimy patina. The brick buildings constructed in the 1950s are crumbling and pockmarked by bullet holes. Thatch and banana leaves cover the broken doors and windows. Women picked through smoldering garbage heaps. On the edge of town stands the shell of an old brick cathedral, with intricate Italian marble flooring and pews constructed from cinder blocks under rotting wooden planks. A painting of a dark-skinned Jesus covers one wall. It's a city evolved from grotesque wealth to crushing poverty.

Rigby and Jesse presented their passports to a customs officer sitting behind a metal desk. He wore a starched khaki uniform and designer sunglasses. The officer scanned their passports, sucked on his lower lip, and shook his head disdainfully. "Where are your international vaccination certificates, gentlemen?" He frowned.

Rigby wondered for a moment and then replied, "What are you talking about?"

"Trying to enter this country without proper vaccinations is a serious crime. You, of all people, should know the rules. I see you're an African." The officer acted like they had committed murder. He snapped his fingers. Two armed policemen stepped forward.

\*\*\*

African jails are nefarious. In most cases, if a prisoner's

family or fellow inmates cannot provide food, an inmate could starve to death. *Kisangani*'s jail was incredibly bleak. Belgians constructed it as a temporary holding pen '*barracoon*' for captured slaves awaiting transfer to the coast. The windowless walls were covered by green moss growing over ancient graffiti. The dirt floor, moistened by decades of urine, was as hard as concrete. Rats and cockroaches were considered food-sources. The tin-roof magnified by the equatorial sun turned the prison into a pizza oven. During the hotter months, the more weakened prisoners were sometimes baked alive.

Rigby and Jesse were befriended by fellow inmates who shared their food, cigarettes, and the accounts of their innocence. A chorus of coughing and snoring made sleeping a challenge. Morning wake-up calls were the wailings from the local Islamic mosque. On the third day of their incarceration, the black dwarf showed up. After berating Rigby for his rudeness at the airport, he arranged their release by bribing the jailer.

\*\*\*

The dwarf accompanied them to a doctor's office. The black physician wore a white lab coat soiled by cigarette ashes. He was hatchet-faced with a stethoscope hanging from his neck. Curiously, he was barefooted.

"So, I understand you gentlemen are in need of yellow fever vaccinations?" the doctor inquired, peering over the top of his half-moons. He had a cigarette dangling from the corner of his mouth. Smoke made his eyes water.

"Yes, that's right," Rigby replied.

"What about typhus?" he asked, squinting.

"I guess so."

"And polio boosters."

"Why not," said Jesse.

"Will there be extra charges, doctor?" Rigby inquired.

"Sir, I am a man of healing, not a thief." He appeared shocked by the insinuation.

The doctor disappeared. When he reappeared, he had two yellow cards with the appropriate vaccination stamps. "That's three-hundred American dollars for me plus another fifty for my assistant," said the doctor acknowledging the dwarf. Jesse paid them. The doctor handed over the certificates.

Rigby and Jesse rolled up their sleeves.

The doctor said, "Oh, I don't give the shots. We just sell the cards. We haven't had proper vaccines in this country for over ten years. Thank you, gentlemen. I hope you enjoy your stay in *Kisangani*."

"Welcome home, Jesse," Rigby said.

"Only in Africa," added Jesse.

After thanking the dwarf, they hired a taxicab. They paid tolls to men impersonating traffic cops at two intersections. The men were raggedly dressed, but they wore official-looking orange vests. Congolese police officers are freelance entrepreneurs.

At one time, their hotel might have been first-class, but the years have not been kind. After booking adjoining rooms for security, Rigby headed to the riverfront to make inquiries while Jesse visited the bank.

\*\*\*

# THE CONGO AFFAIR

The bank manager wore an ill-fitting rumpled suit. His shoes were in desperate need of a shine.

"*Raphael Mutombo*, at your service, sir," he announced, thrusting out his perspiring hand. Nasal French tainted his English. He had jug-handle ears and a face scarred from acne.

"I'm Jesse Spooner. If I'm not mistaken, I have an account here, and you have a letter for me."

"Certainly, sir. May I see your passport, Mr. Spooner?" The manager scrutinized Jesse's passport. "I see you're an American.

What is the purpose of your visit?"

Jesse ignored his snooping. "I'd like to see that letter."

"Very well, Mr. Croxford. I hope you will consider keeping your account with Advans Banque."

Jesse gave him a cautious stare. "What's the account balance?"

Mutombo tugged on his large earlobe. "Perhaps, you require privacy. Can I offer you my office, sir?"

"No thanks," Jesse said, taking a seat.

The manager retrieved a brown manila envelope from his desk. "Your balance, including last month's interest, comes to one- hundred and nine-thousand. That's in American dollars, of course. I can get you an up-to-date figure if you wish?"

Jesse tried to appear calm, but the amount staggered him. "That won't be..." His voice cracked slightly. He cleared it with a cough and tried again. "That won't be necessary. I want you to include this man's name on the account." Jesse handed him a slip of paper. "With the right of survivorship, naturally. Something happens to me-it's his. Something happens to him-it's mine. Please have the documents drafted. Now, how about the letter?"

"At once, Mr. Spooner. Is Mr. Croxford an American?" He handed him a sealed manila folder, which Jesse tore open. Someone has resealed this, he thought. He put the notion to bed before it crystallized.

"He's a citizen of Zimbabwe. Is there a problem?"

"No problem. Is Mr. Croxford here in *Kisangani*?"

Jesse dismissed the question with an impatient wave. "Say, I'm a little pressed for time." You're a nosey son-of-a-bitch, he thought.

"My bank requires his signature. I'm just doing my job, Mr. Spooner."

"You'll have it by the end of the day," Jesse said, still annoyed. The bank manager left him alone.

Jesse read the following letter addressed to him from James Cheatham:

> *To my friend, Jesse Spooner,*
>
> *If you're reading this, I'm pushing up daisies. I got two weeks before I meet the hangman here at Huntsville. My life has been a fuckup from the day I was born. Knowing the end is near gives me comfort. I instructed my lawyer to mail you this letter after I'm buried. You know about the robbery and the missing money and the minerals. Well, they ain't missing. I hid the money in a grave behind a catholic mission. (It's in the grave nearest the largest mahogany tree. You can't miss it). The minerals are hidden in a barge 100 clicks downriver from Kisangani. You'll see lots of rusty barges on the river. The number of our*

*company in Iraq is painted on the stern. If you decide to carry on, I promise you it's all there. You've got one problem. I also told Ray Carson about the money. If he tells you he wants to save those kidnapped schoolgirls, he's a liar. He won't rest until he gets his hands on that money. And if it means killing you or anybody else that gets in his way, he won't hesitate.*

*So be careful, my friend. I'm sorry for involving you, but you're the only man in the world I trust to do what's right. You need to know why I hate Ray Carson. Where do I begin? My mother was worthless. Her daughter and my little sister, Ann Marie, was a good girl who never done a bad thing in her life. I put her through college. She was a school teacher in Houston. Then she fell in with that sweet-talking preacher, Ray Carson. Carson knocked her up, and then he walked out on her. If I wasn't locked-up, I would have already killed him. When the school fired Ann Marie, it broke her. She had no place to turn. My sister killed herself. She left a note asking me not to blame Carson, but that ain't my nature.*

*She wasn't the only innocent girl he ruined. So, there you have it.*

*P.S. Our last security detail together was in this village. Carson knows most of it. You know everything. Good luck. Whatever you decide, I wish you a Good Life. Enjoy the money.*

*Semper Fi*
*James Cheatham*

Jesse crumbled the letter against his chest. The money is in *Ugigi*, he remembered.

The bank manager reappeared. He seemed nervous. "Mr. Spooner, there was a man, an American, asking questions about you. He said he was a friend of yours. He was here yesterday. I thought you should know. He left his business card." He placed the card on his desk and pushed it forward. Reed Cunningham and a telephone number were on one side. The following note was on the other side:

> I'm staying at the Ramela. Call me if you need my help. Good luck.
>
> RC

"Mr. Mutombo, you're certain no one has read this letter?"

"Very certain, Mr. Spooner." The bank manager looked injured. "I assure you, sir, no one has seen your letter." His denial sounded too emphatic.

***

Jesse hired a taxi to avoid the gauntlet of beggars. Invisible bicyclers hidden behind mountains of bananas and skinny women balancing woven baskets on their heads lined the road. Donkey carts slowed the traffic to a snail's pace. A herdsman walked behind some emaciated cows—a man advertised live chickens by waving them in the air, which dislodged feathers. The chaotic intersections were manned by more unauthorized policemen demanding money. This city emitted odoriferous human tangs.

The atmosphere felt dangerous.

Jesse found Rigby in the hotel bar. The walls were stained yellow from tobacco smoke. The patrons included a rogue's gallery of gold prospectors and diamond miners down on their luck. An assortment of ex-soldiers of fortune rounded out the cast of serious drinkers. Cigarette smoke made the air unbreathable.

"So, how'd it go?" Rigby asked between drags.

"Better than expected."

"Jesse Spooner, meet, Wilson Kasonga." They shook hands. "Wilson knows everything in this country worth knowing. We served together in the last Congo War. A damn fine soldier. Sergeant Kasonga saved my life."

Wilson had intelligent eyes and splayed teeth. He looked embarrassed. "I think you saved my life."

Rigby said, "Let's just say, we saved each other and leave it."

Jesse pinched the bridge of his nose. "Brother, we need to talk." Confused, Wilson stared at Rigby, then Jesse, and back at Rigby.

"Same mother, different fathers," Rigby joked. "So, talk. I trust this man with my life." Rigby nodded at Wilson, who stiffened proudly.

A leathery-faced man with a bushy mustache and a wandering eye approached their table. Nigel Birtwistle was as English as fish and chips. He wore an ascot, knee socks, and a British bowler.

"Croxford?" he slurred. He smelled like gin. They shook hands, pulling each other into a warm embrace. "Well, I'll be damned."

"Most of us are, I reckon. I never thought I'd run into you. Jesse Spooner, meet Nigel Birtwistle. Nigel and I go way back," Rigby said. "Still flying helicopters, I presume?" Birtwistle and Wilson acknowledged each other with a familiar nod.

"Indeed. So, what're you doing in paradise?" Nigel asked.

Rigby tossed him a grin. "Oh, just on holiday."

"If you say so, mate." Nigel exhibited disbelieving crossed eyes.

"Nigel matriculated at Oxford. A clever man of letters. People say he's lost the plot. In his defense, most bush-pilots are crazy. I will say one thing—he saved my ass more than once." Rigby's memory revisited a firefight in Angola. His unit was minutes away from being overrun. In desperation, he called Nigel and asked for an emergency evacuation. Against all the odds, Nigel landed in a hail of ground fire.

"To be labeled psychologically unhinged by an absolute lunatic is farcical." Nigel's laughter was cut short by a smoker's rattle. "The first sign of insanity is the total absence of fear. Need I say more?"

"My daughter says I lack the imagination to be fearful," Rigby said.

"Smart girl, your daughter. If I'm not mistaken, Christine's a medical quack."

"Luckily, she inherited her mother's brains."

"Sorry about Helen's passing." There were very few things that Rigby avoided. Talking about his wife was one of them. Nigel got the message.

"Now then, Croxford, why don't you tell me what you're really up to?"

"We're off on the river tomorrow. Headed to *Mongala*, in fact," Rigby said evasively, lowering his voice several octaves.

"You do know there are Mai Mai rebels between here and *Mongala*? Three weeks ago, two Belgian missionaries were captured, tortured, and had their privates cut off and eaten. Their heads were displayed on bamboo spikes. I refer to our local epicureans as the Congolese culinary board."

"Ouch!" Rigby said, grabbing himself.

"But then again, at my age, who needs testicles?" Nigel sighed. "I'm afraid old age has neutered me—bloody awful stuff. I've got more runway behind me than ahead. Please forgive the weak metaphor. It's the pilot in me speaking."

"Now, you sound like Otto Bern," Rigby said.

"How is that old scoundrel?" Nigel asked.

"Alive and well. Otto's divorced for the fourth or fifth time. I've lost track. He's cohabitating with a vervet monkey."

Nigel laughed. "Could there be a subspecies in our evolution? Perhaps, simian winos, given Otto's fondness for drink. Something we share in common."

"Otto warned us about traveling on your river. What about the missionary stations?"

"The missionary stations are no more, casualties of war, I venture." Nigel continued. "Just remember what Melville wrote. 'Better to sleep with sober cannibals than drunken Christians.'"

"So, we'll be on our own, more or less," Rigby said. "I was afraid of this."

Nigel handed Rigby his business card. "Here's my mobile number. Call if you need an extraction."

"Like in the old days, hey, Nigel."

"For Queen and country." Nigel drained the last drops of a gin and bitters. He muffled a belch. "It was great seeing you, Croxford."

"Always better to be seen than viewed. Take care of yourself, Nigel."

"If I don't, who will?" Nigel tipped the brim of his bowler. "Cheerio."

"Cheers, mate."

After he was gone, Rigby turned to Jesse, "You were saying. Before Jesse could respond, Rigby cautioned him. "Not here." Congolese bartenders are notorious eavesdroppers. In a town frequented by desperate conmen, collecting loose-gossip was a marketable commodity. They moved to a table.

A waiter took their drink orders. Jesse waited until the waiter was out of earshot. "Where do I begin," Jesse said this more for himself than his listeners. "Read this." He handed Rigby Cheatham's letter. Rigby read it and then reread it. The first time quickly, the second time more deliberately. He tore the letter into tiny pieces, sprinkled the paper scraps into an ashtray, and lit them.

Nosing his Scotch, Rigby said, "You're attracting some odd characters. The preacher sounds like a world-class asshole. Besides a murder request, what else did you learn? Do you remember the location of the village he referenced?"

"*Ugigi* is a fishing village around two-hundred kilometers from *Mongala*. Before I forget, sign this," Jesse insisted.

Rigby signed without reading it. "Am I signing my life away?"

"Hardly. This document gives you one half of a bank account, which has more than a hundred grand, compliments of the late Mr. Cheatham. Like I told you from the start, we split everything fifty-fifty."

Rigby gave him a low whistle. "Not that I don't appreciate your generosity, but this does make us paid accomplices in a murder-for-hire-scheme. Christ, you can have someone killed in this part of Africa for fifty francs. And it's open season on 'mzungus' white people. Talk about a markup."

When he saw the hurt in Wilson's eyes, he said, "I'm not talking about you. Just generally speaking."

The wounded look fell from Wilson's face.

"There is something else," Jesse confessed. "Reed Cunningham is here in *Kisangani*." He retold the story of meeting Cunningham in Key West and the note at the bank.

At first, Rigby half-listened without interrupting. "I don't trust Cunningham. As I recall, Global Security has a history of throwing people under the bus when push comes to shove. And besides, he may have gone rogue. Money can change a man. Your undertaking is getting complicated."

"What did you find out?" Jesse asked.

"Unfortunately, we just missed Captain Pieter. His steamer set-sail for Kinshasa two days ago. The river is low this time of year, which, according to Wilson, means Pieter won't risk running at night. He'll anchor-up in the middle of the river. Wilson's brother has access to an outboard-powered longboat. Says, we can overtake Pieter in nine or ten days. It depends on how many times Pieter stops." Rigby lowered his voice. "I purchased two AKs and ammo on the black market. They didn't come cheap."

"I thought possessing firearms in this country was a crime," Jesse stated.

"Quite right. But traveling on the Congo unarmed is nuts. I know Otto Bern said we should hire Captain Pieter, but Wilson says Pieter can't be trusted. If and when we overtake him, we'll need to watch our backsides."

"Otto warned us."

"That he did," dittoed Rigby.

# CHAPTER ELEVEN

## A river without pity

**They left** one hour before daybreak. There wasn't time to get properly outfitted. The plan was to buy food and fuel from fishing villages on the river.

The Kasonga brothers occupied the bow and the stern. Jesse and Rigby sat in the middle. The outboard-powered dugout skimmed over the water like a sculling-hull as long as they hugged the leeward shoreline. Submerged boulders and hippos hiding beneath the surface forced them into deeper water. The river was sixteen kilometers wide in places. At times, they lost sight of the shorelines. A lack of morning wind made the river benign, but the calm didn't last. As the sun came up, so did the wind. The longboat, appearing like a speck adrift on an endless ocean, took waves over her bow. Afternoon thunderstorms also slowed their progress.

The next five days were pregnant with monotony. The nights were intolerable. Sleeping in the narrow longboat was next to impossible, but Nigel's warning about cannibals made them cautious about beaching. Instead, they rode at anchor. They took turns bailing. No one slept during the first two nights.

Chilly mornings were brief interludes to long days of sweltering heat and bloodsucking insects. Wilson pulled anchor on the sixth morning. The river was benign. Yellow butterflies fluttered at the water's edge. Gliding African black skimmer birds with their orange lower mandibles extended carved the river's surface, searching for minnows. The eroded riverbanks were topped by soaring ochre-colored cliffs with twisted roots hanging over the edges.

Slowly, the equatorial sun beat them into submission. The air thickened as the sun became more fierce and unrelenting.

The nights were unbearable, but fatigue was taking a toll. They dozed in short intervals. Between napping, Rigby asked Jesse, "So, what's your take on Nigel Birtwistle?"

"I like him."

"Nigel's a gay blade."

Jesse looked confused. "What the hell are you talking about?"

Rigby clarified, saying, "Nigel lives with a man."

"No, shit. Well, he would love Key West."

"Like most Brits, Nigal suffers from the eternal characteristic of habitual understatement, which I find charming. He is fearless in the face of danger."

The seventh night was a repeat of the sixth.

By the eighth day, their drinking water was exhausted. Wilson and his brother drank straight from the river, but

Rigby and Jesse knew their stomachs couldn't tolerate the impurities. Jesse checked his handheld GPS. "According to Cheatham, we're getting close to the minerals barge. Keep an eye out."

One hour later, Jesse sighted what he hoped was the barge abandoned near a fishing village. The rumor of a black American and a white man traveling on the river had preceded them. Wilson and his brother waded ashore to boil water and, if possible, buy gasoline. Rigby stayed with the longboat while Jesse inspected the river barge.

The number of Jesse's military unit in Iraq was hand-painted on the stern. The cargo hatches were bolted shut. When Jesse returned to the longboat, he was ecstatic. "It's the right barge, alright."

Within minutes, grim-faced villagers gathered around the longboat. Rigby tried to start-up a conversation but was unsuccessful.

The village spokesman bared his teeth in a hate-filled smile. "Why are you here? I think you are rich. How much money will you give us?" He pointed. "Do you have gold nuggets in your pockets?"

"I'll give you the square root of fuck-all," Rigby hissed. "Now, bugger-off, before I lose my temper."

"You give us money, or we take this *bateau*." He shook his fist in Rigby's face.

The villagers tightened their circle. A wrinkled older woman tried to touch Jesse. Rigby pushed her hand away, thinking, she's shopping for her next rump-roast. Her smile revealed more gums than teeth.

The Kasonga brothers showed up in the nick of time. The village spokesman addressed Wilson in Swahili. "Why have you not cut these foreigners' throats? Camp here tonight so that I can kill them. We will share their money. We shall be rich."

Rigby had enough. "Get lost, *kumanyoko*."

The spokesman yelled in Swahili, "The *mzungu* called me a fucker of my mother." He charged at Rigby but was stopped short by Jesse's Kalashnikov jammed into his Adam's apple. The screaming villagers scattered in every direction. The spokesman dropped to his knees. Wilson pushed off the longboat and hopped aboard. By luck, the outboard engine sputtered to life on the second crank. They sped away for open water. Emboldened by the distance between them and the longboat, the natives shouted, *'nyama, nyama.'* Jesse aimed his weapon at them, but he didn't fire.

"That certainly went well," Jesse said. "Hey, what the hell does *nyama* mean?"

"*Nyama* means meat in Swahili. Trying to scare us, I reckon."

"It worked. If I wasn't so constipated, I would've crapped in my pants," Jesse said.

"God damn it, Wilson, we need friendlier natives," Rigby demanded.

"Those were friendly natives," Wilson acknowledged.

"Well, that's just fucking wonderful," Rigby muttered.

The night closed around their longboat in a flurry of rainy squalls. Blood-sucking mosquitoes drove them back into the middle of the river. With their fuel reserve empty, they drifted throughout the night and came to rest near another village. Exhaustion bested discomfort; everyone slept soundly.

At first light, the morning mist dissolved into light rain. It was raining cats and dogs when the sun broke finally above the jungle. They were awakened by the sound of children laughing. Rigby crawled out from underneath the canvas tarp. Sleeping in the longboat had stiffened his joints. Working the kinks out of his neck, he yawned loudly. His white face produced a panic. The screaming children vanished into the undergrowth.

After a few minutes, they reappeared with an ancient black priest carrying an umbrella. He wore a black clerical waistcoat with a large pectoral cross hanging from his neck. He was barefooted, and his hair was snow-white. He sounded more like an English headmaster than an African. "Good morning, I'm Father Sebastian, he said, extending his hand. My sons, how can I serve you? Are you hungry? We are very poor, but we will gladly share our food."

"This must be a dream. Are we still in Congo? Rigby said, scratching his chin stubble. "Yesterday, villagers tried to eat us. We're lucky to be alive."

The priest said, "I apologize for my countrymen. Without God, Congo has lost her soul. Poverty is not an excuse, but it is our reality. It's unfortunate. You're safe here. Even the river thugs leave us alone."

"Your godforsaken country is in the Dark Ages," Rigby stated cynically and added, "Bloody savages."

Jesse said, "Father, we need fuel. Can you help us?"

"Of course. Are you sure you are not hungry? My home is modest, but it is dry. Let me show you where I live."

Wilson and his brother stayed behind guarding the longboat. Rigby and Jesse followed Father Sebastian up a muddy jungle path into the steady downpour. Children held their hands as they walked. The priest whistled a tune, but his lack of front teeth made the musical attempt sound like air escaping from a punctuated tire.

The priest's tin-roofed hovel centered the village clearing.

Grass-huts in various states of disrepair surrounded it. Cooking fires smoldered. Scrawny chickens scratched in the black mud. Dogs barked at the sight of Rigby. Hooded individuals lurked in the shadows. Hacking from phlegm-filled chests was heard. A medicinal odor filled the air.

The priest's shack had a dirt floor. Bookshelves covered the walls. The back wall contained a workbench with a microscope and lab equipment. A generator hummed in the background. When the priest clapped his hands, a servant emerged from the backdoor. A hoody partially hid then man's face. The tip of his nose was missing. The priest ordered tea.

The man reappeared, balancing a tray. Tea was served.

"Father, what's the name of this village?" Rigby asked.

"I thought you knew. This is Saint Paul's Leprosarium."

Jesse had just taken a sip of hot tea, which lodged in his throat. He discreetly spit the fluid back into his cup.

The priest smiled. "Leprosy isn't that contagious. It's caused by exposure to *mycobacterium leprae*. You see, I'm also a doctor. I graduated from the London School of Tropical Medicine. Leprosy is quite curable if treated early. We give refuge to the untreated lepers shunned by isolated villages. Congo's greatest impediment is ignorance. Witch-doctoring takes a dim view of modern medicine. Our more pressing issues are hemorrhagic fever, tuberculosis, and HIV. I'm sure you've noticed the lack of older adults. Most died from diseases cured in the industrialized world fifty years ago. Procuring proper drugs in this country is next to impossible. Our mortality rate is dreadful. Twenty percent of all Congolese babies die in the first five years. The majority of our children are orphans. Without Catholic charities, we couldn't survive. Enough said about my world. Why are you here?"

Jesse summarized their mission to rescue the lost schoolgirls. He didn't mention the money or minerals. When he referenced Captain Pieter, the priest's smile curled down into a frown.

Father Sebastian listened intently before interrupting, "You look familiar, Mr. Croxford. Were you ever a mercenary in my country?"

"Yes," Rigby admitted and added sarcastically, "I don't believe I've had the pleasure. But then again, we all look alike."

The priest ignored his sarcasm. "We've had so many soldiers in this country it's hard to keep track. Unfortunately, wars attract foreigners."

"I was born in Africa. Rhodesia to be precise," Rigby acknowledged curtly.

"But, your ancestry is European."

"Don't hold that against me." Rigby conceded. "Is there a problem?" His face showed undisguised annoyance.

"Not for me. I detect hostility, Mr. Croxford."

Jesse appeared upset by the priest's questioning. "In my friend's defense," he said, "He lost his wife recently. Murdered by Africans, I might add."

"Please forgive me. Preconceived impressions are my failing. Surviving in this country has made me insensitive, at times. Even a lowly Catholic priest can make a mistake."

"When it comes to Africa, your God has been on holiday," Rigby said.

"Oh, so it's my God. The priest locked eyes with Rigby, "May I ask you a question? If it's too personal, I withdraw it."

"Go for it."

"Do you believe in the Almighty?"

A grin played at the corners of Rigby's mouth. "Well, in my line of work, I've had a few of those, please God, if I ever get out of this alive, moments."

"And recently?"

"Let's just say we haven't been on speaking terms since my wife passed. And besides, I'm sure I've broken all of the commandments, a time or two. Does that answer your question?"

"Not really."

"Father, I cannot deny the existence of hell. I've seen it," supplemented Rigby. There was heartbreak in his voice.

Father Sebastian steepled his hands. "I shall pray for you, Mr. Croxford."

Jesse and Rigby noticed the absence of fingertips on his left hand. When the priest recognized their interest, he said, "If you remember, I said leprosy is curable. It wasn't when I settled here sixty-odd years ago." He laughed. "Shortened my career as an organist, no doubt."

The priest placed his good hand on Rigby's shoulder. "Now then, you say you're trying to overtake Captain Pieter. I must warn you–the man is a disgusting reprobate. Pieter stopped here three days ago. As is his usual practice, he refused to come ashore and dumped our supplies overboard. We had to retrieve our goods at the risk of being eaten by the crocodiles. To add insult to injury, he overcharges us. I thought Pieter might unload our cargo on the pier because he had an American minister and his wife on board. It didn't happen. That man hasn't a speck of decency."

Jesse asked, "You're sure the minister is American?"

"Very sure. News travels on this river faster than any wire

service in the world. The drums say the minister's wife is much younger. He dresses like an American cowboy."

Jesse and Rigby's thoughts were identical; Reverend Carson is here. They jumped up.

"You needn't hurry off. Pieter will dock at *Mongala* tomorrow night. I can't express how much I've enjoyed your company. Not often, one gets to chat with foreigners."

Jesse said, "Father, you've renewed my faith in the human race. We'd like to donate." Jesse handed him some money. "Only wish it was more."

"God bless you both. You make it difficult for me to ask for a favor." The old priest's smile dislodged his dental bridge. He discreetly pushed it back into place with his tongue.

"Nonsense," Rigby said.

Father Sebastian told them about two children found adrift on the river. Both had contracted malaria. They had recovered and wished to reach *Mongala*, but traveling unaccompanied was too dangerous. When he remarked that they were trying to get home to *Ugigi*, Jesse's ears perked up. "It's settled. We'll take them with us."

"How nice of you. I think you'll find their histories valuable. Before you meet Winnie and Sefu, you should know they have suffered unspeakable atrocities. The boy may have engaged in cannibalism. The girl has been raped and re-raped. The resilience of the human spirit is one of His miracles. Only He can heal them."

Rigby reflected; too bad God didn't prevent the kidnappings. He decided to keep the comeback to himself.

The priest led them to a hut. Winnie Obo and Sefu sat outside in the shade under a lean-to constructed from banana leaves. "Winnie dear, these gentlemen have been sent to rescue your classmates."

Winnie stood up. Her face tightened into a mask of despair. "What took you so long? So many of them have died." She sniffled and wiped her nose with the back of her hand.

"Please, my child," Father Sebastian begged. "For the sake of those still alive, won't you help them?"

Winnie acquiesced with a tearful nod.

Rigby said, "I know it brings back painful memories, but it would help us if you started at the beginning. Tell us about the kidnapping."

Winnie detailed her abduction by Mohamed bin Sali's gang. She described in-depth the gang rapes and the vicious beatings she'd witnessed. Even Rigby, who was no stranger to violence, closed his eyes to hide his revulsion. She avoided her pregnancy and the killing of her baby.

Sefu began to sob. Father Sebastian hugged him.

Rigby raked his fingers through his uncombed hair. "Do you have any idea where Sali might be at this very minute?"

Winnie shivered. "I don't, but Sefu does. Sali moves a lot, but he always camps in the same places."

Rigby said, "Rescuing your classmates might not be hopeless, after all."

Winnie appeared elated.

Sefu, who understood only bits and pieces, looked equally pleased.

The priest made a sour face. "You can't do this. It isn't safe."

"What isn't safe?" Rigby asked.

"Using these children to help you kill that monster."

"Who said anything about killing him? Father, hear me out.

There are risks. I won't deny it. But rescuing those girls without the boy's help is one-in-a-million. And if Mohamed bin Sali gets in the way, well, his days on this planet might be limited. I give you my word on it. I must tell you I'm very good at what I do."

The priest appeared conflicted.

Rigby thought for a moment. "I think you know what I do or have done." His stare was so intense–Father Sebastian averted his eyes.

"*Quieta non movere*," the priest mumbled almost inaudibly.

"I don't think I take your meaning, sir."

"Let sleeping dogs lie," said the priest.

"It's too late for that."

"How can I be sure you won't endanger their lives? These children have endured the unendurable, gentlemen. How will you protect them?"

Rigby proposed a deception used during the Rhodesian Bush War. The Kasonga brothers would pretend to have captured Rigby and Jesse. More to the point, the Kasongas would seek Sali's help in ransoming Jesse and Rigby. Once they gained Sali's confidence, the tables could be turned. They needed Sali to drop his guard.

Father Sebastian said, "So, you're not the good Samaritans you claim to be. You had me fooled, Mr. Croxford. I'll give you that."

"That isn't fair. Sali is a murderer of innocent women and children and Christians, for that matter. He claims affiliation with Islamic terrorists. And like I said, killing him may not be necessary."

As the priest listened, he looked more dejected. "Everything you say is true. My country is overwhelmed by violence. The cycle has to end." He wrung his hands. Finally, he said, "If anything happens to these children, their blood will be on your hands."

"Father, I will protect them with my life," Rigby pledged.

"What makes you think Sali won't shoot you on sight?"

"Curiosity killed the cat. Knowing your enemy is half the battle."

"What about the other half?" the priest asked.

Rigby couldn't answer.

\*\*\*

They left Father Sebastian standing on the pier. The priest shouted, "God protect you and my children, Mr. Croxford." Winnie Obo and Sefu waved goodbye. The shoreline disappeared behind a curtain of smoky haze. Inexplicably, the mist parted, allowing brilliant rays of sunshine to illuminate the old priest. Rigby and Jesse looked at each other. Although they didn't speak, their thoughts were identical.

They headed downriver towards *Mongala*. Rigby tried to engage Winnie, but the aftereffects from malaria had weakened her. Winnie and Sefu slept for most of the day.

Rigby used the time to tell Wilson and his brother about his rescue plan. The Kasonga brothers viewed Sali's downfall as their tribal duty. Sali had victimized members of their tribe. In Africa, settling tribal blood-feuds is a time-honored tradition.

With the sun setting, Wilson cut the burbling outboard letting the longboat slice into some dense river-reeds. His brother handed out bowls of bitter *cassava* porridge and fig bananas. Soon, shrill whining mosquitoes drove them under the tarp. The Kasonga brothers, Winnie and Sefu, fell asleep immediately and began a snoring competition. Like clockwork, it rained during the night. Heavy raindrops pelted the tarp, which worked into the folds. Constant dripping added to their misery.

Rigby and Jesse found sleep elusive. Around midnight, they popped their heads out simultaneously. The insect assault had abated. Jesse quipped, "Another night in paradise. Did you sleep?"

"Not a wink. What I wouldn't give for clean sheets and air conditioning," Rigby whispered hoarsely. "Somebody, please slap me—I can't be having this much fun. The next time you have a bright idea, I beg you not to include me."

Jesse snickered. "Where's your sense of adventure?"

"If I ever get off this stinking river, I'll never eat another banana." Rigby smacked a mosquito on his cheek. "What're you gonna say to Reverend Carson?"

"I haven't crossed that bridge. The minute I read Cheatham's letter, I knew one way or another, Carson would show up. It was never about rescuing the schoolgirls. It's all about the money. As you said, this is getting more complicated by the minute."

Jesse's expression told Rigby that his attitude might be changing, and that made him nervous. "Hey, you're not thinking about going after the money, are you?"

Jesse evaded the question. "He used me."

"Who used you?"

"James Cheatham is using me to avenge his sister's death. Carson might be a piece of shit, but that doesn't mean he deserves to die."

Rigby struck a match on the gunnels and lit a cigarette. "I thought you said Cheatham was a friend." He exhaled smoke to repel the insects.

"I also said he had a disregard for life, more specifically his own. Not to mention, he was off his rocker."

"He didn't give two shits about risking your life," Rigby said.

"Not sure it ever entered his mind. I know one thing, Cheatham had brass balls. He was the guy you wanted on your side in a barroom brawl. I remember one time we were delivering arms to the *Tutsis* during the Rwandan genocidal goat-fuck. These *Hutu* rebels ambushed us. Cheatham jumps out of the truck, and the dope-smoking crazies surround him. They stick their AKs in Cheatham's face and start taunting him."

"So, then what happened?"

"It was one of those holy shit moments. Get this. Cheatham says, 'Which one of you fucking baboons has a light?'"

"What did they do?"

"They couldn't stop laughing. Maybe it was drugs. I damn near shit in my pants. We traded them our old AKs for new ones, and they let us go."

Rigby pointed his finger and mock-fired. "I know one thing. After listening to what Mohamed bin Sali did to these kids, I'm putting him at the top of my endangered list. If I get the chance, Sali is going to meet those seventy-two virgins."

"That's not what you told Father Sebastian," Jesse reminded Rigby.

"Dishonesty in the pursuit of a just cause is acceptable."

"Mm. Did you just make that up?"

"Yup."

"I'm impressed, Croxford," Jesse said. "Hard to stomach Carson getting his hands on the money. These people have been screwed over."

"Ripping off Africans isn't unique."

Jesse continued to make his case. "It ain't right, partner. That's all I'm saying."

Rigby shooed away a zebra-legged insect. "Lots of do-gooders have died on this river."

"Croxford, you could make roses smell like a beer fart."

"Speaking of beer, I could use one about now." Deep in thought, Rigby inhaled deeply on his cigarette and whispered through the blue-grey smoke, "Sleep tight, my black knight in shining armor."

"Nice try, Croxford. Push comes to shove–you always side with the underdogs."

"Goodnight," Rigby said. "Just don't tell anyone."

\*\*\*

Sunrise was windless. The silky-smooth river looked like polished black marble. They woke-up with daylight sneaking into their porous tarp. The graying sky, rinsed by rain, was perfumed by wildflowers. Morning fog clung to riverbanks.

Tree limbs, festooned by different shades of green creepers, hung heavy with dew. They escaped the papyrus reed embrace and nosed out into the river. Wilson fired-up the ancient outboard motor.

Their longboat made progress until the wind freshened. Sefu trailed his hand in the water. Jesse grabbed it and growled. The boy giggled, as did Winnie. As the day evolved, the sun became more unforgiving. The stench of rotting vegetation replaced the tinge of wild lilacs. They doused their faces with the russet-colored water. The river seemed endless. The hours passed slowly. A few times, they overtook dugouts heading in the same direction. The older natives gawked. The smiling children waved.

"How're you feeling?" Rigby asked Winnie.

"A little better," she answered weakly. "Mr. Croxford, can I ask you a question?"

"Sure."

"Have you done wicked things?"

Rigby laughed. "As bad as they come."

"Father Sebastian says all men have goodness in them. But in your case, it might be harder to find."

"Smart man, your Father Sebastian. It isn't that simple. It should be, but it isn't. Let's just say I haven't lived a peaceful life. My daughter says I have an offensive skill-set."

"Have you killed men?" she asked.

Rigby thought for a long moment. "Not by choice, actually. You asked me a question. Now it's my turn. If we find Mohamed bin Sali, do you want me to kill him?"

"I believe deep down–you're a good man."

"Thanks for that. But you haven't answered my question," Rigby persisted.

Winnie stared into space. "If any man deserves to die, it is Mohamed bin Sali."

"I'll take that as a 'yes.'"

She didn't argue.

\*\*\*

After eight hours of motoring, they came within sight of the *Esperance*, which lay captive to her moorings against the commercial jetty at *Mongala*. Wilson eased the longboat against the ferryboat's starboard side. Lines were handed up. Nicolas Pieter looked down at them disdainfully. Reverend Carson, standing next to the captain, gave the impression of being annoyed.

Jesse spoke in a hushed voice, "Looks like Carson and Pieter have become partners in crime. If that Bible-thumper thinks he can trust Pieter, he's in for a rude awakening. Hopefully, they'll kill each other."

Rigby whispered back, "From your lips to God's ears. Hey, I trusted you. Look where it got me. Up this shitty river without a paddle."

Jesse grinned. He yelled up, "Permission to come aboard."

Pieter granted his consent. Jesse and Rigby climbed the boarding ladder. Captain Pieter stood with his hands clasped behind his back, imitating Admiral Horatio Nelson received dignitaries on his flagship, Victory. They shook hands with Pieter. Reverend Carson and his wife, Maria, stayed back at first.

Carson stepped forward. "What's he doing here?" He

# JAMES GARDNER

nodded at Rigby. "This isn't what we agreed to, Mr. Spooner."

"Reverend, you hired me. You don't own me. How I do my job is my business. You violated our agreement the minute you set foot in Africa."

Before Jesse could continue, Winnie and Sefu were helped up onto the deck. Pieter stared at Winnie, drinking her in like a cobra appraising a helpless mouse. He wet his bulbous lips. "I've been waiting for you to leave that filthy nest of lepers, my sweet." Pieter tried to hug her, but she wiggled free. "I paid for you, Winnie Loci. Your father accepted a fine motorboat. I own you, lock, stock, and barrel." He grabbed her wrist. Again, she twisted free.

Jesse intervened. "Back off, friend. Clearly, the young lady is not interested."

Jesse's warning died stillborn. Pieter shot him a menacing glare. "I'll thank you to mind your own business. It's between me and this ungrateful little slut." Pieter's face turned burgundy, matching the mottled veins in his nose. "How many men have had you, fifty, one-hundred? Why you're nothing more than a 'malaya' whore."

Winnie began to tear-up.

"You're making an ass of yourself, sir," Rigby said, putting his hand on the captain's shoulder.

Pieter pulled a switchblade and flipped it open. "Touch me again–I'll gut you."

Pieter never saw it coming. Rigby's crushing straight-right was on target. Pieter collapsed like a pricked balloon. Rigby helped the woozy captain to the gunwale and pushed him over the railing. Pieter did a back-flip, landing on his belly. He surfaced, gasping for air.

The crew rallied to Pieter's defense. At first, Rigby and Jesse seemed to have the upper-hand, but they were outmanned and overwhelmed. During the melee, Winnie and Sefu managed to slip away unnoticed. Rigby yelled to Wilson to take them back to the mission. Jesse was relieved to see the longboat heading back upriver.

The captain had to be carried onboard. He was beyond furious. Pieter ordered his men to tie Rigby and Jesse to the masthead. "When I'm finished with you two, the crocs can have what's left."

Pieter pummeled both men. Rigby took the brunt of it. A kick broke his nose, and another one opened a deep gash above his right eyebrow. Pieter turned his attention to Jesse, but fatigue had sapped his strength.

Reverend Carson seemed fascinated by the brutality. Carson's wife ran into the wheelhouse, crying. Pieter's rage masked the injury he received from the fall. Pieter sucked on his pudgy knuckles, stretched his back, and winced. Crewmembers carried Pieter into the wheelhouse. He cried out, "Better if you die tonight than face me in the morning. Pleasant dreams."

\*\*\*

The night was moonless. As ordered, Rigby and Jesse remained tied to the masthead. Except for the rats scurrying on deck, it was ominously still. The crew members went ashore to spend the night with their insignificant others. Pieter, Carson, and Carson's wife, Maria, stayed on board. As the night progressed, heavy drinking ensued in the wheelhouse. Maniacal laughter replaced loud arguing and then silence.

Rigby whispered, "Hard to believe we're going to die of thirst floating on the second biggest river in Africa. I wish we had some bananas. God, I hate rats."

Jesse said, "Hard to believe I got you into this mess. I'm sorry."

"Don't blame yourself. My daughter says I have a death-wish. Didn't want my tombstone to read, here lies a man who never lived. Well, anyway, it was nice getting to know you, Jesse."

"This trip hasn't been a Kodak moment."

"Scarcely." Rigby laughed and then grimaced from the pain. "We're not totally fucked, at least not yet."

They saw someone moving in the darkness. Rigby muttered under his breath. "Looks like our friend, Captain Pieter, is back for more fun and games."

Maria Carson stepped out of the shadows. She gave them long swigs of water. Then she cut their bindings. Both massaged their wrists. Maria handed them thick slices of bread covered in *cassava* paste, followed by more sips of water. She shined a flashlight in Rigby's face and gasped.

Rigby straightened his broken nose groaning as it popped into place. "How do I look?" He asked Jesse. Fresh blood poured from his nostrils.

"Like you rejected the sexual advances of a gorilla," Jesse whispered.

"Maria, you better get back. If they miss you, there'll be hell to pay."

Maria said. "I mixed pain pills in their whiskeys."

"What about your husband?" Rigby asked.

"My good-for-nothing husband lost me in a card game to Captain Pieter. When I refused to sleep with that pig, Ray beat me. He doesn't care about me. He never did. I should've listened to my mother."

Rigby thought, if Pieter gets his hands on that money, he'll kill your husband. That way, he keeps everything, including you. Or maybe it goes the other way. Poor kid, either way, your future isn't worth a sixpence.

Maria whimpered. "I just wanna go home."

Pieter anchored his ferryboat offshore as a defense against would-be robbers. The crew had commandeered the ferryboat's dinghy. Their only option was to swim ashore.

Rigby asked Maria, "Can you swim?"

"Not so good." She shivered.

Jesse and Rigby's thoughts were identical; they envisioned crocodiles.

Jesse said, "I've got a better idea." As instructed, Rigby walked to the bow and engaged the windless retrieving the anchor. Jesse started the Lister engine. Maria gathered up some clean clothes, reclaimed Jesse's money belt and his mobile. She shoveled her husband's money into a purse. Pieter and Carson didn't stir when Jesse shifted into forward and idled towards the land. The *Esperance* coasted until the bow bumped gently against the pier. Rigby made her fast to the dock. Jesse shifted into reverse. The bowline stretched as taut as a banjo string, but it held-fast. They jumped off the bow. Jesse released the bowline letting the ferryboat back away. The *Esperance* merged into the night with its two passengers sound asleep.

"Bon voyage," Jesse whispered, saluting.

Rigby dialed Jesse's cell. "C'mon Nigel, answer your damn mobile."

He did answer, albeit in a huff. "This better be important."

"Croxford here. I need that extraction we talked about."

"Where are you?"

*"Mongala."*

"There's an abandoned school at the other end of town. The soccer field is a perfect LZ. See you at first light. I'll be inbound low, and hot. Don't want to give the bad boys a heads-up. How many passengers?"

"Three."

"Perfect. Am I flying you to the airport in Kinshasa? Are you going home?"

"Negative on both. Saint Paul's is our drop-off."

"It's your funeral. See you when I see you."

"Cheers, mate."

***

Except for a mangy dog, they walked to the Catholic Academy unseen. They found refuge in the same administration building where Loci Obo had been murdered. Lime could not mask the death stench. Jesse and Maria hunkered down. Rigby concealed himself outside in some cedar trees to stand watch.

Maria whispered to Jesse, "How old is Mr. Croxford?"

"I'm not sure. Why do you ask?"

"He's different. I feel safe with him."

Jesse said, "Hey, how old are you?"

"Old enough to make him happy."

"Sounds serious."

"Do you think he likes me?"

Instead of answering, Jesse started snoring.

***

Rigby heard thumping rotors seconds before a Jet-ranger popped out of the greyish fog. Nigel Birtwistle's helicopter skimmed the treetops, banked into a light breeze before touching down in the middle of the soccer field. Maria, Jesse, and Rigby scrambled on board. Nigel lifted off, dipped the helicopter's nose, and headed straight for the river.

They flew over Pieter's ferryboat, which was hard-aground and heeled over. A massive mud-slick encircled the steamer. Captain Pieter directed his crew laboring to free her. Reverend Carson, standing next to Pieter on the ship's fantail, shaded his eyes as the helicopter swooped overhead. Maria gave him the finger. Idiotically, he waved back.

Rigby pointed at Carson, yelling in Maria's ear, "Not enough bloody pain-killers. Damn shame if you ask me." She nodded.

During the flight, Rigby noticed Maria Carson staring at him. "Anything wrong?" he asked her.

"You saved my life," she yelled over the engine drone.

"We're the ones who should be grateful." He touched her shoulder. She grabbed his hand and kissed it. "What you did for us took guts," he added.

She held his hand and closed her eyes.

***

Father Sebastian waited on the edge of a clearing. Winnie and Sefu stood next to him. The helicopter hovered momentarily before touching down. Before the rotors stopped spinning, Winnie ran out to greet them. She threw her arms around Rigby's neck and hugged him. Disregarding the priest's warning, more squealing children joined Winnie.

Rigby shouted to Nigel, putting his hand on Maria Carson's shoulder, "I need her on a flight back to the States."

Maria grabbed Rigby's neck and kissed him hard on the lips. Caught off guard, he blushed.

"I love you to pieces," she yelled.

"Yes, yes, and I love you," Rigby shouted back without considering the unintended implication. He believed her affection stemmed from being freed from a joyless future. Her interpretation was very different.

"Get her to the Kinshasa Airport," Rigby said.

"Consider it done," Nigel said.

"Thanks, awfully, Nigel. I won't leave Congo without paying you for this. You always said God was an Englishman. Now, I believe you."

Nigel shouted back, "This one's on the house. For old time's sake. Be safe and go well. Don't want to be airlifting body-bags."

"You bet. And thanks again, my friend."

"Cheers, mate."

Nigel gave him a thumbs-up. Maria blew Rigby a kiss and mouthed, I love you. Rigby and Jesse coaxed the children back to the edge of the clearing. The Jet-Ranger spooled up and lifted off. Within seconds the disappearing helicopter was soundless.

The passengers waded into the crowd. Father Sebastian shook his head. "Dear God in heaven, what has that animal done to you? I warned you."

"You did, indeed."

"Did Winnie give you the news?" the priest queried Rigby.

"News about what?"

The priest spoke, examining his eye. "On her trip back from *Mongala*, Winnie recognized two men in a motorized launch. She is sure they work for Mohamed bin Sali. Your eye will require sutures, Mr. Croxford."

"So, you're saying Sali is nearby?" Rigby asked.

"Sefu says he knows the location of Sali's camp. I tell you this with grave misgivings, Mr. Croxford. By the way, I owe you an apology."

"Concerning?"

"Winnie told me what happened between you and Captain Pieter. A priest should never condone violence. In this case, I hope God will forgive me. Well done, Mr. Croxford."

"No apology needed. Father, you can't stitch-up my eye, at least not yet."

***

Nigel Birtwistle landed his Jet-ranger at the Kinshasa Airport. He booked Maria Carson on an Air France flight to Paris, connecting with a transatlantic flight to JFK and then back to Dallas, Texas. The problem was the first scheduled flight departed in five days. Kinshasa is one of the most crime-ridden cities in the world. Leaving a young white woman to fend for herself was unthinkable. He opted to fly

Maria Carson to his home base. The plan was to return to Kinshasa a few hours before her flight departed.

Maria was enchanted. She believed her destiny was with the man of her dreams, Rigby Croxford. Her fantasy was, of course, delusional.

***

Nigel maneuvered his whirlybird above a walled-in compound that included living quarters and a workshop. Two armed security guards protected the entrance. Razor-sharp glass shards topped the walls. He hovered momentarily before starting a descent. A dust plumb obscured the touchdown spot. He used a tamarind tree to judge his distance to the ground. The Jet-ranger touched down as gently as a dragonfly, landing on a pond. As soon as the copter spooled down, line-boys descended on it like hyenas feeding on a carcass. One boy secured the rotors to prevent windmilling. Another boy hand-pumped jet-fuel into the fuel tanks. Two more boys polished the fuselage. A mechanic started his visual inspection. Congo did not have a labor shortage.

Two yelping crossbreeds vaulted off the veranda and greeted Nigel as he exited the helicopter. The cottage was typically English, whitewashed with a reed-thatched roof. A heavy-set black man stood on the stoop with his clenched fists resting on his hips. He wore a turquoise *pagne* and matching scarf.

Many expatriated Europeans have a history of keeping illicit paramours, both male and female. Nigel started the relationship under those preconditions, but after thirty years and raising four adopted daughters, their bond was unbreakable. The man handed Nigel a gin and tonic.

"Mrs. Carson, this is Imani." Maria gave Imani a double-take.

Imani's intelligent face radiated affection. He kissed Maria's hand. "I am delighted to meet you." He spoke in a soft, welcoming tone.

A housemaid showed Maria to her bedroom. Exhaustion overwhelmed her. She flopped onto the bed and fell asleep the second her head hit the pillow. She would not move for ten hours.

After dinner, Imani and Nigel sat together on the veranda listening to Giuseppe Verdi's opera, La Traviata. Citrusy smoke from insect candles scented the air. Nigel smoked a cigarette through an opera-length holder between sips of brandy. Imani read a week-old newspaper. Their two mongrel dogs slept under the chairs. The distant cackling of hyenas alerted the dogs. They scurried into the house and crawled underneath a bed.

Nigel discussed his upcoming charters. He was scheduled to pick up two German geologists at the Kinshasa airport and fly them to a mining camp on the Katanga Plateau. Later in the week, two men representing an American company chartered his helicopter. When he queried them about the flight plan, they were elusive. It wasn't a secret that their company was a front for the CIA.

In the past, when Imani cautioned Nigel about doing business with unsavory characters, Nigel reminded him that unsavory characters were the backbone of his charter business.

"Say what's on your mind," Nigel insisted.

"Does this charter involve your friend, Croxford?"

"Odds are, there's a connection," he answered. "I'm sure the Americans are spooks." When he saw the anxiety, he elaborated, "They work for the American Government."

Imani changed the topic. "Mrs. Carson is very beautiful."

Nigel baited him. "Is she? I hadn't noticed."

"A blind pilot is unusual," Imani snapped.

"Like the poet said, 'And oft, thy jealousy shapes faults that are not.'"

Amani pouted under his reading glasses. "This woman has lived with much sadness in her life. I can see it in her eyes. What do you know about her?"

"Not much. I think the woman's husband mistreated her."

"Most Congolese husbands mistreat their wives," Amani observed.

"What about me?" Nigel asked.

Imani patted his hand, saying, "You are different."

\*\*\*

# CHAPTER TWELVE

**Ignoring Father** Sebastian's forewarning, Rigby and Jesse said goodbye for the second time in three days. Like many Africans, Sefu possessed a mental compass. Following his instructions, they crossed the river and skirted the shoreline for ten kilometers. Heavy rain drenched them to their cores. A mangrove island obscured a waterway, which they entered and idled into the jungle. As they motored deeper, the shorelines were more foliated by squat palms and papyrus reeds. Overhanging fig trees limited the sunlight.

As the tributary narrowed, Rigby's anxiety escalated. A giant blue heron took off, squawking in protest. Jesse and Rigby grabbed their weapons. The Kasonga brothers ducked. Sefu and Winnie giggled.

Rigby ran his mind's eye over an ambush. "Jesse, I don't like this. We're sitting ducks."

"You're reading my mind," Jesse said.

"Winnie, ask the boy, how far is Sali's camp?" Rigby said.

Winnie translated Sefu's answer. "He says, not so far."

Rigby half-rolled his eyes. The African definition of not so far can mean fifty kilometers or fifty meters.

"Ask him how long to walk there."

"He says two hours, maybe less."

Water hyacinths clogged the outboard motor. The jungle stream became impassable. Wilson shut down the engine. Using their paddles, they pushed and prodded the longboat until it hit dry land.

Wilson's brother would stay behind with Winnie and Sefu. If they didn't return by sundown, Wilson's brother would return the children to Father Sebastian's mission. Both Winnie and Sefu became emotional. Rigby tried to reassure them, but his eyes hinted uneasiness.

Wilson hacked a pathway through the bulrushes. A well-trodden trail paralleled the stream. Jesse and Rigby fell in behind him. Wilson carried one AK with the other weapon slung over his shoulder. Tie-wraps secured Rigby's and Jesse's hands. The locking devices had been jimmied–one hard pull would free their hands. The men's faces showed injuries inflicted by Captain Pieter, which would hopefully deceive Mohamed bin Sali.

The trail opened onto a cleared landing. Smaller native dugouts had been hauled out and overturned. An outboard-powered canoe was partially beached. The bigger boat could possibly expedite an escape.

Wilson searched for clues as they moved deeper into the jungle. Broken twigs and a smashed anthill were signs; they weren't alone. After two more hours of hard slogging, Wilson found a footprint.

"How old?" Rigby asked, kneeling for a better look.

Wilson whispered, "The spoor is fresh."

"I must be getting old. I need a break," Rigby said, lighting two cigarettes and handing one to Spooner.

After taking a puff, Spooner spoke through the exhaled smoke. "The girl is head over heels for you."

"What, girl?"

"Aren't we the coy one? I'm talking about the reverend's wife."

"Poor kid is confused," Rigby said almost to himself.

"What a body."

"Spooner, that's the difference between you and me. I'm..."

Wilson hushed them. He scanned the jungle sifting the silence. Goose-flesh rose on Rigby's arms. Wilson and Jesse glanced at each other. It became eerily still. Screeching cicadas were quieted. Birds stopped tweeting.

They continued, stepping noiselessly. The canopy was so dense, only dull shafts of sunlight escaped. Wilson held up his hand and froze. He used his weapon's barrel to lift a mat of laced palm fronds covered by leaves. The pit contained sharpened bamboo spikes meant to impale careless trespassers. They circled the booby trap and kept moving.

The jungle became more fused with danger. Again, Wilson stopped dead in his tracks. He smelled something so putrid, his forehead furrowed. Three round objects impaled on bamboo spikes blocked the trail. Squirming white maggots covered whatever they were. Only after Wilson shooed away the blowflies were the objects identified as human heads. The eyeballs had been plucked out. Severed penises had been stuffed into the mouths. The faces were ghoulishly distorted, but the middle head drew Jesse's attention. As they moved nearer, Wilson saw something shiny on the ground. He picked up a pair of wirerimmed glasses and handed them to Jesse. The lenses were cracked. Someone had died so violently his eyeglasses had been crushed. Jesse held his breath and leaned in for a closer look. The hair texture and eyeglasses were proof-positive. It was Reed Cunningham's decapitated head. Jesse fought the nausea building in the pit of his belly.

Wilson's tone lacked confidence. "Should we turn back?" he asked Rigby.

"Has old age turned you into a woman?" Rigby answered.

The reproach worked. Wilson straightened himself, took the point, and marched off into the jungle. As they followed him, Rigby thought he saw movement in the shadows.

The first sign of Sali's camp was tendrils of campfire smoke in the treetops. Out of nowhere, two armed boys stepped out from behind a tree. Behind them, two more boys blocked their escape.

Wilson yelled, but his voice lacked volume. He tried again, "I have business with Mohamed bin Sali."

Armed boys bookended them. After marching for another thirty minutes, the path showed heavy traffic. More children appeared lurking in the shadows. Harsh undulating rap music broke the stillness.

As Rigby, Jesse, and Wilson entered the encampment; they were taunted. A boy poked Rigby with a stick. Jesse's makebelieve handcuffs loosened. He did his best to retighten them, but he knew a careful examination would expose the ruse.

Rigby made mental notes. Grass-huts surrounded what appeared to be a command tent. The air was permeated by ganja smoke. Weapons were stacked in pyramids. Two half-naked girls tended iron kettles suspended over a crackling fire. Boys congregated under trees playing cards. Rigby counted six grown men, all of them sleeping. The rest were children, but high on drugs, they could be unpredictable. Earsplitting native rap music blared from a shortwave radio.

A guard pulled back the tent-flap and motioned them in. Mohamed bin Sali sat behind a makeshift field-desk. He was bare-chested and wore mirrored sunglasses. His shaved head glistened from beads of sweat. Behind him, a naked girl sat lotus-style on a cot. The smell of unwashed genitals filled the tent. No man who looked at Sali face to face for even a moment would doubt his fondness for violence.

"Why are you here?" Sali questioned. Smugness crossed his lips. He squeegeed perspiration from his brow with the back of his hand and flicked it.

Fear made French slippery on Wilson's tongue; he switched to *Bantu* mixed with Swahili. The exchange became heated. Jesse guessed it wasn't going well. Agitation wrinkled Sali's forehead. Rigby whispered in English, "God damn it, Wilson, what's he saying?" A guard struck Rigby from behind. The blow staggered him, but he didn't fall.

Sali addressed Wilson. "You ignored my warnings. You bring outsiders into my camp. Either you're very brave or very foolish. Which is it?"

"We should become partners," Wilson stuttered, ignoring the condemnation.

"Praise Allah, the *mzungu* we killed was carrying a great deal of money." He held up a wallet to support his claim. Sali grinned, fanning a stack of crisp one-hundred-dollar bills. "Maybe your prisoners also have money." He eyed Wilson suspiciously.

"All Americans are rich. His family will pay to keep this one alive." He smacked the back of Jesse's head.

Sali squinted, assessing Rigby and Jesse's injuries. "I could use a man like you. But kidnapping foreigners is a dangerous business."

"We can make big money." Wilson shifted nervously from one foot to the other.

Sali crossed his arms over his chest. "Maybe so, but your venture is too risky for me. And besides, the drums say a reward is already on the table."

Wilson swallowed dryly. "Reward? I know of no reward."

"A friend will pay for their heads. Maybe you've heard of him? Captain Nicolas Pieter?"

"Good. Then it's settled," Wilson said. His jumpiness accompanied a hard-faced smile.

"You should join us. I have everything a man desires in life." He noted the naked girl and held up a plastic bag containing a white powdery substance. "Do you want us to kill your hostages, or will you do it." Sali discharged the girl with a dismissive wave. She scrambled out of the tent.

Wilson answered Sali in pigeon English. When Sali seemed puzzled, they switched back to *Bantu*. Rigby heard enough to know Sali's intentions.

Wilson improvised, biding for time. He confessed that he had, in fact, stolen money from Rigby and Jesse. The cash was in a safe place, and he was willing to share it as a sign of good faith. Sali was all ears and seemed pleased. When Wilson asked for something to drink, Sali ordered a guard to fetch some water. One guard left the tent. The odds had improved.

Rigby whispered to Jesse, "It's now or never."

Rigby grabbed Wilson's spare AK and vaulted over the desk. He hit Sali squarely between the eyes with the rifle butt, and then he wrapped the sling around his neck. Wilson shot one bodyguard point-blank and wounded another one as he reentered the tent. Jesse picked up the discarded AK, just as a small skinny man, not much bigger than his weapon, burst into the tent. Jesse hesitated. The man fired, dropped his gun, and ran. Gunsmoke cut visibility.

Rigby dragged Sali out into the open. Girls exited their huts, some of them in various states of nudeness. When Wilson ordered everyone to raise their hands, they complied. Wilson gathered up the firearms. Three unarmed boys ran off. Nothing was done to stop them.

Wilson waved his weapon yelling in Swahili, "Men and boys face down, hands behind your backs." They obeyed. Wilson secured their hands with tie-wraps. In support, Rigby fired his weapon in the air.

The girls huddled together, moaning. They seemed transfixed, without emotions.

"Winnie Loci has sent us to bring you home." Rigby's words didn't register.

Wilson tried. "We are here to rescue you." The girls still didn't respond.

Rigby knew there was one way to break the spell. After conferring with Wilson, he calmly walked over to Sali, who had regained consciousness and was screaming death-threats.

Sali hissed, "I will piss on your grave, mzungu."

"Not in this life, you won't." Rigby placed his rifle's muzzle on Sali's foot and pulled the trigger.

Sali grabbed his foot, shrieking, "Kill these infidels." His men didn't move a muscle.

Wilson fired his weapon. The shot hit Sali just above the left temporal lobe. A blood geyser following buttery brain-matter spurted from the hole. Sali fell over convulsing. His unblinking eyes stared at the sun. He stopped twitching and lay still.

"Hear me. Mohamed bin Sali will never hurt you again," Rigby yelled. He snatched Sali's morbid necklace and tossed it into the campfire.

After a few anxious moments, the girls begin to wail, but this time, unlike so many times before, their weeping was joyful. Wild cheering erupted.

And then the pent-up fury exploded. The girls grabbed anything they could get their hands on and began to beat their tormentors. The men received the lion's share of their anger. The older boys were not granted pardons. Only exhaustion ended the beatings.

Rigby yelled, "Spooner, you need to see this." When Jesse didn't respond, he panicked.

Rigby found Jesse sitting in a pool of coagulated blood. His face was grey, his breathing labored.

"How bad is it?" Rigby asked as Wilson stuck his head into the tent.

"I've had better days," Jesse panted. His teeth were bloodied. Rigby gently lifted Jesse's hands away from his stomach. The entry wound looked innocuous, but the exit hole was the size of a man's fist. Rigby had seen enough combat-wounds to know Jesse would bleed-out, and there was nothing anyone could do to save him.

"Why didn't you shoot, Jesse?"

"I don't know why. I..., I couldn't pull the trigger." Rigby swabbed the sweat from Jesse's brow.

"I can have a copter here in one hour, maybe even less," Rigby said. His lower lip quivered.

"We both know it's too late for that." Jesse unzipped his money belt and handed it to Rigby.

Wilson appeared with the shooter. The man had a rope around his neck, and his hands were tied. He had soiled his pants. "You want me to shoot this hyena turd?" Wilson asked, holding his nose.

"Get him out of my sight," Rigby said.

Jesse motioned to Rigby to come closer. "Promise me..." He struggled to speak. "Promise me you won't let the crooked bastards get their hands on that money. It ain't right."

"If that's what you want, consider it done." Jesse started to fall forward; Rigby righted him.

"That's what I want. Croxford, you're the best man I've ever known. I want you to know that." Jesse's teeth chattered. "Damn it to hell–I'm freezing."

"I thought you didn't trust white Africans."

"We had a shaky beginning, but you grew on me," Jesse said, attempting a puny smile.

"As I remember, you had a huge chip on your shoulder."

"Guilty as charged." Jesse's voice had grown weaker.

"Never thought it would end like this. What a lousy way to die. See you on the other side."

If there is another side, Rigby said to himself.

Jesse closed his eyes. He saw himself crossing the Gulf Stream at the helm of his sport-fisherman. Slanted sunrays escaped dark, tumbling clouds on the horizon. The cresting cobalt-blue swells were white-bearded. Salty air filled his lungs. The Hatteras buried her bow into a steep wave jettisoning rainbow-colored spray. Flying fish scattered. Her engines rumbled. Pure exhilaration made him shiver. The glint in his eyes faded. His body wilted in Rigby's arms. A final breath exhaled from his lips. You didn't deserve this, Rigby thought, closing Jesse's eyelids. An overpowering sadness washed over him.

When Rigby emerged from the tent, he went straight for Jesse's killer. He yanked the hangman's noose lifting the man into the air. The man thrashed and kicked. His eyes bulged. The color drained from his face. He released the rope letting the man collapse at his feet. Rigby waved his AK, shouting, "I ought to kill all of you."

A boy yelled, "He is not one of us. He works for Captain Pieter."

"Is this true?" Rigby asked the shooter. The man nodded, keeping his eyes closed. His lips mimicked an Islamic prayer.

"Wilson, untie the prisoner."

Wilson pleaded, "Let me kill him."

"Untie him," Rigby ordered.

Rigby supported the man's chin with his gun barrel. "I have a message for your Captain Pieter. You tell him, I could have killed him on his boat. Now, it will be my distinct pleasure to watch him die. My only regret is, I can't kill him twice." The shooter vanished down the jungle path on a dead-run.

Rigby sat down on a tree stump. A chill raised the hair on the back of his neck. A trembling spasm raced through his body. Why am I so cold, he wondered? Soon, he would know the reason.

Wilson lit two cigarettes and handed him one. Rigby smoked it thoughtfully. A sultry breeze swept in from the river. The trees rustled. It looked like it might rain. Terrible loneliness overshadowed his discomfort. Conflicted memories raced through his brain. He heard Father Sebastian's words, 'Congo has lost her soul.' Then he remembered Otto Bern's confession, 'That's when I decided to play God.' Suddenly, everything became crystal clear.

There was only one way this would end.

"Wilson, help me dig a grave for Jesse."

"What about the Arab?"

"Let the hyenas eat him," said Rigby.

Wilson hissed like a mother crocodile protecting her eggs. "Sali is too foul for hyenas. Maybe the vultures will pick his bones."

"After we finish here, I want you to march these kids to the landing. Wait for me there. Keep the boys handcuffed until I join you."

"What about them?" Wilson asked, indicating the men on the ground.

"What happens to them doesn't concern you."

After they laid Jesse Spooner to rest, Wilson led the children to the landing. He kept the girls and boys segregated. Waiting for Rigby, he rolled a cigarette. When he saw smoke billowing above the trees, he knew Rigby was burning the camp. He was destroying the evidence of Mohamed bin Sali's existence. Wilson heard four consecutive gunshots. He felt overjoyed. In Africa, there is no honey sweeter than revenge.

A few minutes later, Rigby stumbled out of the jungle. His face and clothes were blood-soaked. He shrugged out of his shirt and used it to wipe his face and hands. He addressed the boys as Wilson cut their bindings. "I have decided to free all of you. Use these dugouts to return to your villages. But if I learn that one of you has returned to a life of crime, I shall kill all of you. As God is my witness, the last thing you will see in this world will be my face. Mohamed bin Sali told you he couldn't be killed. Said he was a god. Well, he wasn't a god. Sali is dead, and so are his men. Remember my words. Now go, before I change my mind."

The boys scrambled down the embankment and into the dugouts. They paddled furiously and never looked back.

Wilson's brother saw the smoke and heard gunfire. He arrived at the landing with Winnie and Sefu. Winnie and her classmates were reunited. They cried at first, then danced in circles. The news about Jesse dampened Winnie's spirits. Grief cast a dark shadow. The mood turned somber.

Rigby handed Jesse's money belt to Wilson. "Give this to Father Sebastian. Tell him to use the money to help these girls. What's left goes to the mission. That's what Jesse would have wanted."

"Where are you going?" Wilson asked.

"To *Ugigi*, like I promised Jesse."

"Then, I shall go with you," said Wilson.

"Oh, no, you won't."

"To abandon, you would dishonor my wives. I beg you, don't do this to me."

After a moment, Rigby relented. "Your brother can take

the girls back to the mission. Don't say I didn't warn you. And no complaining, thank you."

"You will not be sorry," Wilson said and added, "Have I ever complained?"

"Not that I can remember. Tell your brother to get moving." The sadness returned. "I can't believe he's gone," Rigby said aloud.

Sensing his sorrow, Wilson said, "We Congolese have a saying. 'If you want to go fast, go alone. If you want to get there, go together.'"

Rigby said, "Our enemy is more cunning than a wounded leopard. You must stalk him with all of your God-given skills."

Wilson clicked his heels together and saluted. With the possibility of vengeance coursing through his veins, his face glowed like a harvest moon.

"Are you ill?" Wilson asked.

"Me? No, I'm fine. I just need to rest awhile." Wilson helped him to the ground. Rigby curled into a fetal-ball and passed out cold.

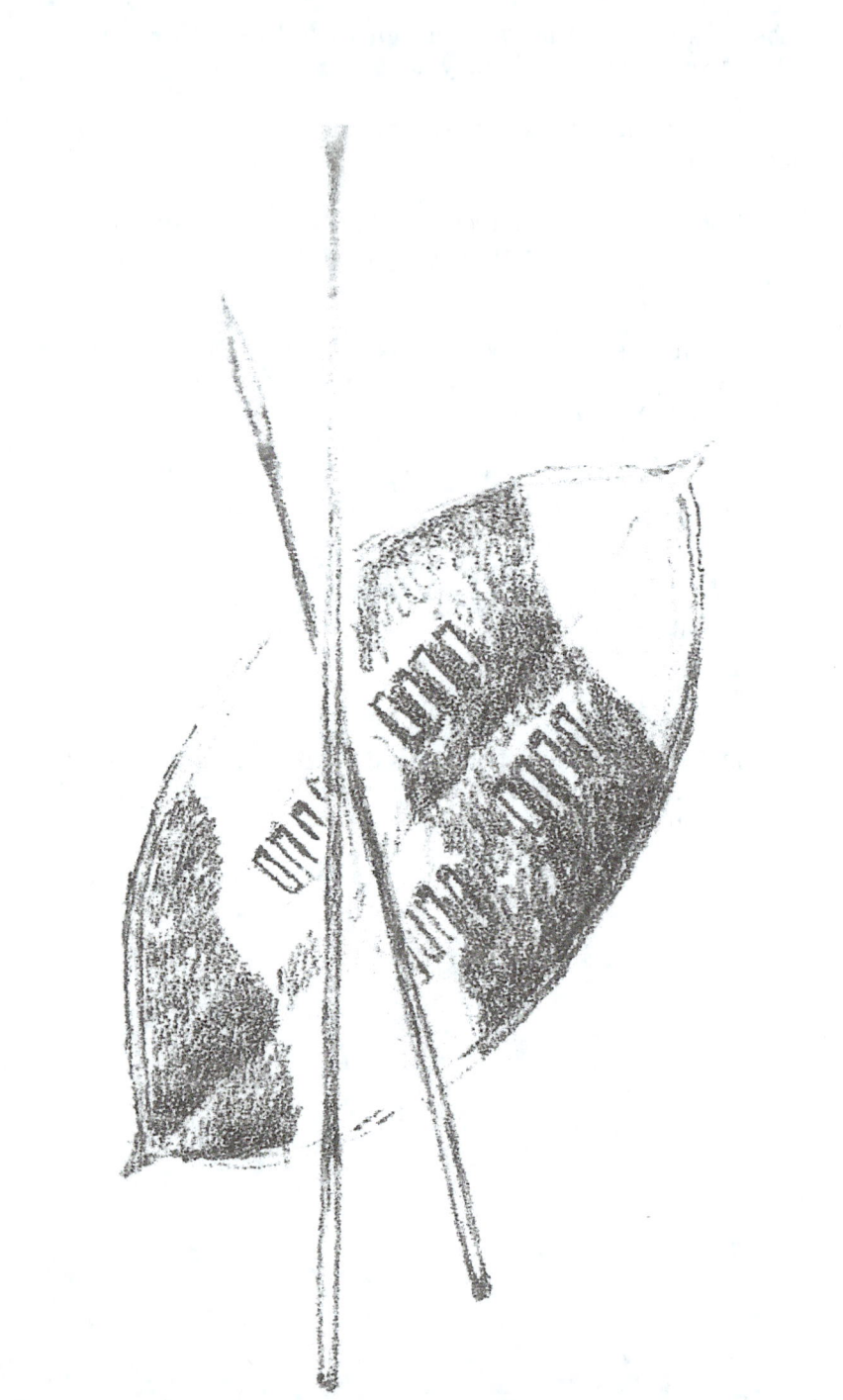

# CHAPTER THIRTEEN

## Reelection Campaign Headquarters
## Washington

Winston Churchill on China:
"Beware of the sleeping dragon. For when she awakes, the earth will shake."

**The following** is a redacted transcript of a meeting attended by Washington political insiders. The goal was to shed light on China's activities in Africa. The primary purpose was to avoid controversial issues detrimental to their candidate. The attendees included the chairman of the presidential reelection campaign, an expert on central Africa, a retired general, two U.S. congressmen, an economist, and the deputy director of the CIA. Identities withheld.

The chairman clicked his water glass with a ballpoint. "Gentlemen, I've asked the professor to bring us up to date on central Africa. More specifically, on Congo's strategic significance. Before he speaks, I want you to read the excerpts from his article, entitled, Sino-African Blueprint." He handed out copies that read:

> Are we so mesmerized by his tweets; we cannot see the forest? Economists and stock market pundits are wringing their hands over the trade war with China. Are we

missing the bigger picture? What is China's endgame? Are they pursuing a long-term strategy for world domination? Will trade restrictions help to slow down their efforts to replace us as the world's economic juggernaut? The jury is out. The last thirty years have been reminiscent of Neville Chamberlain's misguided placation of the Nazis.

I have made twenty trips to African over the last fifty years. After my trip in 1968, I had the honor of meeting Senator William Fulbright, then serving as chairman of the Foreign Relations Committee. He asked me what surprised me most about Africa. I told him the number of Chinese ships I observed in Mombasa and Dar es Salaam. China has had Africa in her crosshairs for decades. Americans are shortsighted. China is playing the long game.

One million Chinese live in Africa, and another five-hundred reside there on work permits. Africa is an integral piece of the Chinese domination puzzle. China has backed African coups. Are they the humanitarians they claim to be, or was their involvement self-interested? A continent plagued by poverty and corruption is ripe for exploitation. It's the perfect recipe for China's playbook.

America's consumption of strategic minerals is escalating. A disruption in the procurement of those minerals will adversely impact the technology industry, which is the mainframe of the American economy.

The professor stood up. He received mild applause. "Questions, gentlemen?"

An attendee asked, "Is China or Russia the key

provocateur?"

"I'd say China. But Russia can't be underestimated. Given the natural resources and Congo's location, Russia and, more specifically, China are flexing their muscles in central Africa. Both countries are supporting various Islamic terrorist organizations operating throughout the Congo Basin. *Boko Haram*, *Al-Shabaab*, and *Al Qaeda* are causing the most havoc, but there are over thirty other terrorist groups operating within and around the region."

A congressman interrupted. "Can you summarize the current status of Sino-African relations? And what are our adversaries' endgames?"

"China's goal is to impede America's procurement of rare earth minerals, not to mention copper, oil, and high-grade uranium. Above all, China wants to diminish America's influence on the continent. In the past, Russia was just being Russia. Payback for sanctions. Lately, Russia has increased her ties to Africa, more specifically, in the Central African Republic. The ruling government is weak, which makes the CAR an easy target. China invested 220 billion dollars in Africa last year. Russia is playing catch-up with a limited bankroll."

"What's Russia's motivation?" the congressman asked.

"The Kremlin sees Africa as a supermarket for arms sales. African wars are never in short supply. And they enjoy putting burrs under our saddles. Keeps our noses out of their mischiefs."

"Crimea?"

"Among others."

The economist chimed in. "Hydraulic fracking has crippled Russia's economy. Besides energy, weapons manufacturing is their only revenue source."

The professor continued, "Think of China as the parasite and Africa as the host. China is the bigger dog in this fight."

"The administration is pressuring China to throttle North Korea. For the time being, they have a free reign in Africa and other places. They pretend to help us. We look the other way. It's a smart play, on their part," added the other congressman.

"Like their man-made island in the South China sea?" asked the general with heavy sarcasm.

"Exactly."

"So, you're saying the Chinese are intensifying their quiet war against us. China is probing our initiatives on multiple African fronts and testing our resolve to stay the course, as it were. How has the ambush in Niger affected our African policy? I mean politically. We had four special operation soldiers killed by ISIS fighters. Not our finest hour."

The deputy director raised his hand. "China and Russia are funding Islamic terrorists in the region. It's a safe bet the ambush was orchestrated indirectly by either Chinese or Russian operatives."

The general slammed his fist on the table. "Gentlemen, I hope those responsible will be held accountable. Nixon opened the door to China as a buffer against the Russians. Another case of unintended consequences."

The other congressman intervened. "The senator from Kentucky is spearheading a movement to reduce our military footprint in the region. Says, he was shocked to learn we had eight-hundred soldiers stationed in Niger."

"You mean the senator who looks like he's wearing a French poodle for a hat." Everyone laughed.

The economist piped up, "Niger has vast high-grade uranium deposits, fourth largest in the world. Fifty percent of the nuclear power plants in France are fueled by the uranium mined in Niger. Abandoning Niger would be a major mistake. Like the Willie Nelson song goes, 'Turn off the lights, the party's over.'"

"France gets drawn into this—we would have to be with them, like it or not."

"A past administration sold twenty-percent of our uranium reserves to Russia."

"For millions contributed to their foundation plus an obscene speaking fee."

"Only in America," stated a congressman

"Tell that to the families of the soldiers who died," said a congressman more bitter than the others.

"Gentlemen, can we skip the partisanship? Let's stay focused. If we draw down our military presence, what are the long-term ramifications? Worst case scenario?" asked the chairman.

"Disastrous," answered the general.

Both congressmen nodded in agreement. One asked, "How so?"

"Well, for one thing, the void would signal a green light for China in the Congo basin. Once they gain control of the Congolese government, Willie's party is most definitely over."

"How long before our technology companies feel the squeeze. In other words, can they purchase strategic minerals from other markets?"

"At what cost?" injected the economist. "China has forty percent of the world's rare earth mineral deposits. Last year, they mined ninety percent of the total production. Their goal is to exclude us or make our procurement cost-prohibitive. It's not just the Congo basin. China is gobbling up mineral concessions all over Africa."

"What about Japan's offshore venture?"

"Unlimited deposits, but expensive," replied the economist.

"How many years before they see results?"

"Best guess, three."

"Unacceptable. Those minerals are indispensable to our tech industry."

"Offshore mining has obstacles. It could be even longer."

The attendees mumbled their disappointments.

The general asked, "Can we discuss long-term military scenarios? We've had success operating reaper and predator drones from our base in Djibouti."

"The distance between Djibouti and Kinshasa is over 3200 kilometers," said the professor.

"So, what country in central Africa affords us the best possibility for building and maintaining an airbase? And is operating a base even feasible?"

"General, the countries within acceptable response times are unstable. The governments would jump at the opportunity. It's a matter of security."

"Northrop Grumman has successfully tested drones using a carrier as a platform. They're working around the clock. The drones require beefed-up landing gears and tail-hooks, but the technology is identical. I'd say we could have a carrier on station in say, six months."

# THE CONGO AFFAIR

The chairman said, "As of now, it looks like our best option is a flattop."

The general agreed. "We've effectively eliminated targets in Somalia, but the terrain is different. It's arid flat terrain versus jungles. Quicker response times are a necessity. In Somalia, you can run, but you can't hide. Not so, in central Africa. A carrier is our best option. We could have a drone over a target in minutes."

"Sir, fifty percent of the Congo Basin has been designated for logging. China's insatiable appetite for lumber is denuding central Africa. Eventually, Congo will look like Somalia."

"Gentlemen, eventually, we may end up in a shooting war with China. This country's future is technology."

"Are we jumping the gun? Military intervention may never be necessary."

"China's ultimate goal is economic domination. The Chinese constructing an air and naval base next to our base in Djibouti is proof-positive–they're not going away. Not to mention, there are ten-thousand Chinese companies presently doing business in Africa."

"I think most of us agree with that assessment. It's only a matter of time."

There were no dissenters.

The chairman announced, "On that happy note, I move we adjourn."

The attendees filed out of the room.

*** 

By prearrangement, a closed meeting between the deputy director and the chairman was scheduled after the conference.

"What's the latest on Reed Cunningham?" the chairman asked.

"Nothing, yet." His disappointment was palpable.

"So, the DNA didn't match. It wasn't him." His disappointment was equally apparent.

"He's still missing. That's all we know."

The chairman sighed deeply. "Talk about a mess."

"We thought we had the situation contained. We get the embezzlement charges expunged. Cunningham retires quietly. End of story."

"Reed violated the eleventh commandment. He got too greedy. So, where do we go from here?"

"Intelligence gathering in central Africa is sketchy. We lost two agents in the last three years. We've asked the Congolese to help us."

"You overlooked his digressions. He disappears. Not hard to figure."

"We thought we could use him until we found a replacement."

"Make sure there's no connection to the administration," the chairman demanded.

"Of course."

"The two agents we lost. They were citizens of...?"

"Nigeria."

"God damn it, we give Congo millions in foreign aid. You

would think the people in charge would help us."

"That's the problem. No one's in charge."

# *PART TWO*
# CHAPTER FOURTEEN

**Rigby Croxford** lay dying in Saint Paul's Leprosarium. When Maria Carson learned that the man she credited with saving her life was critically ill, she rushed to be at his bedside. Ignoring Father Sebastian's reprimand, she pinned his naked body against hers to restrain his malarial convulsions and prevent detachment from the intravenous blood transfusions supplementing his failing kidneys. Rigby's mumblings were conversations with his departed wife.

Winnie and Sefu had elevated Rigby's status to godlike. They slept on the floor at the foot of his bed. Wilson, who provided the life-giving blood keeping Rigby alive, rested in a chair. Father Sebastian administered the last rites.

This was the final day of their vigil.

\*\*\*

*Am I dead? I hear voices discussing the odds of me surviving. I know the verdict is grim. They say I have malaria. I've had* malaria before, but this time it's black-water fever. Not many survive blackwater fever.  Usually, I feel the onset, but this time I was caught off guard. Maybe the beating I received from Pieter masked the warning signs. Yes, of course, that's it. The injuries from the beating disguised the symptoms. One minute I'm freezing, and the next minute I'm on fire.

My dreams are so real. Helen is here, sleeping next to me. I can feel her breasts pressed against my back. I can smell her sweetness and the thrill of her touch. If I keep my eyes closed, maybe this dream will never end.

I see myself and my father standing behind the outhouse on our farm. I'm seven or maybe eight.  I look sad. My father says, "Son, God has chosen us to look after the munts. They're a helpless lot, more like children. It's not the path we chose, but it's all part of His plan. When you abuse them, you offend God. The boy you hit couldn't defend himself. Lord knows blacks in this country have been killed for striking a white. Would you beat a newborn calf?"

"No, father," I said. "I could never do such a thing."

"Of course, you couldn't. Son, I hope this will teach you the error of your ways. After we finish, I want you to apologize to the boy you struck and his mother. Will you do that for me?" He said, undoing his belt.

"Yes, father," I said, dropping my pants and bending over. I don't remember the pain, only the humiliation. I was too busy rehearsing my apology.

I found Sammy sitting under a tree in front of his family's hut. His brown face was streaked white from dried tears. The blood-nose had stopped bleeding. His mother did not look happy.  She glared at me.

"Sorry I hit you, Sambo. If you want to sock me, I won't fight back. And I promise I won't tell anyone." I stuck out my chin.

"Why would I punch my best friend?" Sammy said, with

tears flooding his eyes. His words pierced me like a dagger. I choked back my tears. I threw my arms around Sammy's neck and hugged him. "Let's never fight again. Promise me–we'll always be friends."

"Friends until we die," he vowed. His mother put her arms around us. A gentle smile replaced her frown. The makeup was blissful.

The childhood memory merged into a war dream. I see myself standing at attention in front of our commanding officer. We had just finished a twenty-kilometer night run. Sam is standing next to me. There is a pile of stones at my feet.

The CO says, "Mr. Croxford, you are without a doubt, an absolute disgrace to Rhodesia and your late father, a decorated war hero at El Alamein, I might add. Always taking the easy path will not win this war. We thought you might discard the rocks you were ordered to carry. That's why we painted them red. Are those rocks red, Mr. Croxford?"

"No, sir," I answered regretfully.

"And why aren't they red, Mr. Croxford?"

"Because I dumped the red ones over a cliff, sir."

"Over a cliff, you say? You collected unpainted stones after you finished the run?"

"Yes, sir."

"Bloody bad show, Mr. Croxford. I put the following to you. You've engaged the enemy. A fierce firefight ensues. Mr. Mabota has been seriously wounded. You must evacuate him from the battlefield to save his life. Would you conveniently dump Mr. Mabota over a cliff?"

*"Never, sir," I announced, coming to attention.*

*"For Mr. Mabota's sake, I hope you're telling the truth. You shall repeat the twenty-kilometer run without delay. We've doubled your stones as punishment. Carry on, Mr. Croxford."*

*"Sir, can I join him?" Sam asked.*

*"I put to you both the following. This selection course was designed to fail nine out of ten applicants. We only want the very best this country has to offer. Selous Scouts is not for slackers. As you've been told, you can quit anytime. As a matter of fact, we encourage you to throw in the towel. Better to unveil a man's shortcomings before it's too late. Is what I'm saying make any sense?"*

*"Yes, sir," we answered in unison.*

*"Very well, Mr. Mabota, you may accompany Mr. Croxford. But you are not under any circumstances to aid him. Do I have your word on this?"*

*"Yes, sir," Sam said, saluting.*

*"Very well," the CO said, twisting a tip of his waxed mustache. Puffs of pipe smoke accentuated his words. "By all means." Puff. "Gentlemen." Puff. "Carry on."*

*That unfortunate episode fast-forwarded to our graduation day. We had just finished the infamous ten-day survival course. They deserted us in the bush without weapons or food or even a compass. Of the original one hundred volunteers, only thirteen remained. Three men had sustained broken bones. They would resume their training after their injuries healed. My clothes were shredded. My stomach growled. My feet were covered in blood blisters. I was so weak I could hardly stand at attention. It was the happiest day of my life. I knew without Sam; I could never have passed.*

*The CO announced, "At ease. Congratulations are in order. You have proven yourselves to be the best of the best. We* welcome you as Selous Scouts. As you can see, we have prepared a banquet fit for a king to honor this prestigious occasion." He pointed at a table laden with frosty mugs of beer, steaming chops, and juicy steaks. I smelled the fresh bread. My mouth watered. "But first, you must eat that." He pointed at a rotting baboon corpse hanging from a tree. Bon appétit, gentlemen."

We cooked the baboon and had eaten most of it before the CO interrupted our first real meal in ten days. "So, Mr. Croxford, was the baboon to your liking?"

"A bit chewy, especially the toenails, sir."

The CO labored to hide a grin underneath his handlebar mustache. "I put the following to you. You've been in the bush for twenty days without the benefit of resupplies. You're near starvation. You happen on the remains of a leopard-kill hanging in a tree, a rotting baboon to be precise. This exercise proves that if you cook rotten meat and eat it immediately, it will not make you sick. Wait fifteen minutes until the meat cools–you will not enjoy the aftereffects. Your graduation dinner awaits you, gentlemen. You've earned it."

Over the next two years, Sam and I ate so many baboons; it's puzzling why we didn't grow tails.

Our first operation, Nyadzonya, was hailed as an outstanding success by Rhodesia's allies, which were few, and a genocidal slaughter by our enemies, which were many. Eighty-four scouts disguised as enemy combatants crossed the border illegally into Mozambique. We attacked a terrorist camp of five-thousand, killing over one-thousand trainees in fifteen minutes. We lost one man to a snake bite. At that time, I rejoiced. Now, I have doubts.

That dream was interrupted by the day I realized we could lose the war. We had parachuted in behind enemy lines. Our third was a stocky Shona I nicknamed Jack, after Jack the Ripper. Jack had fought for the enemy before we converted him or rather blackmailed him into joining our side. Sam detested violence, but Jack, a natural-born killer, relished it *like a Frenchman savors a fine Burgundy.*

*We were on a night patrol. Our mission was to recce a friendly village being harassed by the gooks. (During the Rhodesian Bush War, enemy combatants were referred to as gooks).*

*Sam asked, "Should we investigate or wait?"*

*"HQ says we wait for reinforcements," I answered, scanning the village with binoculars.*

*Sam and I took turns standing watch and keeping an eye on Jack. We never trusted Jack. It was a stunning night. I remember looking up at the panoply of stars. Crickets serenaded us. I dozed off listening to the haunting yelps of a jackal. Two hours before daybreak, we heard gunshots. The village below us burst into flames. The night-sky turned red. Then we heard screaming.*

*"Bugger HQ, let's go," I yelled, grabbing my rifle.*

*We fanned out and started our descent down the mountainside. By the time we reached the village, the grass huts were reduced to smoldering ashes. The remnants of a wooden chapel occupied the center of the village. The bodies of villagers and the priest who died defending their church littered the ground. I entered through what had been the front door. Sam followed me in. As usual, Jack was busy scavenging the village for valuables. I remember the scorched wooden pews stacked in a heap. Beneath the pile, we found a tangle of tiny bodies burned beyond recognition. In desperation, parents had hidden their children under what became a funeral pyre to protect him. Sam was overcome by grief, but Jack showed no emotions. He picked through the rubble, searching for more spoils. Most Africans are experts at hiding their feelings. Sam was different.*

*At that moment, I feared the worst. In Africa, ferocity triumphs over timidity. The world had turned her back on us. We didn't have the military resources to wage war. As the war* intensified, my premonition became painfully clear; we were losing. I should have warned Sam. We were fighting for a lost cause.

The war pressed on. Our deployments increased. Assassinating collaborators, blowing up bridges, or harassing the enemy became routine. Sam's demeanor changed so much, I hardly recognized him. He never smiled. I used whiskey to dampen my qualms. The war was taking a toll on us. We were helpless.

I remember the day my presence was requested at HQ. The CO stood with his back to me. He was looking dreamily through a window fogged by drizzle. He seemed smaller. "At ease, Mr. Croxford. Let me be blunt. I put the following to you. We have a security breach within the Scouts. Damn embarrassing, to say the least."

"I don't understand, sir," I said.

"Oh, it's simple enough. We have irrefutable evidence that either Sam or Jack has gone over to the other side." He held up his hand to stop my answer. A fly had crawled across the window. He retrieved a swatter from his desk, and after striking it, he swept it from the sill. "You were saying."

"Sir, it has to be Jack. I'd bet my life on it."

The CO waved his unlit pipe at me. "Don't be so sure. This war has turned the most diehard patriots into traitors. I know you grew up with Mr. Mabota. Don't let that friendship cloud your judgment. As you're about to learn, your life will hang in the balance."

"How did you obtain this intelligence, sir?" I asked.

"I'm not at liberty to say. What I can tell you is that your next assignment has been compromised. You will be walking into an ambush. There's a hefty price on your head, Mr. Croxford. A testament to your efficacy, I suppose." He sucked on his pipe until it made a low gurgling sound.

"No way it's Sam," I reiterated.

"We shall see about that, Mr. Croxford."

"It can't be him."

"Before we get into the plot to expose this...this filthy maggot in our ointment, I need to know if either man wears something or does anything that would identify him at a distance. For instance, does he carry his weapon a certain way? There must be something."

I visualized Jack for a brief moment. "Sir, as of late, Jack has been sticking guinea fowl feathers in his cap. Says they're for good luck."

"Yes, yes, sounds like you might have pinpointed our traitor. Now, let's go over the plan to expose him."

The purpose of the covert mission was to interrogate a tribal headsman. His modus operandi was planting Chinese landmines around the white-owned farms. A farmer's teenage daughter had recently lost her leg to one of his insidious devices.

On the march to the village, we stopped at a livestock water tank to refill our canteens. As Jack doused his head, I discreetly removed the feathers from his cap.

I pointed. "Jack, the village is beyond those hills. You take the point. Sam and I will cover you. Intelligence says we won't receive fire. Our job is to question the headsman and, if necessary, arrest him."

Jack was panic-stricken. "What's the problem?" I asked.

"The feathers. I need my feathers," Jack stuttered, searching the ground.

"We're wasting time. Let's get cracking."

*Instead of covering Jack, we raced around a hill and outflanked him. Sam and I peeked over the rim. Below us, four armed men lay in wait. Jack ran at them, yelling, but gunshots muted his words. As soon as he fell, the ambushers revealed themselves. They were fish in a barrel. We cut them down. Jack was still alive, but not for long. The headsman begged for his life. War hardens men, especially the losing side. We executed him with extreme pleasure.*

*After two more years of fighting, as I had predicted, we lost the war. I spent the next two years exiled in Israel. Sam stayed behind to face the music. Considered a conspirator, he was shunned by his country, his tribe, even his own family. He never complained. Sam deserved a better friend.*

*A mental picture of Sam's mutilated body, killed in a lion hunting accident, was replaced by an apparition of Helen, murdered by political assassins. He censored that vision with the happiest day of his life.*

*I saw Helen standing on the veranda at Willie's farm in South Africa. The bush war was in full swing. I was on leave and very drunk. The soft glow from a lantern illuminated her face. She was the most beautiful woman I had ever seen.*

*"I'm Rigby Croxford," I said, extending my hand.*

*"I'm...,"*

*"I know who you are," I slurred. "It's beautiful, isn't it?"*

*"The stars are brilliant tonight," she said.*

*"No. I mean, the silence. I detect an American accent. So, what brings you to Africa?"*

*"I'm a Peace Corps volunteer," she said.*

*"It must be wonderful, being so, so virtuous," I snapped.*

*"I detect hostility, Mr. Croxford."*

"*Your country is boycotting my country. Without arms, Rhodesia could lose the war. Let's see how the world likes dealing with a communist government in the heart of Africa.*"

"*Vaccinating children doesn't make me the enemy. I suggest we continue our discussion when you're in a more civil mood. And with that, I bid you goodnight. On second thoughts, I hope our paths never cross. Goodbye, Mr. Croxford.*"

"*Can I say something?*" I said.

"*By all means, please do. I'm breathless with anticipation,*" Helen said sarcastically.

"*Someday, we shall be married,*" I said.

"*You don't say. How startling. I never intended to remain single for the remainder of my life.*"

"*I mean, we'll be married to each other.*"

"*What? I'm confused. Do explain yourself, Mr. Croxford.*"

"*I know this may come as a shock. But someday we'll be husband and wife.*"

"*And how do you know this to be true?*" She asked.

I smiled. "*Only an African can know these things. Fortune telling is a gift from God.*"

"*I'll say one thing. You are, without a doubt, the strangest man I've ever met.*"

"*Does this mean you'll consider my offer?*"

"*Not a chance. Do you always get this drunk?*"

"*Depends on how hard I try.*"

*"I doubt you'll recall a word you said tomorrow morning."*

*"Don't bet on it."*

*"Goodnight. Oh, and drink lots of water."*

*I saw myself sitting at the head of a long table. Everyone seated has gone over to the other side. Sam is on my left. Helen is on my right. Jesse is at the opposite end. My parents and all the friends I lost in the war are there. I'm ready to join them. Black spots blur my tunnel-vision. And then I saw a blinding white light. So, this is how it ends.*

Father Sebastian spoke using a penlight to dilate his patient's pupils. "Can you hear me, Mr. Croxford?"

Rigby nodded weakly. His complexion had turned waxy. His eyes dulled by fever were unfocused. A wet blanket stuck to his body. He fought to marshal his thinking.

"You gave us quite a turn, Mr. Croxford."

A long silence grew longer. Finally, Rigby answered, "I thought I was dead."

"You were most definitely knocking on death's door. Fortunately for you, your disdain for God has not altered His mercy. Despite your cynicism, your resolve to live is quite strong."

Rigby managed a whisper. "How long..., how long have I been out?"

"Five days. I won't bore you with the pathology. But the probability of surviving *malarial hemoglobinuria* or *blackwater fever*, as you know it, is not good. Renal failure is almost always fatal."

"I can't thank you enough," Rigby muttered after taking a

deep breath. Wilson and his brother, Maria Carson, Winnie, and Sefu, were gathered around his bed.

"Keeping you alive has been a team effort. I would like to speak to Mr. Croxford." The priest made a shooing motion. After they were alone, he said, "We have a delicate situation, or rather you do."

"Situation?"

"I am talking about Maria Carson's infatuation. Poor girl never knew her father. She has been mentally and physically abused by men her entire life. Not to mention the flagitious scoundrel impersonating a man of God. I believe you have done nothing to encourage this..., this fixation. Despite my repeated warnings, I found her in your bed as naked as the day she was born. She claimed it was necessary to keep you warm. I hope your intentions are honorable, sir."

Rigby shrugged expansively. "I don't know what to say." His expression registered innocence.

"I may be a Catholic priest, but I am not ignorant to the ways of the world. Women have been rewarding men with their bodies since Adam and Eve. Need I say more? Men twice your age marry women half her age in my country, but that does not make it proper in God's eyes."

"Father, is there a way to re-infect me? I prefer dreaming."

Father Sebastian looked down at the floor and then at Rigby. He placed his fingerless hand on Rigby's shoulder. "When you are well enough, I shall organize transportation to Kinshasa. From there, you can fly home. In the interim, I advise you to disentangle yourself. Tact is paramount."

"First of all, I have something that needs my attention."

The priest spoke. "Jesus said, 'Put away your sword. For all who take up, the sword shall perish by the sword.'"

"I made a promise to Jesse. I'm a man of my word."

"Perhaps, you should reconsider. For some reason, God has chosen to spare you. Only a fool would tempt Providence so soon. Shame to throw your life away."

Rigby countered. "Death is a robe every man has to wear." He rubbed his temples. A throbbing headache made him grit his teeth.

The disappointment in Father Sebastian's voice was evident. "Your motivation is greed. You're wondering how I know about the money. Your dreams were informative."

"You wound me, Father. You think you know my motives, but you don't. I'll leave it at that."

"Your decision is what I expected. I have already made the necessary arrangements. You will be happy to hear–Captain Pieter's steamer is still dry-docked in Kinshasa. It seems the grounding did extensive damage."

With Father Sebastian's guidance, Wilson and his brother had reconfigured the longboat. They constructed a convalescing bed with a sunshade and mosquito netting. Provisions included anti-malarial medicine, ample food supplies, and disregarding the priest's displeasure, the AK-47s.

The loose-end was dealing with Maria. Rigby decided to confront the problem head-on. "Father, I'd like to speak to Mrs. Carson in private."

Rigby waited until he was alone with her. "Mrs. Carson, you keep saving my life," he said, taking her hand. "I...I don't know what to say, except thank you."

"Sorry about your friend," she said, teary-eyed.

Unable to speak, he looked away. Sensing his discomfort, Maria said, "Hey, thanks for reminding me I'm married to that bastard. Why couldn't I have married someone like you?" She kissed his hand before he could withdraw it.

"I'm flattered. Not often, an old man gets this kind of attention, especially from a beautiful young woman."

"First of all, you're not that old. And second, I'm not as young as I look. My mother lied about my age to try to get money from Ray. Looking back, I only ran away with him to get away from her. When I told him the truth, he beat the hell out of me. How could I have been so stupid?"

"We all make bad choices," he said.

A silken strand of hair fell across one eye. She blew it aside, whispering, "At least now I met a man I would die for."

Her candor left him searching for words. "Excuse me?"

"You heard me," she said. "Am I making you nervous?"

Rigby said, "Mrs. Carson, I mean Maria, as soon as I'm well enough, I aim to hunt down Captain Pieter and your husband. Even if I have to sacrifice my life."

"Take me with you."

"That could get us both killed. This isn't a game."

"If anything happens to you, I don't want to live," she said.

Rigby felt his throat tighten. "Now, you're just acting silly."

She chewed on her bottom lip and then, in a shy voice, asked, "You said I saved your life. Was that silly of me?"

"Of course not," he admitted.

"I don't expect you to feel about me the same way I care about you." She pouted haughtily. "Has something I said upset you?"

He said, "I was thinking about something else."

"Like what?" she asked.

"Like you've got your whole life ahead of you. My time is limited," he said, trying hard not to hurt her feelings.

She undid her loose-fitting *dashiki* letting it fall around her ankles. Her bronzed body was so flawless, Rigby was tongue-tied. She turned around. Her back and buttocks showed purple bruises and raised welts.

Rigby said, "He did this?"

She lowered her eyes. Her expression revealed she enjoyed his discomfiture.

Finally, he whispered. "I wouldn't want Father Sebastian to find us like this."

Maria struggled to pull the dress up over her breasts. "You do what you have to," she said. "I'll wait for you here until hell freezes." Her mutinous eyes softened.

Rigby's mind drew a blank. He could barely bring himself to believe he had survived, and now this. Fatigue scrambled his thinking. He slowed his speech and closed his heavy-lidded eyes. Feigning sleep would give him time to think. She tucked the blanket under his chin and kissed the top of his head. After she closed the door, he opened his eyes.

*Now, what do I do*, he pondered.

***

# CHAPTER FIFTEEN

**Father Sebastian** was troubled watching the *Esperance* swing lazily on her anchor. The crew had threatened mutiny when Captain Pieter ordered them to dock at the mission's wharf. The fear of leprosy ran deep. After the *Esperance* anchored, the Congolese police launch escorting the tramp steamer, secured lines to her port side. Sebastian tried to see who disembarked, but his eyesight failed him in the downpour.

As the launch came into view, he recognized Pieter. It was a safe bet that one of the two white men accompanying Pieter was Reverend Carson. The other white man was unknown. Sebastian was familiar with the policeman in charge, a man more interested in breaking laws than enforcing them. The priest prepared himself for an ugly confrontation.

The police officer spoke French. "Father Sebastian, you are charged with harboring a known criminal. And you are holding this man's wife against her will. You will produce them at once." The backup policemen raised their weapons.

"Sir, I am not a mind-reader. Who is this so-called criminal? And who is this woman, you reference?"

"Let us not play games. You know the man's name is Croxford. It is this man's wife of which I speak—he answered, glancing at Carson. "Like you, Reverend Carson is a man of God."

Father Sebastian pointed his collapsed umbrella at Carson. "That man has battered his wife." The priest believed Maria's account of her husband's abuse, but in Congo, wife-beating is normal. "And I'll thank you not to soil my reputation by comparing me to this masquerading impostor."

Reverend Carson, who didn't understand a word of French, smiled stupidly.

Not mentioning Jesse Spooner was telling. Croxford was right. Pieter was responsible for Spooner's death, the priest realized. Who is the white man wearing sunglasses and the slouching hat? He attempted to find out by stating to the man in English, "Whoever you are, you seem unaware of the insidious company you keep, sir. Consider yourself warned."

The mystery man didn't answer, but he was in charge. He whispered to the police officer, who responded by shouting, "Father, if you do not produce these fugitives at once, I shall have my men burn your mission to the ground. Is this your wish?"

"Perhaps, you should reconsider your threat." The priest clapped his hands. Dozens of lepers appeared on the shoreline. They disrobed, which highlighted their deformities. Some were missing appendages. Like a herd of Cape buffalo attacked by lions, Captain Pieter bolted first, and his men broke ranks. They almost capsized the launch as they scrambled on board. Unguarded, Reverend Carson and the nameless man made a run for it.

As the launch pulled away from the pier, Father Sebastian yelled, "Next time you visit, I hope you will stay for tea and biscuits."

The lepers jeered the deserters.

\*\*\*

Maria Carson, Father Sebastian, and the lepers stood together watching Pieter's steamer weighing anchor. Pieter barked orders at his deckhands. Black exhaust puffs belched from the *Esperance*'s smokestack as she got underway. A prolonged blast from the ship's horn confirmed the steamer's intention.  The police launch headed off in the opposite direction.

Unbeknown to Sebastian, Maria had hired a guide with a motorized boat. She was preparing to leave the mission that night. Maria Carson was determined to warn Rigby Croxford about Captain Pieter's sudden appearance.  Her fantasy was becoming more delusional by the minute.

\*\*\*

Reed Cunningham wasn't concerned. He relaxed in the captain's quarters as the *Esperance* chugged her way upriver towards *Ugigi*. Captain Pieter had assured him that Mohamed bin Sali could handle Jesse Spooner and Rigby Croxford. Spooner's death was a setback. Now, he must deal with Croxford, but he believed he was leaving that problem in his wake. He had enlisted Pieter and Reverend Carson from the beginning. Now, he saw them for what they were, dim-witted greedy buffoons. For the time being, using them was the best option. In the end, he would have to kill them.

Before Reed Cunningham disappeared into central Africa,

he worked as a CIA operative. Most criminals justify their crimes. He had sacrificed for his country. A forced retirement was the straw that broke the camel's back. The government he swore to defend had turned its back on him. This was how he rationalized his transgressions. Truth be known, he was, by any measure, mentally unhinged. Ten-million was a powerful aphrodisiac. It wasn't about just the money; it was about getting even, or that's what he told himself. There was no turning back.

\*\*\*

The river was benevolent for two days. It was the calm before what turned into a biblical storm. Rigby's condition improved as they made their way upriver. Winnie and Sefu's spirits were lifted. Father Sebastian had highlighted the friendlier villages on a chart. They had no trouble obtaining fuel and drinkable water.

On the third day, the river turned hateful. The morning started normal, but by midday, fast-moving clouds darkened the sky. The afternoon deluge turned into a savage storm. Howling wind and torrential rain lashed Rigby's party into capitulation. They sought refuge with the other native dugouts rafted-up on the leeward side of an unnamed island. Continuous white lightning strikes fissured the purple sky. Bellowing thunder was as nerve-racking as receiving artillery fire. It took constant bailing just to stay afloat. It was as if God meant to punish the land. The sunshade disappeared as did the mosquito netting, both by wind-gusts. They huddled together at the bottom of their boat, praying for the pitiless weather to pass.

Even the *Esperance* wasn't immune. Her bow rose and slammed, discarding angry sheets of white spray. The metal seamed hull creaked and groaned in protest. Captain Pieter tried anchoring, but soft holding ground caused his vessel to drag her anchor. Pieter engaged the Lister engine to prevent drifting onto snags. Terrified, Reverend Carson and Reed Cunningham stayed in their cabins. Unsecured objects flew. The windows rattled. With zero visibility, the crew remained on deck as lookouts. They shielded their eyes and cursed Pieter's callousness.

# THE CONGO AFFAIR

Maria Carson and her guide had slipped past Pieter during the night. She was only three kilometers behind Rigby when a rogue swell swamped her dugout. With the outboard motor inoperative, her tiny boat bobbed like a cork. As swiftly as the storm started, it ended.

After the weather cleared, Maria Carson's dugout drifted with the current and into the path of the *Esperance*. Captain Pieter wasn't in the habit of rendering assistance to vessels in distress, but the white woman piqued his curiosity. Maria and her guide were too weak to climb the boarding ladder. Crewmembers lifted them over the guardrail. If Maria had not been delirious, she would have refused the rescue.

"*Enchante, madame,*" Pieter shouted down before recognizing her. "What have we here?" His face lit up. "Seems your long-lost wife has returned, Reverend Carson."

Ray Carson, who was dead drunk, yelled, "Judah said, 'Bring the harlot forth and let her be burned.'" He took a slug straight from the gin bottle.

Captain Pieter was like a bulldog sniffing a bitch. "Reverend, I run a tight ship. I'll ask you to mind your manners, or I'll have you put ashore. I won your wife fair and square with two queens and a ten of spades. Come hell or high water, I aim to collect my winnings, sir." I will have my pleasure, he thought, licking his lips

Reed Cunningham watched the proceedings from the wheelhouse. His blue eyes enlarged behind thick bifocals. When he took off his glasses, the world looked better. He pinched the bridge of his nose with his thumb and forefinger. What filthy pigs, he thought. Any qualms about killing them had vanished. Indifferent, Cunningham reopened a book.

"Take her to my cabin," Pieter ordered, spitting fruitfully over the railing.

***

Maria Carson woke up, face down and naked. Pieter had tied her spread-eagle to the bunk-bed posts. He was taking her doggy style, grunting with every thrust. His massive weight impaired her breathing. She had dreamt she was making love to Rigby. Her reality was stomach-retching. She suppressed the urge to vomit. She could feel his hairy belly bumping against her buttocks. He smelled like diesel fuel and ammonia. He drooled profusely. It ended with one final plunge into her. His body wilted as he emptied himself.

Pieter whispered in Maria's ear. "I'm not finished with you yet, my sweet. I intend to enjoy what's owed to me. Fucking you is like sticking my prick into a corpse. No wonder your husband dumped you. What you need is stimulation." He used his leather belt to beat her mercilessly. As her screaming increased, so did the severity of the whipping. He licked her buttocks, thrusting his tongue deep into her crack. He bit down hard, taking a mouthful of flesh.

Maria's agonized screams grew ever louder. Her suffering fueled his arousal. He increased his bite pressure until blood spurted. Then he remounted her placing his belt around her neck. He had never experienced such intense pleasure. He ejaculated, jerking on the belt. His convulsive climax ended with the sickening sound of bones breaking. Her body quivered one final spasm. Maria's face was frozen in a silent scream. It took him a few seconds to realize she was dead.

***

After he dumped her overboard, Captain Pieter burst into the wheelhouse. "Your wife jumped into the river while I was sleeping. So, help me, God. He peered into the night, throwing up his hands. "I knew she was crazy from the minute I laid eyes on her."

Ray Carson sobbed hysterically. His performance was a little too theatrical. He mumbled the last words of the Lord's Prayer but passed out before he could say amen.

Cunningham looked up from his book. Disgust etched the

corners of his mouth. Everyone heard Maria Carson's pitiful screaming. Even her husband, who cared nothing for his wife, deadened her sobbing with gin. There was no doubt in Cunningham's mind; Pieter had murdered Carson's wife. Killing them will be such a joy, he thought, reopening his novel.

\*\*\*

# CHAPTER SIXTEEN

**The heavens** wept incessantly after the storm passed. Most of their dry goods were soaked beyond salvage. Keeping their clothes dry was next to impossible. Wilson and Winnie hovered over Rigby like mother hens. The conditions did not slow his recuperation. Rigby seemed in better spirits with each passing hour. His yellowed complexion cleared. He was chattier, which they saw as a hopeful sign.

"When this is over, what will you do?" Rigby asked Winnie.

"I don't know."

"Will you go back to school?"

"My school has closed."

"Weren't you studying to be a nun?"

"Yes."

"Are you still interested in becoming a nun?"

Winnie burst into tears. Mentally, she believed she was tainted. She sobbed uncontrollably. Her body shook. "Captain Pieter was right about me. My life was stolen by Mohamed bin Sali."

"Winnie, listen to me. God won't hold you accountable for things done to you." He held her chin and daubed her eyes. She sniffled.

She asked, "Mr. Croxford, are you married?"

"My wife died. I have a daughter. She's a medical doctor in Zimbabwe."

Her eyes widened. "Your daughter is a doctor."

"I guess you find it hard to believe someone so wicked could have an accomplished daughter."

"You are not wicked, Mr. Croxford."

"And you're as worthy as the bishop of Rome."

"I think you were right about us. We are alike, in some ways," she said, wiping her nose. "But I'm an African, and you're white."

"I was born here. I may be white on the outside, but my heart beats to an African drum." He pointed at his heart.

"Then, we are the same."

"I take that as a compliment," he said.

Wilson knew rougher water was slowing them down, and that meant Captain Pieter's steamer was closing the gap. He listened to the 'talking drums' from the villages they passed. The *Esperance* was running around the clock, albeit at slower speeds after dark. Death on the river wasn't unusual and rarely newsworthy. He was shocked to learn a white woman's partially consumed body was discovered floating in the river. Wilson had seen one white woman, the missionary's wife, Maria Carson. Hours later, the drums confirmed his suspicions. He wanted to tell Rigby but decided to wait. Rigby wasn't himself, at least not yet. Seeking revenge could get his friend killed. Wilson was never good at hiding his emotions. His eyes never lied.

Usually talkative, Wilson went uncharacteristically mute. He screened his eyes, searching the horizon for signs of the *Esperance*. He busied himself, rearranging their depleted stores. He avoided eye contact. Wilson had a well-earned reputation for such longwinded dissertations; his listeners entertained thoughts of suicide. Now, he barely uttered a sound. The change did not go unobserved. Rigby confronted Wilson. "What's bothering you. Something's not right here."

Wilson shrugged his shoulders.

"Speak to me, damn you."

A terrible sadness filled Wilson's eyes. He looked away.

"Are the drums saying something has happened to Father Sebastian?" Rigby asked.

"No. It was a white woman."

"What white woman?"

"The missionary's woman. The one who nursed you," Wilson divulged, crossing himself.

Rigby was dumbfounded. "What about her?"

"She has passed to a better place."

"Let me get this straight. You're telling me Maria Carson

is dead? I don't believe you. She's at the mission."

Wilson shook his head. "Her body was found in the river."

"You're sure it was her?"

Again, Wilson nodded sadly. "The drums say she was thrown off Captain Pieter's ferryboat."

Rigby tried to clear his brain. Sorrow gave way to anger. She didn't deserve this, he told himself. His eyes blazed. He clenched his fists. His jaw tightened. Rigby asked Winnie, "How many days before we reach *Ugigi*?" She held up four fingers.

"And how many days before the *Esperance* overtakes us?" Wilson held up two fingers.

"So, we can't outrun her. We have a choice–we either fight or make a run for it," Rigby said aloud, knowing the answer as he said it. "We shall attack the *Esperance*."

Wilson was dumbfounded. "But we are small, and the enemy is much bigger."

"What you say is true. Just remember, the lion who roars is never the lion that kills. The element of surprise evens the odds. They're in for a rude awakening. That I promise you, my friend."

Wilson scratched his head, trying to fathom the attack.

"In all the battles we fought, have I ever let you down?" Rigby added.

"Never," Wilson said, swallowing his apprehension.

"Then find us a safe place to hide. We have two days to prepare."

The challenge was teaching Winnie how to operate the outboard motor. They stripped the dugout, making her light and more maneuverable. With everything in place, they rested for the next two days. Wilson concocted an insect repellant made from the sap of an Olon tree. It worked like a charm; the mosquitoes left them alone. They huddled together in companionable silence, listening to the river. The new moon cast only the barest of illumination on the water. Wilson or Rigby didn't miss this benefit.

Rigby addressed Winnie through cigarette smoke. "Captain Pieter says he traded a motorboat for your hand in marriage. Is this true?"

Winnie quipped, "If you were my father, would you let me marry Pieter?"

"I withdraw the question. Do you think your father is still alive?"

"If God answers my prayers, we will find him in *Ugigi.*"

"I think we do have a lot in common, you and me. So many of our friends have died," Rigby acknowledged.

She said, "I'm glad we are friends. I wouldn't want you as an enemy, Mr. Croxford." She curled up next to Sefu.

Rigby stared at the clearing sky, abandoning himself to his thoughts. He couldn't erase Maria Carson's face from his mind's eye. His thirst for revenge was overwhelming. Poor kid never had a chance, he thought. The thought of killing Pieter made his heart race. Father Sebastian was right about me. He fretted for a few seconds, then buried his concern.

As Wilson had predicted, the telltale smoke from the *Esperance* came into view right on schedule. The steamer emerged from a rain shower like a ghost ship lost at sea. Its silhouette appears dark and ominous. Soon the *Esperance* could be described in detail.

They plunged the longboat into a thick stand of river reeds and ducked. The *Esperance* motored past them, disappearing into a fog bank and then reemerging from another.

***

Daylight was fading fast as they exited the reeds. The longboat slithered over the invisible river, bumping into a light chop. To avoid detection, Winnie gave Pieter's steamer a wide berth hugging the shoreline. On cue, Pieter slowed down to avoid hitting the sandbars as the visibility decreased. The lookout's warnings carried on the water. A few times, the *Esperance* was forced to reverse her course. The best she could do was idle ahead.

It was time to launch the attack. Winnie closed the distance, steering the longboat directly behind the *Esperance*. Sefu took his place standing in the bow, ready with a mooring line. Rigby and Wilson held on. The dugout wallowed in the steamer's wake and almost broached. Water poured over the starboard side. Winnie fought for control as it lurched and cork-screwed. Sefu nearly fell overboard, but he regained his footing.

Winnie tried again. This time she was better prepared. She gunned the outboard, letting the bow nudge up against the steamer's stern. Sefu launched himself, grabbing the handrail. He hung precariously over the churning water for a split second, then managed to pull himself up over the gunwale. He secured the mooring line umbilicaling the longboat to the steamer. Sefu climbed back down into the longboat. Wilson and Rigby climbed over the railing. Both had the AKs strapped to their backs. Wilson undid the line letting the longboat drift back into the night. They heard the outboard motor and saw its wake contrasted against the black water. Winnie was following the *Esperance* at a safe distance.

Wilson and Rigby froze, letting their eyes adjust. Chests heaved in sympathy with racing pulses. Trickling sweat burned their eyes. Rigby vaguely remembered the steamer's layout. He would advance with Wilson acting as a rearguard.

# THE CONGO AFFAIR

The deckhands were preoccupied on the bow watching for snags. They could hear them grumbling about the weather. Pieter was in the pilothouse with his first mate at the helm. Reverend Carson was also in the pilothouse, but he was sleeping.

Rigby worked his way forward and ducked silently into the pilothouse unseen. "Good evening, Captain Pieter," Rigby said, raising his voice above the thumping engine.

Pieter spun around. "You!"

"You and I have unfinished business." He pointed his weapon at Pieter.

"My men will tear you to pieces. They'll feed you to the crocs."

"Perhaps, but you'll be the main course." Rigby unlocked the safety.

Pieter yelled, "Wait, wait. Look, there's enough money for everyone."

The commotion stirred Carson out of his stupor. He seemed disoriented. "What's he doing here?" He bobbed off before he heard the answer.

"Settling an unpaid debt," Rigby answered.

Rigby saw a red laser dot dance on the bulkhead a second before he heard, "You must be Croxford? Place your weapon on the floor," the man said. "That's better. Now, turn around very slowly. I wouldn't do anything foolish if I were you. I'm an accomplished marksman and at this range. Well, let's just say, missing you would be difficult."

"For God's sake, man. Shoot him," Pieter shouted.

"I believe Mr. Croxford could be useful. I guess you're wondering what happened to what's his name?"

"You killed Wilson," Rigby charged.

"Not if Wilson's a decent swimmer. I believe the late Mr. Spooner entrusted you with the exact location of the money and those unrecovered minerals."

"Maybe he did, maybe he didn't," Rigby answered.

"Wavering is not in your best interests. My arrangement with the Congolese authorities is based on retrieving those minerals, which by the way, have doubled in value since the incident. We're talking twenty-million. I or rather we get to keep the money in exchange for those minerals. Are you following me so far?"

Rigby nodded. "I take it–you're Reed Cunningham?"

"That's what it says in my passport."

"Mind telling me the name of the man who died in your place? We found his head. I forgot to ask Sali before I shot him."

"I have no idea. At any rate, I'm confident the world can survive without Mohamed bin Sali."

"The Lord is a jealous God filled with…" Carson's quote was cut short by Cunningham yelling, "Shut him up."

Rigby lowered his arms.

"Not so fast, Mr. Croxford." Rigby re-raised his arms. "That's better. You know what they say, 'Three is a party– four is a crowd.'" Cunningham locked the laser dot on Rigby's forehead. "Sorry about this, eeny-meeny-miny-moe."

Rigby held his breath. The detonation startled him. He opened his eyes. The perfectly placed shot hit Reverend Carson squarely between his eyes, which were wide open and vacant.

"Fuck!" Pieter screamed. "Why?"

"It's simple, even for a man of limited intelligence. Carson was an expendable irritant. Mr. Croxford, on the other hand, could have value."

Pieter hissed, "Leave him alone with me. When I'm finished, I'll own him."

Cunningham slapped his demand away. "I've conducted difficult interrogations–you haven't. Your mistake is judging Mr. Croxford by your weaknesses. He doesn't fear death as much as you do. This man has served his country with distinction. The concept of honor is foreign to you."

"You're making a big mistake," Pieter growled.

"Let me do the thinking, Captain Pieter. I'm trying to make you rich."

As ordered, the crew threw Reverend Carson's body overboard.

\*\*\*

# CHAPTER SEVENTEEN

**Like a** sailor buried at sea, Rigby's bindings were so tight he could scarcely breathe, let alone move. He was imprisoned in the captain's quarters adjoining the pilothouse.

Heavy rains swelled the river, which caused deeper water, and that meant Pieter could maintain a higher cruising speed until night-fog concealed the sandbars, which were unseen at one-hundred meters. The long wedge of *Esperance*'s wake broke on the shorelines. An inexperienced master wouldn't slow down, but the river had been Pieter's life, and as such, he knew it as well as he remembered his mother. He turned the steerage over to his first mate, a tall ink-black *Bantu*. Pieter hunched over a nautical chart like a ravenous bulldog protected a bone. The *Esperance* motored upriver. "Back to idle, come five degrees to starboard," Pieter barked. "Not port, turn to starboard, you idiot." He cuffed the man with his opened hand. Frustrated, the mate righted himself.

"A baboon could steer a straighter course," Pieter scoffed, pulling the gear shifter into neutral.

"Why are we stopping?" Cunningham asked.

"I cannot risk running aground," Pieter answered after he belched. "We'll anchor until the fog lifts." His breath fused the air with the smell of rotting teeth and tobacco.

Cunningham, who had been teetering on the edge of seasickness, ran to the railing and regurgitated. Pieter smiled. Reed Cunningham reentered the wheelhouse wiping his mouth.

"This isn't rough. I worked on a fishing trawler in the North Atlantic. Thirty-foot seas. Now, that was rough," Pieter said contemptuously.

Cunningham said, "Mr. Croxford, before I retire, I must warn you. Don't waste your time trying the old divide and conquer routine. I'm talking about inciting Captain Pieter against me. I think it's safe to say, Captain Pieter and I don't trust each other. We don't even like each other. Our arrangement is based solely on mutual interests. I need him and his vessel to transport the minerals to Kinshasa. He needs me and my contacts to complete the transaction. Our success can only be achieved by cooperating. Do I make myself clear?"

Rigby nodded.

"I'm glad we understand each other." Cunningham turned to face Pieter. "With that, I bid you a bonne nuit. Oh, one final thought. If I find this man has been mistreated, I will hold you responsible. I need Mr. Croxford in one piece."

"He killed my friend, Mohamed bin Sali."

"I doubt you have friends. You disobeyed my orders. I wanted Mr. Croxford and his friend delivered to me unharmed. Your lack of common sense killed his friend, not to mention, the reverend's wife."

"She killed herself," Pieter said.

Cunningham shot Pieter a sideways glance. "Please don't insult my intelligence. Everyone knows what happened. I suspect your sadistic proclivities killed her. What's done is done. I will not let your stupidity jeopardize my plans."

Pieter sulked. Cunningham retired.


Rigby's thirst for revenge was unquenchable. He laughed internally at the absurdity of asking God to spare his life long enough to kill Pieter. There was little doubt; Cunningham planned to kill everyone in the end. There could be no witnesses, not for a man intending to disappear with ten million dollars.

*** 

When Rigby woke up, he could hardly believe he was still alive. Cunningham had relieved Pieter. The armed guard had fallen asleep with his head resting on his hand. He awoke with a start when his elbow slipped.

"I need to piss," Rigby shouted.

"Piss in your pants."

"C'mon, man. You're armed."

Cunningham addressed the guard. "Untie the prisoner." He supplemented the order with hand gestures. "Be warned, Mr. Croxford, I won't hesitate to shoot you."

He kept his weapon trained on Rigby. When Rigby glanced aft into the darkness, he thought he recognized the outline of a longboat slipping in and out of the fog.

After ushering Rigby back into the pilothouse at gunpoint, Cunningham sat down across from him. It was evident he wanted to start a conversation, but he just stared as the seconds dragged on. Finally, he said, "I know a great deal about you, Mr. Croxford."

"Oh?" He lowered his voice, forcing Cunningham to lean in closer. "Enlighten me."

"Well, for starters, I know about your decorated record in the Rhodesian military. After your farm was confiscated by the Mugabe regime, you worked as a professional hunter and then as a mercenary. I understand your father named you after the Rigby Firearms Company. We do extensive background checks before we employ what I refer to as soldiers of misfortune. Sometimes we worked for the same people, not always mind you. I'm guessing you knew."

"Do you know how I lost my wife?"

"No."

"My wife was murdered because of her political activism.

"I'm sorry."

"Why are you involved in this?" Rigby asked. "The money?"

"Not in the way you think." Reed Cunningham's thin lips compressed, and the wrinkles crisscrossing his forehead deepened. His hands shook. His bloodshot eyes darted. Rigby realized that he was at his wit's end, and that made him dangerous. Cunningham started a rambling harangue by comparing their histories. Like Rigby, he had served his country with distinction. He felt they both had been deserted by their respective governments.

"Criminals kidnapped my country," Rigby said. "Our histories aren't the same."

"I can tell you know nothing about what's happened to the United States."

"I'm listening."

"My congratulations, Mr. Croxford. By engaging the abductor, the victim becomes more humanized, thereby making it difficult for the perpetrator to harm the victim. Captain Pieter, on the other hand, is a psychopath. I'm sure he intends to kill me, and you, for that matter."

"The head I found, wasn't your doing, was it? What about killing Jesse Spooner?"

"Your friend's death was unnecessary," Cunningham said, avoiding the first question.

"One question. Did Pieter kill the Carson woman?" Rigby asked.

Cunningham nodded. "His kinky persuasions killed her. I had no inkling. If I had known, I would have protected her."

Rigby showed abhorrence.

"I suspect inflicting pain gives him pleasure," Cunningham said.

"Killing Pieter would give me pleasure," Rigby confessed.

Cunningham's gaze became unfocused. It was clear his thoughts were far away. Out of the blue, he said, "By now, my detractors know the DNA from the head you found doesn't match. I'm a dead man walking. I'll never leave Congo alive."

"Why are you telling me this?"

"Oh, I don't know. You strike me as a good listener. And I'm running out of options. I need someone to help me right some wrongs, both done to me and by me."

"You work for the CIA. That means something, even in this shithole."

"Not in my case," Cunningham explained that the Central Intelligence Agency, once the bastion of patriotism, had taken sides in the upcoming presidential election. The outgoing director tried to damage a presidential candidate. The 'deep state' leaked misinformation about the candidate. The mainstream media added fuel to the fire. When he exposed the ex-director, his future with the agency was fait accompli.

Otto was right. Things don't add up, Rigby reasoned, remembering Otto Bern's forewarning.

Sensing Rigby's skepticism, he elaborated. "I sacrificed my ideals for the greater good, or so I thought. The institution I worked for betrayed me. I went to bed, believing I was a puritanical defender of our Constitution. I woke up with police officers banging on my door. I was arrested for having kiddy-porn on my computer. Naturally, the evidence was planted. There wasn't a rock big enough to hide under. Retractions are always in small print. To add insult to injury, I had to register as a child molester. I lost my friends–even my family looked at me differently. They said they believed me, but there would always be an element of suspicion. It was either kill myself or disappear." He waved expansively, indicating his surroundings. "*Voila.*"

"So, what happens now?"

"I'd be half a man if I didn't compensate the families I destroyed. I spent twenty-five years ruining lives, some because of misguided loyalty. I did to others what was done to me."

"I doubt Captain Pieter shares your noble intentions."

"Pieter's a cold-blooded psychopath. But for the time being, he's indispensable. I was counting on your friend Jesse to run this..., rust-bucket. Your friend's death was a setback. Pieter couldn't risk a replacement captain. He's an evil son-of-a-whore, but he's not stupid."

Cunningham eyed Rigby thoughtfully for several moments without uttering a word. He looked like he was weighing options. "If I thought I could trust you, we might come to an arrangement." He pressed the cold barrel of the pistol against his cheek.

"What kind of an arrangement?"

"Have each other's backs. Pieter wanted to kill you. I saved your life."

My choices are limited, Rigby thought.

"We haven't much time. Do we have a deal?" Cunningham demanded.

"For what it's worth, you have my word."

"Mr. Croxford, for some reason, I trust you. If things go wrong, promise me you'll use my share of the money to compensate the people on this list." He held up a sheet of paper and then stuffed it back into his breast pocket.

"Assuming I'm still alive. And the money is where it's supposed to be?"

"I have faith in your survival skills, Mr. Croxford."

"Question? What happened to my weapon?" Rigby asked.

"I gave it to Pieter after I removed firing-retaining-pin. "Only a matter of time before Pieter makes his move. Why make it easy. What did Jesse Spooner tell you about me?"

*Jesse said you were a liar*, Rigby remembered. "Not much. He talked about your fishing trip in Key West. Before Rigby could continue, Cunningham gave him a slight head shake and rolled his eyes. Rigby realized that Pieter had reentered the pilothouse and was standing directly behind him.

"I trust you rested well, captain?" Cunningham said.

"I'd rest better if you would let me deal with him." He bit down on his lower lip, pointing at Rigby.

Hatred raged on Rigby's face. "Like you dealt with Maria Carson, you fucking pervert?"

"You would not believe the things I have done to men," Pieter snarled. "The beating I gave you was just a taste." He swung his fist, but Rigby managed to duck, averting the full force of the blow. The unhealed gash above Rigby's eye reopened.

Rigby challenged him. "Why don't you untie me?"

An evil grin crossed Pieter's lips. "You know, I've been thinking. If the *sauvages* recover her body, she could end up in the cooking pot. There's a shortage of fresh meat these days."

Rigby struggled against his bindings.

Cunningham stepped between them. "Captain, you seem determined to prevent me from making you rich. Let it go. I know what I'm doing."

Pieter sucked on his disastrous teeth. He leaned the AK against the bulkhead. After starting the engine, he yelled at the men standing in the bow. "Weigh anchor and be quick about it, you hairless apes." Pieter engaged the Lister in and out of gear until the anchor was onboard and catted.

The *Esperance* crept ahead. As the fog thickened, Pieter decreased the cruising speed. When they rounded bends, Rigby tried to see if the longboat was following, but a bulkhead blocked his vision.

Cunningham inquired, "Captain, what's our ETA for

*Ugigi?*"

"With decent weather, three days, at the latest."

"Will we anchor here?" Cunningham asked.

Pieter looked like he was addressing an imbecile. "Well, I guess that depends on how much you enjoy the company of cannibals. The *Hema* tribe controls this part of the river. They have a sweet tooth for human meat."

Cunningham grimaced. "Captain, we are in your hands."

"We will run upriver. Ride the hook until sunup. The natives won't venture that far out, not in their flimsy *bateaus*. We don't want to be their dinner guests."

After two hours of idling, they dropped anchor in the middle of the river. A deckhand used the dull side of an ax to knock the holding pin from the anchor shackle. The chain rattled through the hawsehole until the anchor found the bottom. The thumping engine was replaced by the sound of waves lapping against the hull and a clacking halyard.

Before Cunningham and Pieter retired to their staterooms, they exchanged glances that were fraught with meaning. Rigby heard them speaking in low voices. He couldn't make out their dialogue but guessed they were scheming.

The crewmembers slept on deck in hammocks. The guard assigned to Rigby fell asleep almost immediately. Rigby gave up struggling against his bindings. Succumbing to exhaustion, he slept dreamlessly for a few hours. And then he revisited a nightmare.

*I was on an anti-poaching patrol. I remember scanning the rolling hills with my binoculars, searching for movement. The tracker crouching beside me didn't need field-glasses. Bushmen's eyesight is legendary. We discovered rhino tracks two days ago, and now the wounded female lay dying below us. I knew the poachers wouldn't relinquish the horn. Sooner or later, they would show up.*

*It was a waiting game.*

*I crawled down the hillside. The ranger was snoring peacefully. "You're up," I whispered. He yawned, then crept up the hill, joining our Bushman tracker. Circling vultures dotted the sky. I needed a cigarette, but smoke could alert the poachers. I closed my eyes.*

*My cat-nap was interrupted by the ranger tossing pebbles at me. The ranger pressed his finger to his lips, pleading for silence. A spark of understanding passed between us. After reclimbing the hill, I peeked over the rim. The poachers had encircled the rhino. Too exhausted to run, she collapsed on all fours. She snorted a final death-bellow. A blow from an ax ended her life. The poachers went to work, chopping out her horn.*

*Our ambush gave the poachers a chance to surrender. If they refused, our plan funneled them into a killing zone. They were five. We were three.*

*A smile played at the corners of the Bushman's mouth. The finale of any hunt always excited him. He had been honed into a perfect hunter by evolution. There wasn't a better tracker in Africa. He placed his fingers in his ears to protect his hearing.*

*The ranger ran at the poachers screaming in Shona, "Get down." They were so occupied with butchering; they were caught off guard. Four complied, but one bolted. I had positioned myself as the blocker. The poacher ran past me. I took a bead, but before I could pull the trigger, the ranger fired. The bullet tore into the poacher's back, rolling him into a heap.*

*And then, out of nowhere, a helicopter appeared. The news of Helen's death changed my life.*

Something startled him awake. He saw nothing and closed his eyes. A faint sound renewed his attention. From a porthole, he saw Sefu's face. Someone pushed him up into the porthole. Only a small child could squeeze through the opening. Barefooted, Sefu eased to the floor without making a sound. He tiptoed to Rigby, took the knife he carried between his teeth, and cut the bindings. The guard snorted. They froze for what seemed like an eternity. The guard shooed away a troublesome mosquito.

Rigby unlatched the dog; the hatchway swung open, screeching in protest. The guard stirred, but he didn't wake up. Wilson was waiting in the companionway. Moonshine illuminated his toothy smile. Rigby reentered the wheelhouse, grabbed an antique rifle from a gun rack, and slipped out into the passageway. They made their way to the stern only to find a night watchman urinating over the side. He had a double-barrel shotgun slung over his shoulder. They climbed the ship's ladder to the poop deck over the stern. They were now crouched directly over the deckhand. He concluded his watering with a loud fart. Sefu giggled nervously.

Wilson shushed him.

They gave the midnight urinator time to retire before descending the metal stairs. Rigby pulled a life-ring from the bulkhead and handed it to Wilson, who gave it to Sefu. Wilson had one leg over the railing. The man shined his flashlight on Sefu and then on Rigby. Rigby unlocked the rifle's safety. The crewmember hesitated, and then inexplicably, he extinguished his light. It was a Mexican-standoff in total darkness. The deckhand guarding the bow yelled in an unfamiliar language. The man answered him, and then he pushed past Rigby, whispering in Swahili, "Go in peace, my brothers."

They climbed over the railing and plunged feet first into the cold dark water. The current swept them aft. All three hung to the life ring. Rigby balanced the rifle on his head. Winnie was waiting in the longboat. They climbed up into the longboat. Rigby panted, "I didn't know you could swim."

"I just learned," Wilson said.

"When did this happen?" Rigby asked.

"Yesterday. When the '*shetani mweupe*' white devil struck me, I woke up in the river. Swimming is not so difficult. Fear of filling a crocodile's belly was my teacher."

"My friend, I can't tell you how happy I am to see you."

Wilson said, "Did you recognize the man who let us go?"

"No."

"He shot your friend, Jesse."

Instead of answering, Rigby questioned himself, how loyal were Pieter's crew? The answer could be critical.

They hugged the shoreline, slipping past the *Esperance* riding peacefully at anchor. The weather and wind were favorable. Running downwind and around the clock, Wilson pushed the longboat to her limits. Rigby disassembled the antique Springfield, drying and lubricating each part with outboard oil. He polished the five corroded cartridges with a canvas rag.

On the first day, they made one fuel stop without a problem.

The villagers on the second day were not as friendly. The village headsman demanded ten-times the going rate for gasoline, which Rigby paid without complaining. As a disincentive, he displayed his Springfield. The warning did not go unnoticed. The headsman looked hard at the rifle. Rigby noted a bamboo cage under a dead ebony tree. The cage contained a juvenile female chimpanzee. There was no relief from the sun.

Rigby said to Wilson in English, "Ask him, how much for the chimp?"

Wilson obeyed. The headsman answered him in *Bantu.* "Does the *mzungu* wish to buy her for a wife?" The villagers laughed. "If this is to be a marriage, he must pay me the '*mahari*,' dowry."

Rigby replied in fluent Swahili, "If I take her as my wife, does this mean we shall be related? Surely, she must be your mother."

The villagers' hilarity was not shared by the headsman.

After some haggling, they agreed to five-hundred thousand francs, which included the cage. Rigby handed his rifle to Wilson, whispering, "If the headsman misbehaves, shoot him." He walked over to inspect his purchase. The chimp rattled the cage smacking her lips, both signs of aggression.

"She has injured three men," a woman hollered." Be careful, mzungu."

"Unlock the cage," Rigby insisted.

"Do not be foolish," another woman cautioned.

"Open it."

She complied. The villagers scattered.

Squatting down, Rigby crawled into the cage and closed the door behind him. The young chimpanzee crouched in the far end, panting from the oppressive heat. Rigby offered her a banana without making eye contact. When the chimp refused, he peeled it and took a bite. After a few minutes, the chimp moved closer. She reached out guardedly accepting the peace offering. He repeated this act two more times. Each time the chimp moved a little closer. In the end, she jumped into his lap, putting her hairy arms around his neck. When he exited the cage, the villagers gathered around him, praising his courage. The chimp rolled back her lips threatening the onlookers.

After loading the chimp and her cage, they pushed off

from the reedy embankment. As they were pulling away, the headsman shouted, "Be careful, *bwana*, your new girlfriend has sharp teeth." He held up his bandaged hand as proof.

"Perhaps she attacked you because she found you so ugly."

The villagers hooted. Even the headsman seemed amused.

\*\*\*

They motored throughout the night, taking turns steering the longboat. As they neared *Ugigi*, Rigby and Wilson discussed the ambush. The *Esperance* had five crew members plus Pieter and Cunningham. Rigby assumed they would all be armed. Somehow, he needed to divide the crew. Nickolas Pieter seldom ventured ashore. As Wilson pointed out, this was the reason why Pieter managed to stay alive for so long. According to Winnie, the *Ubangi* was wide, but her village was on a tributary narrowed to less than three hundred meters. A plan began to formulate in Rigby's imagination.

Wilson said, "So, they are seven, and you have five bullets. The odds will be even, two against two."

"As easy as that, is it? I'm not sure this old Springfield will even fire," he replied, holding up the weapon. "The rifling is buggered. If it does fire, it won't be accurate."

"You always find a way," Wilson said.

"Nice to know you're so bloody confident."

"There is an African saying, 'One arrow can bring down an elephant,'" Wilson said.

"Elephants don't return fire."

Wilson shrugged it off.

They entered the *Ubangi* River at sunrise. The morning mist evolved into a shower. Rigby noted the floating vegetation islands drifting past them, some supporting parasitic trees. Could these islands be used to steer the *Esperance* into a trap?

Two hours later, Winnie directed Wilson into a narrow waterway. Towering *kapok* and ebony trees reinforced the heavily foliated riverbanks. The channel, circumventing shallow sandbars, was marked by bamboo poles. As they rounded a bend, *Ugigi* came into view. The reed-roofed grass huts were partially obscured by mahogany trees. Banana groves bordered the village. Fishing nets hung draped over drying racks. Overturned dugouts, some of them in disrepair, spotted the shoreline. An outboard powered dugout lay tethered to a mooring ball.

Wilson cut the outboard engine allowing the longboat to caress a rickety dock. Two skinny dogs announced their arrival. Winnie's face showed anxiety. Would she find her father alive, or had he shared her brother's fate?

"Shall I go with you?" Rigby asked Winnie.

She feared a white man's appearance would panic the village. "I must go alone."

Winnie walked up the footpath and disappeared. As they waited, Sefu and the chimp played together on the beach. Wilson searched for a tree with a clear view of the river. Rigby was antsy. The *Esperance* would arrive in two days. He was eager to explore the graveyard, but desecrating gravesites was unimaginable for Africans. They feared retribution from the departed whose graves had been vandalizing. Rigby would need to get permission from the village chief. Overshadowing everything was avenging Maria Carson's death.

An hour had elapsed before Winnie returned. Cheering

villagers, most of them women, surrounded her. Constant waring has thinned Congo's male population. Even the old witch joined the fête. Winnie's father, Stanley, and Rose were overjoyed. The villagers paid tribute to Rigby and Wilson by touching their faces. Rose lifted Sefu into the air like he was a ragdoll. Stanley kissed Rigby's hand.

Rigby hated to wet-blanket the festive mood, but time was running out. His announcement that Captain Pieter's steamer would arrive in two days silenced the crowd. The atmosphere turned somber. The villagers retreated to their huts to gather up their belongings. Safer to vanish into the jungle than face Pieter, whose penchant for violence was renown. Stanley Obo and Rose decided not to run. For them, Nickolas Pieter was the devil incarnate. Lust for revenge dispelled their fear. Disregarding her father's pleading, Winnie and Sefu would not leave Rigby's side.

Rigby's plot involved two delaying strategies. The first one entailed moving the bamboo channel markers, which would hopefully guide the *Esperance* into shallow water. A floating vegetation island towed into place would hide a sandbar, which might ground the steamer. The backup plan called for a rope stretched across the channel, which would foul the ship's single screw. Winnie and Rose braided ropes and vines into a thick hawser. Delaying the *Esperance* ensured that some crewmembers would stay behind working to free her. Either Cunningham or Pieter and maybe one crewmember would use the launch to come ashore.

With the traps set, Rigby was eager to search the graveyard. The problem was avoiding a village insurrection. He listened to Winnie describe her captivity to the villagers. Winnie avoided the depraved parts. Winnie's recollection of her brother's death cast a dark shadow. Stanley and Rose wept.

# CHAPTER EIGHTEEN

**By questioning** passing natives, Wilson learned that the *Esperance* lay anchored at the mouth of the *Ubangi* River. It was a safe bet that Pieter would not venture into uncharted waters without proper sunlight. Rigby used the time to discuss the subject of digging up the grave. He started circuitously by asking Stanley about the shootout.

"So, you do remember the shootout?"

"Sure. We all ran away, but I crawled back. I hid over there," Stanley said, pointing at some banana trees.

"What did you see?"

"There were three white men and some soldiers. When the shooting stopped, two of the whites and the soldiers were dead."

"And then what happened?" Rigby asked.

Stanley shivered. "One white man was only wounded. He rolled the soldiers into the river. Then he dragged the bodies of the two white men to where we bury our dead."

"In the Catholic graveyard?" Stanley nodded cautiously.

"What else did you witness?"

"Nothing. I was afraid the *mzungu* would see me."

"Was there a barge? What happened to the truck? Did you see the wounded mzungu leave in the 'mashua' boat towing the barge?"

Stanley stared at Rigby quizzically, thinking how does he know these things. "There was a big truck loaded with many barrels."

"You said the soldiers died. Who moved the truck?"

Stanley looked frightened. Rose, who had been listening, said, "Tell him the truth."

Stanley confessed that when he came out of hiding, the white man did catch him. The man forced him to help drag the dead bodies to the graveyard. Then they loaded the barrels onto the barge. When the man's wounds reopened, he gave up. He warned Stanley that if the police found the truck, they would make big trouble for the village. After the wounded man left in the mashua, Stanley moved the lorry. Then he walked home.

"Was the truck ever recovered?" Rigby asked.

"The police never found the lorry," Stanley explained that the roads were muddy. The truck kept getting stuck. He rolled the lorry into a ditch and covered it with limbs and leaves. He appeared puzzled. "The barrels contained worthless dirt," he explained.

Precious minerals that could come in handy as a bargaining chip, Rigby thought.

"One more question. Did you see the wounded man throw anything into those graves, besides the bodies?"

"No. How do you know these things?" Stanley queried.

"The man who survived the shootout told my best friend. He was killed by Mohamed bin Sali."

Stanley asked, "What happened to the wounded man."

"Died in an American prison for killing his girlfriend. He found her with another man."

Stanley appeared conflicted. In central Africa, killing a promiscuous girlfriend is not a crime.

Stanley's tone sharpened. "Sali killed my son and dishonored my daughter. The drums say you killed him. For that, I owe you my life."

"This man had a hand in killing Sali," Rigby said, recognizing Wilson. Stanley shook Wilson's hand vigorously.

"What I need from you will take great courage," Rigby told Stanley about the stolen money hidden in the same grave where James Cheatham buried the two white men. The idea of desecrating a grave caused Stanley's face to register fear. Seeing his distress, Rigby tried a different approach. He mentioned that Captain Pieter was coming for the money, which had the desired effect. Stanley fixated on avenging his son's death.

Without consulting Stanley, Rose exclaimed, "We will help you."

"It would mean digging up that grave," Rigby cautioned, thinking if you want work done in Africa, you must find a woman to do it.

"Come, we are wasting time," Rose said.

*I was right about her*, Stanley realized. *She is a serious woman.*

The gravesite was where Cheatham had claimed. They used digging sticks and hoes to excavate the red-earth beneath the giant tamarind tree. Stanley's digging was compromised, but Rose burrowed like an anteater unearthing a termite mound. As Rigby had hoped, the grave was shallow. Cheatham's injuries prevented him from digging deeper. The six duffel bags were on top of the corpses, but that didn't mask the stench. Wilson passed the bags up to Rigby. He opened a duffel bag and whistled. Rigby tunneled his hand through the bundles of currencies until he felt the diamonds.

The old witch fumed, watching them desiccate the gravesite. Vandalizing the graveyard would indeed cast an evil spell on her village. She waved her fist at the graverobbers shouting incoherent threats. Rigby walked over and handed her a bundle of Euros. The witch was instantly pacified. She stuffed the cash between her sagging breasts. She even helped them refill the grave. They bowed their heads as she recited an abbreviated Swahili prayer. After thanking Rigby, she limped away humming. Rigby worried about hiding the money. The solution was to hide each duffel bag under an overturned dugout.

With the sun setting in a few hours, Rose cooked catfish and yams on an open fire. Attracted by the smell, villagers re-emerged from the jungle-like zombies.

There was nothing to do but wait. Winnie recounted her river experience. When she described Rigby's escape from Pieter's steamboat, the villagers cheered. Rigby whispered to Stanley, "You must be very proud of your daughter. Maybe now she'll get married. Start a family."

Rose replied before Stanley could. "Congolese men will never marry her. She is a marked woman."

"But that's crazy," Rigby said.

"Men are like foolish children," Rose said, grabbing Stanley's hand. "Not all men," she added.

A helicopter flew overhead. Helicopters are harbingers of death. Screaming villagers disappeared into the jungle. Rigby shaded his eyes, looking up. Rose and Stanley stood their ground. Wilson, Sefu, and Winnie didn't move.

After hovering, Nigel Birtwistle landed his Jet-ranger on the shoreline. The landing kicked up the embers from the campfire. After the rotors stopped spinning, two white men carrying briefcases disembarked behind Nigel.

"Terribly sorry, old boy," Nigel apologized. "This wasn't my idea."

"Who are they?" Rigby asked, indicating the men standing behind Nigel.

Nigel turned to the passengers. "I'd tell him if I were you. Mr. Croxford doesn't have a sense of humor."

"We work for the American government," one of them answered.

"To what do we owe the honor of this visit?" Rigby said, raising his rifle.

"Do we have a problem?" the other man asked curtly.

"That depends on your answer," said Rigby, engaging a cartridge.

"Take it easy. We're looking for an American," he answered, holding up his hands.

"That would be Reed Cunningham."

The Americans glanced at each other. "You know, Reed?"

"Quite well, in fact."

"So, he is alive?"

Rigby nodded, but thought, not for long if you find him. His memory drifted back to his past dealings with CIA agents. They had one common trait; they never told the truth about anything. "Maybe he is, maybe he isn't. Alive, that is."

"I detect antagonism," one of them said.

"I lost two friends this week. Both Americans, I might add."

"Would you mind pointing that antique in another direction? These might come in handy," he said, handing Rigby a briefcase, which he opened. It contained an Uzi submachine gun with a pistol grip. The other American gave Wilson his briefcase. It contained an identical weapon. "And yes, they're both loaded." Wilson mock fired the gun skyward.

Rigby inquired, "Sorry, I didn't get your names." The American waved off the request.

"Okay. How about answering my dumb questions?"

"Shoot," said one American.

"Not the best response for someone holding a firearm. Does Reed Cunningham work for American intelligence?"

"Past tense. Next question."

Rigby threw up his hands. "You know, I've been soldiering for thirty years. I've dealt with guys like you before. One thing stands out–you're all habitual liars. Why should I believe you?"

# THE CONGO AFFAIR

"Can't say I blame you. Let me start at the beginning."

Rigby sat down on a log. The Americans leaned against an overturned dugout facing him.

"Can you excuse us?" the American asked Nigel.

"Nigel's been my friend for thirty years. He stays."

The Americans glanced at each other. "Fair enough."

"Before you get started, Reed Cunningham says you guys are gunning for him. Says, he expects to die for the crimes you invented."

"Is that so? Mr. Cunningham has a vivid imagination. Let's talk about him for a moment." He started by praising Cunningham's early career. As Reed neared retirement, he started skimming, which they defined as siphoning monies destined for causes in central Africa. They allowed his minimal digressions to continue because he was their most useful asset in Africa. The 'good-life' was Reed's Achilles' heel. Cunningham had numbered accounts in Switzerland and the Cayman Islands.

As Rigby listened, he realized his suspicions about Cunningham were correct; he was a liar. He was unmarried, and he lived in Cape Town, South Africa, with his mistress. Cunningham's account of the attempt to frame him was bullshit.

"Wait. You're not telling me the whole story. You could have stopped Cunningham before things ran amuck," Rigby said.

"We made a mistake on that one," the American admitted.

The other American added, "Our assignment was to identify a mole working for the Chinese Communist Party inside the Congolese government. We screwed up."

"Your screwup killed two innocent people."

"I'm sorry. Look, here's the bottom line." He summarized the behind-the-scenes struggle underway between China and the United States on the African continent. The payoff was controlling Africa's natural resources. "We believe our country would be a more benevolent caretaker."

"Your country has made a mess of Africa. That includes killing this country's first black leader, Patrice Lumumba."

"An unsubstantiated allegation, Mr. Croxford."

Rigby opened his mouth and then shut it as he rehearsed what he was about to say. "Tell that to the billion Africans who believe otherwise."

"So, you think China has Africa's best interests at heart?"

"It's no secret—China is a curse on Africa. How about Africans as the caretakers?" Rigby suggested."

"Tell that to the Chinese."

"There's an old African proverb. 'When two bull elephants battle, it is the grass beneath them that gets trampled.'"

"Mr. Croxford, in this battle, the whole world could get trampled. Let's hope it doesn't come to that."

"You still haven't told me why you didn't step in."

The Americans glanced at each other. One of them admitted that Reed Cunningham had initiated the mineral transaction as a means of identifying the mole working for the People's Republic of China. The screw up was the shootout. Cunningham saw the botched robbery as his golden parachute.

"What was James Cheatham's involvement?"

"A hired hand, nothing more." Cheatham murdering his girlfriend was an unforeseen event, as was his involving Reverend Carson. The man speaking added that Cunningham had to think he was the luckiest man in the world. All roads were leading him to a pot at the end of a rainbow. The Chinese were hellbent on protecting their mole working for the Congolese Government. Our side still had hopes of identifying him. Cunningham was our means to that end.

"So, you were playing Cunningham," Rigby said. "Even after you knew he was only interested in the money."

"Yes. By this point, Reed was hellbent on feathering his nest. A government pension could never satisfy his lifestyle. We believe he viewed this as his swansong."

Rigby speculated. "I reckon Cunningham's shelf-life is past due."

"Not really." He revealed that Reed Cunningham would have taken steps to protect himself by threatening to go public with specific top-secret intelligence. It was the indemnification ploy used by other compromised agents.

"What happens now?"

"We make a deal. We get Cunningham. You keep the money. It's the least we can do. We know the *Esperance* will show-up sometime tomorrow. We even the odds." Both Americans opened their windbreakers, revealing holstered pistols. "I assume you've recovered the robbery money?"

Rigby didn't answer. "Just out of curiosity, what's in Cunningham's future?"

"Reed? He lives out his life with his mistress in exile. Comfortably, but not lavishly. He forfeits his passport. And he's watched around the clock. We call it lifelong house-arrest."

"Sounds bloody awful," Rigby said, looking at Nigel.

"Most unpleasant," Nigel acknowledged wrinkling his nose.

Rigby held out his hand. "You've got a deal under one condition."

"Which is?"

Rigby described his efforts to waylay the *Esperance*. He concluded by demanding, "The captain's name is Nickolas Pieter. "When this is over, he's mine to do with as I wish."

"Fair enough.  I'm guessing you know the location of those minerals."

"I do."

"Any chance…?"

Rigby shook his head.

"Didn't think so."

***

# CHAPTER NINETEEN

**Nigel repositioned** his Jet-ranger in an abandoned maize field behind the village. As the daylight faded, they huddled around the campfire. The Americans retired to an abandoned hut to sleep. Rose and Stanley did the same. Winnie, Wilson, and Sefu slept underneath overturned dugouts. Rigby and Nigel sat alone, staring at the glowing coals. Light from the campfire flickered on their faces. Moths drawn to the campfire attracted bats. Occasionally a spark ignited. They shared a bottle of Gordon's gin.

"What's your read on the Americans?" Rigby asked Nigel in a low whisper. "Cheeky bastards, they are."

"Candidly?"

"Yes."

"I'd take their promises cum grano salis," Nigel added between sips straight from the bottle.

"Translation?"

"With a pinch of salt."

"That's what I thought." Giving me the money was never their intention, Rigby reiterated to himself. "Nigel, when push comes to shove, can I count on you?"

"They chartered my helicopter, not my honor. Surprised, you'd have to ask."

"Figured as much," Rigby said, passing him the bottle. "No offense."

"Apology accepted."

Rigby walked away from the campfire. Nigel thought he was taking a leak. Rigby returned, dragging a duffel bag. "Nigel, I've decided to purchase your helicopter."

"For what purpose?"

"What bloody difference does it make? Who knows, maybe I'll take up flying."

Nigel's right eye stared left, and his other one gazed right. "You do know there are more expedient ways to kill yourself.'"

Rigby said, fixating on Nigel's shiny nose. "Tell me when to stop." He tossed bundles of Euros into Nigel's lap.

"That's enough for three helicopters plus my retirement."

Grinning, Rigby said, "Good, then it's settled. I own you and your bird."

"What now, milord?" Nigel asked.

"If I survive tomorrow, can you fly me back to Zimbabwe?"

"That would be difficult."

"Difficult doesn't mean impossible."

"Lots of obstacles. Some could be insurmountable." Nigel explained that the distance between Congo and Zimbabwe was two-thousand kilometers. The flight would require fuel stops, which entailed illegally crossing borders because they would be smuggling a large amount of money. And they would be unarmed. Getting caught transporting weapons meant facing a firing squad. "God forbid, we have a mechanical. Your venture will be fraught with dangers."

"So, are you in or out?" Rigby asked.

"In, of course. I wouldn't miss this for the world. We could depart before the hostilities."

"Not before Nickolas Pieter gets what he deserves."

"Like Hipolito said, 'I do applaud thy constant revenge.'"

Rigby outlined his strategy. Nigel reminded him that many native villages had suffered attacks during Congo's never-ending civil wars. And as such, most villages had well-established escape routes. If *Ugigi* were assaulted from the river, the villagers would merely disappear into the jungle. Reed Cunningham had a military background. Pieter had endured Congo's turbulent warring. It was a safe bet that either Cunningham or Pieter would approach the village using an escape route. To avoid getting trapped in a crossfire, Rigby needed to amend his plan.

"Nigel, when this is over, I'm gonna miss you. Can't say I'll miss your country."

"Oh, I don't know. It grows on you.

"So does skin cancer. Ever consider Zimbabwe?"

"You mean trade pandemonium for bedlam?"

"I've habituated to the chaos," said Rigby.

"Croxford, you thrive on unpleasantness."

"Maybe so. I'm having the most god-awful nightmares. What about you?" Rigby waited for a response. Sleep had crept up on Nigel. He dozed lightly.

Rigby gave him a nudge, "Wakeup, Nigel." Nigel yawned.

"Quickly, my lord. I need my beauty rest."

"Why do the people around me keep dying? And why have I been spared? It doesn't seem fair."

"It is not in the stars to hold our destiny but in ourselves."

"Not sure I take your meaning. But thanks, anyway."

"Don't thank me. Thank the Bard of Avon. Sweet dreams."

As Rigby stared into the star-peppered sky, he felt re-energized. Looming violence always heightened his senses. Most combatants feel immortal before going into battle. Warring requires it, he reasoned. His dreaming drifted back in time to a distant land.

He envisioned himself in Sudan.

*I remember lying in wait for the Janjaweed to attack. Jesse hunkered down beside me. The desert moon was bright. The night air was chilly. Hyenas' giggling dominated the pitiful sounds of an animal being eaten alive.*

*"What the hell was that?" Jesse whispered.*

*"Spotted Hyenas. Someday, I'll end up in a hyena's belly. Only fitting, I reckon."*

*"Let's hope tomorrow isn't the day. Hey, that reminds me, what are the rules of engagement?" Jesse asked.*

*"Rules? This is Africa. The only rule is to shoot the enemy before he shoots you. Were you an officer in the Marines?"*

*"How did you know?"*

*"Just a wild guess."*

*"Is that a problem?"*

*"Not for me."*

I knew the Arabs would use an attack helicopter. *"Everything depends on you taking out their gunship. Jesse, I need you at the top of your game."*

*"Gotcha covered,"* he said, caressing the barrel of his Barrett fifty-caliber.

***

The desert was featureless at dawn. And then, like a mirage, the exhaust fumes of an attack helicopter wavered on the horizon. Black Arabs dressed in flowing robes riding war camels and decorated horses lined the far side of the wadi. One Arab carried a green Islamic pennant. Their high-pitched tongue trilling raised the hair on my arms. My ragtag Sudanese natives stirred restlessly. I sensed their fear.

*"Jesse, if we don't do something, the first shot will scatter them."*

We slid down the face of the dune and dropped our pants. Baring our asses and jeering the enemy was contagious. Our first-time warriors followed suit, hooting and hollering insults. Their insolence enraged the Arabs, who believed they were unbeatable. They viewed the Africans as cowards. How could they lose? They charged down into the wadi. The trap was sprung.

I had ordered the soft-sand cliff protecting our foxholes steepened. Their camels and horses tried to charge up the face, but it was useless. Some somersaulted backward, crushing their riders. We had the high ground with the rising sun at *our backs. It was like shooting chickens in a coop. Camels bellowed. Stampeding horses bucked off their riders—panic spread.*

*And then the attack helicopter joined the firefight. The first strafing run was off the mark. Bullets hit all around us. We ducked into our foxholes. I could see the snarling lion painted on its fuselage as it roared overhead. We jumped up and returned fire, but our small calibers only ricocheted. The pilot banked around for another run. This time, he flew straight at us. I could see the pilot's face.*

*"Jesse, it's now or never," I yelled. "Fire, damn you."*

*Jesse held his ground. The helicopter's twin twenty-caliber cannons blazed. Ricocheting rounds kicked-up sand on either side of him. He didn't flinch. Jesse fired at the last second. The fifty-caliber shell shattered the canopy. I saw the pilot wince as the bullet went through him. The helicopter hovered momentarily before spinning out of control. An orange fireball filled the sky, followed by black smoke. Unspent ammo ignited.*

*A dying camel's death throes refocused the fighting. The downed helicopter seemed to sap the Arabs' will to fight. Wild cheering on our side erupted. The Arabs retreated. It was over.*

*"Jesse," I yelled. "If you weren't so bloody ugly, I'd kiss you."*

*"Aw shucks, 'tweren't nothin','" Jesse said. He tried unsuccessfully to light a cigarette.*

*I steadied his shaking hands. "Jesse, if you had waited for another second, I would have shit myself. Brilliant shot."*

*We knew the Arabs would come again. But on this day, we celebrated.*

\*\*\*

Rose shook Rigby and Nigel awake, whispering, "It is

time, my brothers." She handed them gourds of hot weed-tea. It took Rigby a few seconds to collect his thinking. Nigel rubbed the sleep from his eyes.

Nigel handed Rigby a satellite telephone. "I can get back here in one hour."

"Save my ass one more time, hey, Nigel?"

"God, willing."

The first order of business was to load the money into the helicopter. At first light, Nigel would fly the money to Father Sebastian's mission for safekeeping. The fear of leprosy offered more protection than a bank. After delivering the money, Nigel would wait for Rigby's call.

"Rose, do you trust these Americans," Rigby whispered, glancing at the hut where they slept.

"No. The eye never forgets what the heart has seen."

Rigby rehearsed his plan internally. He hoped the *Esperance* would run aground, which would divide Pieter's crew. The sticking-point was Pieter. He remembered Cunningham's uncanny warning, '*Pieter is a psychopath, but he's not stupid.*' It was a safe bet that Pieter and Cunningham planned to double-cross each other. He had advised Wilson to keep an eye on the Americans, whose intentions were hazy. My plan has too many moving parts; he voiced to himself. Too late to change it now.

Nigel lifted off at daybreak, reduced power, and banked away from the river. Rigby watched the helicopter disappear. He felt vulnerable.

\*\*\*

# CHAPTER TWENTY

**Captain Pieter** waited for daylight before weighing anchor and entering the Ubangi River. As a precaution, he sent a scouting party ahead in the motorized launch. The sun couldn't penetrate the tannic-colored water. He was running blind in uncharted waters. A deckhand tossed a leaded sounding-line from the bow, calling out the depths. After two hours of idling, Cunningham encouraged Pieter to pick up speed.

Pieter pointed at a submerged boulder. "The last grounding cost me one-million francs. Will you cover the damages?"

"After tomorrow, you can buy a yacht and move to the West Indies."

"Quiet!" Pieter shouted, raising his hand.

The crewmember yelled, "One and a half fathoms, captain."

Scanning with binoculars, Pieter said, "Steady as she goes. Keep an eye out."

The helmsman obeyed, wiping sweat from his eyes. "Aye, aye, captain."

Deeper water was defined by the misplaced channel markers. The *Esperance* zigzagging between two markers churned up mud. Pieter grabbed the ship's wheel, but not in time. A loud bumping sound was followed by silence. Pieter ran to the starboard side and looked overboard. He was dragging the braided hawser that fouled the propeller, which strangled the diesel engine. She coasted for a few meters before striking the sandbar. Pieter grabbed the handrailing as the *Esperance* jolted to a standstill.

Pieter yelled, "Run faster, you said. Lucky for you, I didn't listen."

Cunningham looked sheepish. Pieter followed him into the wheelhouse. He spread a land-map over the binnacle. "We are here. *Ugigi* is three kilometers upriver," he said, pinpointing both spots.

Cunningham rubbed his temples. "Now, what do we do?"

"After we clear the running gear, we back her off and precede upriver."

"What if Croxford shows up?"

"He's already here," Pieter said.

"How can be sure?" Cunningham asked.

"Trust me, stranding us was his doing. He wants to separate us." Pieter turned to his first mate. "Don't just stand there. Get divers in the water. I want the propeller sorted."

"What about the crocs?" the first mate asked, searching the riverbanks with bug eyes.

"Deal with the crocs or me. Which would you prefer?"

A lookout shouted, "Captain, the launch is returning." Lines were tossed down.

Pieter barked, "Whose idea was this?" The men pointed at each other, trying to escape the blame. "Well done." They both smiled, trying to take credit. Winnie Obo's elbows were tied behind her back. "This does change things." He looked upriver, musing to himself. It's your move, Mr. Croxford.

*** 

They didn't have long to wait. "Captain," the lookout yelled, pointing at the approaching longboat. Rigby stood in the bow with Wilson at the tiller. They pulled alongside.

"So, we meet again, Mr. Croxford." Pieter turned to his crew, "If he doesn't obey me, shoot the organ grinder and his monkey. Keep shooting until I tell you to stop."

Rigby yelled, "Let her go, Pieter. I'm the one you want."

"As I see it, three hostages are better than one."

Pieter addressed Reed Cunningham. "You claim you know where the money is buried. It's time you earned your keep. I'm giving the orders now. Kindly exchange places with Mr. Croxford. I can give you two of my men. I will remain on board. He glanced at Winnie, unconsciously licking his lips. "Cunningham, returning without the money is not in your best interests."

"What about the villagers?" Cunningham asked.

"Blackies scatter at the sound of gunfire," Pieter replied.

"You have weapons. Use them."

Rigby followed Wilson up the boarding-ladder. *He doesn't know about the Americans. You split your force. The wrong move,* he told himself. Cunningham set off in the launch with two armed guards. Rigby, Wilson, and Winnie were held in the wheelhouse. An armed crewmember guarded them.

The commotion attracted crocodiles. The water was alive with yellow eyes. Inquisitive, they zeroed in on the divers. The divers clung to the tangling rope-ladder. Pieter was incensed. He fired a warning shot. The divers wouldn't budge.

A blood-curdling scream startled them. A crocodile had latched on to a diver's foot–dragging him off the ladder. The second diver levitated up the rungs. The croc's death-roll twisted the man's leg off at the knee joint. More crocs were attracted to the blood. A massive male engulfed the diver's torso in its jaws and swam away. Smaller crocs harried the monster tearing off bitesize pieces of shredded flesh. The water boiled red. The crocs raised their heads, swallowing the chunks.

Pieter yelled, "Enough! I want the *mzungu* and his *Rafiki.*"

Rigby and Wilson were led on deck. Pieter said to Rigby, "Your *kaffir* will clear my running gear." He handed Wilson a machete. "In the water, and be quick about it." The crew looked relieved. They raised their weapons.

"He can't swim," Rigby said, taking the machete. "I'll do it." Wilson didn't argue.

"Very well," Pieter said. His smile showed more gums than teeth.

Rigby removed his boots and shimmied down the ship's rope-ladder. Bits of flesh and blood clouded the water. The feeding crocs were preoccupied, but he knew they would lose interest once the body had been eaten. He filled his lungs and slipped beneath the surface. Visibility was so restricted; he had to use the hawser to pull himself down to the running gear. Something bumped against his leg. He spun around, thrusting the machete like a spear. What he envisioned as a crocodile was the rudder. His brain craved oxygen. He reemerged gasping for air. After hyperventilating, he tried again. This time, he locked his legs around the propeller shaft. The razor-sharp machete cut through the braided-hawser quickly. After yanking the loose strains free, he popped to the resurface and scaled up the ladder.

"Good work," Pieter said. "Let's see if you can make it to the shore. Rigby knew if he got past the crocs, the crew would use him for target practice.

"Back in the water," Pieter ordered.

Rigby said, "Cunningham won't find it."

"By it, you mean the money?"

"Yes."

"How do I know you're not trying to save yourself?"

"I reburied it, " Rigby answered defiantly. To support his claim, he retrieved a diamond from his breast pocket and tossed it to Pieter.

Pieter showed exasperation. "If you've lied to me, I'll kill you and your *kaffir* friends." He wet the diamond with saliva and held it up to the light.

He ordered his first mate to restart the ship's engine. Emitting puffs of black smoke, the diesel thumped back to life. Reversing backed her off the sandbar.

They idled slowly upriver. Rigby noticed the absence of wading birds. The monkeys were silenced. Nothing stirred.

Deckhands used the *Esperance*'s crane to hoist the lifeboat over the side. Pieter said, "You two, come with me." Then he turned to the man he thought he could trust. "While I'm gone, you're in charge. The *mzungu* may have a trick up his sleeve. If you hear gunfire, I want you to shoot the hostages. Do you understand what I'm saying?" Rather than answer, the first mate nodded.

"After you, Mr. Croxford," Pieter said, motioning to the lifeboat.

They secured the lifeboat to a mooring stake. Rigby led them up the muddy trail to the village. Pieter positioned himself behind Rigby with the crewmembers protecting his flanks. Even the dogs had vanished. Campfires still smoldered. Kettles contained uneaten food. The evacuation appeared hurried.

Rigby stopped in front of the previously dug up gravesite. "I reburied it here," he said, straightening the crooked cross.

Pieter squatted and picked up a handful of freshly turned soil. He sifted the red dirt through his fingertips, addressing Rigby. "God, help you if we don't find it."

The village witch halted the excavation. She hobbled out of her hut, screaming at the desecrators. Horrified, they dropped their digging sticks. Having lived most of his life in Africa, Pieter wasn't immune to superstitions. Her mantra was fever-pitched. White foam gathered at the corners of her mouth. Her performance was award-winning. Pieter and his men were mesmerized. The Americans exited the hut unnoticed.

Regaining his senses, Pieter shouted, "Don't just stand there, shoot her," His men picked up their weapons, aimed, but then they hesitated.

Rigby blocked the shooters. "Pieter, even you can't kill her. She's a harmless old fool."

"Oh, no. Watch me," Pieter yelled, grabbing an AK.

Rigby saw the Americans move out of the corner of his eye. Both had leveled their pistols. Instinctively, he knew they were about to open fire. He jumped between Pieter and the Americans, waving his hands. "Don't shoot."

An American yelled, "Get down."

Rigby shouted that two hostages would be executed if gunshots were heard. Everyone lowered their weapons. Pieter and his armed guards retreated to the river. Rigby and the Americans did nothing to stop them. The ceasefire was maddening. Both sides had lost, or so it seemed.

The Americans produced Reed Cunningham with his hands bound. He looked reconciled to his fate. Rigby found the slip of paper in Cunningham's breast pocket. Cunningham had insisted it contained the names of individuals he wanted to compensate. As expected, it was blank. They did not speak. There was nothing to say.

Standing on the shoreline, Rigby watched Pieter's men stow the lifeboat. Wilson, I hope you know what you're doing. Wilson claimed that Pieter's first mate did shoot Jesse, but he was following orders. The man wouldn't harm Wilson because they were members of the same tribe. Wilson's persistence conquered Rigby's misgivings.

\*\*\*

Safely on board, Pieter bellowed at the first mate, "After we get underway, throw the hostages overboard. Let the crocs do our work."

"What about the girl?"

"I'll do her myself," Pieter said.

Pieter didn't see Stanley standing in the shadows. When he did, he rubbed the scar on his cheek, saying, "What's this? The thief has come for his whoring daughter. More food for the crocs. Not here. Dying can be messy." He stuck the gun-barrel into Stanley's back, shoving him towards the doorway.

"I trusted you," Pieter snapped, pushing his first mate behind Stanley. "You betrayed me."

Rose was waiting outside. She struck with the swiftness of a mongoose attacking a cobra. Her honed machete severed Pieter's hand as cleanly as a surgeon's scalpel. Pieter stared at the twitching hand as if it wasn't his. The stump sprayed blood. Pieter screeched like a woman giving birth.

His crew did not intervene. Years of maltreatment had hardened them.  Thoughts of sharing the robbery money had vanished. Their indestructible captain had been hood-winked. Four crewmembers commandeered the launch and abandoned the *Esperance*, leaving the first mate and Captain Pieter to fend for themselves.

*** 

Rigby tossed a rope down to Wilson. Wilson directed Rigby to the wheelhouse. The first mate looked petrified. He looked up at Rigby, and with a trembling voice, begged, "Please, don't kill me."

"Wilson has convinced me to spare you." The man fell to his knees, grabbed Rigby's hand, and kissed it.  He helped him to stand up. "I need a promise from you."

"Anything," he gushed.

Rigby told him that Pieter's wife, Rose, was the new owner of the *Esperance*. Rigby concluded by asking, "Will you help Rose and Stanley with their new venture?"

"I promise to do my very best," he said, looking confused by the implication.

"Wilson will report to me. You do not want to disappoint me."

"I live to serve you, *bwana*."

"Then, go well."


Rigby ordered everyone off the *Esperance*. There could be no witnesses. He walked to the stern, where Pieter sat in a pool of blood. A belt tourniquet had staunched the bleeding. Pieter and Rigby didn't speak until they were alone. The minutes droned on painfully.

Finally, Pieter stammered, "I...I give you my money. You let me go. I'm nothing to you."

Rigby shook his head.

Pieter croaked, "You..., you call yourself a Christian?"

Rigby laughed without humor. "No one ever accused me of being a Christian."

Pieter said, "We are not like these *noir sauvages*. We are *blanc hommes*."

Rigby said, "I need to know how the Carson woman died."

"An accident. I swear before God," Pieter sobbed, crossing himself with his mangled remnant.

As he listened to Pieter change Maria Carson's death by suicide to accidental, he envisioned her face. Something clicked in his head. His eyes narrowed. Pieter recognized the change. He knew he had only seconds to live. Too weakened to run, he cried out for help. No one answered.

Fueled by hatred, Rigby slammed into Pieter, lifting

him over the railing. Pieter seized the guardrail with his left hand and hung on. Rigby tried prying his fingers loose; then, he gnawed on Pieter's thumb. A spine-chilling scream ended with a splash. Pieter's floundering was feeble. The current swept him away.

Crocodiles slithered down the riverbanks. The water churned into a jumble of snapping jaws and twisting bodies. As quickly as the feeding began, it ended. Calm replaced carnage. An oily slick marked the spot.

Villagers mingled at the water's edge to celebrate Captain Pieter's death. The witch recounted her performance to enthusiastic applause. Rigby introduced Rose as the new ferryboat owner. He knew Rose would be successful. Rose had spunk, and she had Pieter's first mate and Stanley to support her. He paid Wilson and his brother generous bonuses, making them wealthy by African standards. At his insistence, they signed on as deckhands to help Rose get started with her new venture.

Life at *Ugigi* returned to normal. The women went back to work. The men gossiped and drank palm wine. A Congolese military helicopter airlifted the Americans and Reed Cunningham to Kinshasa. They left without saying goodbye, which Rigby found odd. Nigel Birtwistle was due in two hours.

Rigby took Winnie aside. "Did you do what I asked of you?"

"Yes."

"You're sure they didn't see you?"

"They were sleeping."

"And what you hid will not be discovered?"

"Everything was done as you asked," Winnie said

He placed his hands on her shoulders. "Winnie, you did well."

\*\*\*

# THE FINAL CHAPTER

**Waiting for** Nigel gave Rigby time to reflect. He thought about Jesse Spooner and Maria Carson and his wife and how their deaths were unwarranted. Rigby remembered arguing with his daughter. Who said life is fair, he asked her? My life has been a series of random tragedies. It has to get better.

Rigby shaded his eyes, watching Nigel's helicopter land in the maize field. Rose and Winnie cried. Stanley and Wilson became emotional. Everyone said they would meet again. No one believed it would happen. Rather than shut down his Jet-ranger, Nigel lifted off before Rigby could tighten his seatbelt. Rigby gave the villagers a thumbs-up.

Nigel zoomed out over the anchored *Esperance*, banked sharply down the *Ubangi*, and headed straight for the Congo River. It was safer to fly in the middle of the river. Taking potshots at aircraft was a Congolese pastime. An engine failure meant autorotating into the river. If they didn't drown, the crocs would eat them. But flying over the jungle was even more dangerous. Surviving a crash-landing into giant trees was doubtful.

"Why the long-face, Nigel?"

Nigel motioned to use his microphone. Rigby complied, asking, "What's wrong?"

Nigel said an informant working for the Congolese military told him that when the Americans landed at the Kinshasa Airport, Reed Cunningham was not a passenger. Rigby proposed that they dropped Cunningham off. Nigel conceded that they dropped Cunningham off. The question was, from what altitude was he dropped. There was little doubt; Reed Cunningham was dead. Cunningham might have been a psychopath, but his death prophecy was real. Both knew they had not seen the last of the Americans. Surrendering the money was never their intention.

Touching down, they were met by cheering lepers. The drums had relayed the news of Captain Pieter's death. Father Sebastian reprimanded the unchristian behavior, but his eyes told a different story. Nigel and Rigby were shepherded into the priest's shack. A pile of duffel bags occupied the middle of the room.

Father Sebastian pointed, saying, "It's all here. Not a penny is missing."

Rigby announced, "It's yours."

The priest stumbling over his attempt at English before reverting to French. "*Excusez moi*?

"The money is yours. All of it."

"Are you certain, Mr. Croxford?"

"Quite certain, actually," Rigby replied.

"I don't know what to say."

Rigby explained that the money belonged to the Congolese

people. He added that Jesse Spooner had intended to return the money. Truth be known, he was doing what he guessed Jesse would have wanted.

"I'm speechless. Mr. Croxford, I misjudged you."

"Don't go overboard, father. One good deed doesn't make the man. My sins would make Satan blush."

The priest ignored his self-deprecation, saying, "Do you have any idea what this means to these people?"

Nigel interrupted their exchange. "Croxford, if we don't leave this very second, your sainthood will be bestowed posthumously."

"Cheers, father," Rigby said, jumping up.

"I shall pray for you every day, my son." They shook hands. Nigel and Rigby waded through the applauding lepers.

"Let's get cracking." Nigel raced through the preflight checklist. As he was spooling up, Father Sebastian stooped underneath the spinning rotors and insisted Rigby open his window. The priest handed him Rosary beads and motioned for Rigby to put them around his neck. The priest mouthed the words; *God bless you.*

They lifted off. Rigby looked down. Father Sebastian and his flock were on their knees with their hands laced in prayer. The crowd waved goodbye. The helicopter disappeared behind some low-flying clouds.

They flew for an hour without speaking. Nigel switched radio frequencies, communicating in French. He fussed with the GPS.

At last, Rigby asked, "Are we lost?"

"Heavens, no. Just checking our position."

"Were you surprised? I mean about the money."

Nigel's answer followed a momentary pause. "Not in the least. You did a good thing, my friend."

"I must tell you, being a millionaire, even for a few hours, felt bloody wonderful. And besides, keeping the money put bullseyes on our backs."

Nigel responded. "Funny, I can't see you as a millionaire. No man is rich enough to purchase his past."

"Does your husband slash wife find you as annoying as I do?" Rigby asked

"Undoubtedly." Nigel's hearty laugh merged into a smoker's cough. "How long have you known?"

"Thirty years."

Sunglasses hid Nigel's surprise.

Landing at the compound went smoothly. Nigel and his mechanic removed the backseat and installed a reserve fuel bladder. The extra fuel increased the helicopter's range to nine-hundred kilometers. The radio scuttlebutt was disturbing. The Americans had been making inquiries about Nigel's whereabouts. The news rushed their departure.

With everything loaded onboard, the burdened helicopter struggled to gain altitude. The flying distance to Luanda, Angola, is five-hundred kilometers. Nigel's flight plan called for following the Angolan coastline giving them access to the towns servicing Angola's offshore oil rigs. Hopefully, buying fuel wouldn't be a problem.

The flight to Luanda took three hours. Nigel was a frequent visitor at the Quatro de Fevereiro International Airport in Luanda. He was on a first-name basis with the Angolan customs officials. He spoke Portuguese. That didn't stop them from strip-searching his Jet-ranger. They even removed the front seats and the reserve fuel tank. Someone had tipped them off, saying they were transporting money, which was false. In the end, the customs officials apologized for the inconvenience. After arranging hangar space for the Jet-ranger and topping the fuel tanks, Nigel and Rigby hired a taxi.

"That was nerve-racking," Rigby said, getting into the cab.

"Raather," agreed Nigel using a toothy Etonian accent.

Luanda is a city of slums and modern skyscrapers. Angola's mineral wealth has not filtered down to its eight-million inhabitants. Once the epicenter of the slave trade supplying Brazil, Luanda has suffered from a twenty-five-year civil war.

"I vote for a libation," Nigel said.

"Music to my ears," agreed Rigby.

Nigel's favorite watering hole was identical to the bar in Kisangani. Loud Portuguese replaced French, which was backgrounded by laughter. Feeble air-conditioning struggled against the cigarette smoke and tropical heat. For the most part, the patrons were the same assortment of alcoholic misfits. Nigel seemed to know everyone. Within minutes, he was holding court. They had just ordered their third round when Nigel received a mobile call. He stepped outside for better reception.

When the call ended, he looked troubled. He slumped onto his barstool.

"Bad news?" Rigby asked.

Nigel sighed. "Dreadful, actually."

"Let me guess. Your better-half dumped you?"

"We are standing on the edge of the abyss, and you're making jokes. Need I remind you of Reed Cunningham's fall from grace." Nigel detailed the call he received from his Congolese informant. The Americans had departed Kinshasa two hours ago in a chartered helicopter. They were scheduled to land in Luanda in one hour.

"Enjoy your drink. Cheers, mate. Here's to growing old disgracefully."

"You're up to something. You look like the proverbial cat that swallowed a canary," Nigel proposed.

"I want you to call the Portuguese customs authorities at the airport. Listen carefully." Rigby told him to say that two Americans would be landing within the hour. If they claimed diplomatic immunity, their passports were forgeries. They were diamond smugglers, armed and dangerous.

"You see where I'm going with this?"

"I think so." When Nigel questioned him about the diamonds, he admitted instructing Winnie to hide diamonds in their briefcases. She removed them while the Americans slept. The diamonds were sewn to the linings.

"That'll put a lid on it. Splendidly fitting, I might add." Nigel raised his gin and tonic. "*Saude*! Are their passports forged?"

Rigby responded. "What difference does it make?"

"None, really. Any other orders, my lord?"

He asked Nigel to call his Congolese informant and say that he knew the exact location of those missing rare earth minerals. He was willing to trade that information for one assurance. He wanted two Congolese citizens granted authorization to immigrate to Zimbabwe.

"I presume you're referring to Winnie Obo and Sefu?"

"They might have futures in Zimbabwe. They have none in Congo."

"Your compassion overwhelms me, sir."

"Let's not get teary-eyed. I have one final request."

"And what might that be? Your wish is my command."

Rigby opened his safari jacket. Packets of Euros were taped to his chest. "Our traveling money. Only the finest hotels and the best restaurants, if you please. After you make those calls, we are officially on holiday.

Nigel said, "As it says in the movies, 'I think this is the beginning of a beautiful friendship.'"

Rigby laughed. "With separate hotel rooms, thank you. Wouldn't want you to get any ideas."

"Croxford, you're impossible."

# ZIMBABWE

## One year later

**Rigby Croxford** resumed his anti-poaching patrols. From his tented camp on the Zambezi River, he watched feathery clouds float lazily over the emerald green hills of Zimbabwe. Beyond those hills, the mist from Victoria falls evaporated into an azure-colored sky.

Winnie and Sefu had arrived six months earlier. Winnie was working with his daughter, Christine, at the medical clinic. Rhodes University offered Winnie a scholarship. She would leave in the fall to pursue her dream of becoming a doctor. Sefu and Michael were inseparable. Jesse Spooner was never far from his thoughts.

He relived the savagery he had witnessed, and the risks men were willing to take to satisfy their greed. The distant trumpeting of an elephant interrupted his daydream. He knew there would be adversities. Surviving Africa was becoming more challenging. But for now, he was at peace.

# HISTORICAL EPILOGUE

**A dissertation** on African history must include slavery. Africans were engaged in the slave trade for a thousand years before the first Portuguese slaver set foot on the Dark Continent. Aggressive natives coveting cloth, iron tools, and muskets preyed on more passive tribes. Their currency was ivory and humans. Europeans played the middlemen in the West African slave trade. The end-users were the plantations in the New World. On the east coast of Africa, Arabs transported captured Africans as far east as China. Arabs fearing the "black seed" castrated the men. Black women were sold as concubines. Mixed babies were euphemized.

Slavery still exists in Africa. In 2017, an African sold for 400 dollars in a Libyan slave market. In 1860, the average price paid for a slave was 800 dollars. Why has the market price declined? In 2019, the average African earned 1 dollar per day.

In 1885, King Leopold of Belgium, under the guise of ending slavery, sent his envoys to claim what was ironically christened 'The Congo Free State.' Leopold's three-million square kilometer claim was the most massive land grab ever recorded.

Two years later, Leopold hired the famous English explorer, Henry Morton Stanley, to investigate Congo's potential. (Stanley's first expedition in 1869 was to rescue Dr. David Livingstone.) Stanley's epic three-year 8700 kilometers march across the African continent is legendary. Three adventurous Europeans and 200 hundred of the 300 porters accompanying Stanley died. The natives he encountered named him "Bonsongo," meaning albino. His men dubbed him "Bula Matari," the breaker-of-stones. Dunlap's invention of the inflatable tire and Edison's discovery of electricity fueled the world's insatiable appetite for rubber. Rubber grows naturally in the Congo Basin. Harvesting rubber resulted in the deaths of an estimated five-million Africans. The "Rubber Terror" made King Leopold the richest man in the world. (Henry Stanley survived Africa, but his legacy was soiled by his inhuman treatment of Africans. His unwavering support for King Leopold further tainted his reputation. Even today, his London grave is desecrated by vandals.)

In Joseph Conrad's novella, Heart of Darkness, and later portrayed in Francis Coppola's epic Vietnam War film Apocalypse Now, the character Kurtz, played by Marlin Brando, is seen as a mentally deranged rogue. Conrad's inspiration for Kurtz was fashioned after a captain in Leopold's Force Publique, known as Leon Rom. Rom displayed human heads in the flower gardens surrounding his residence in Stanley Falls. Rom's madness was further evidenced by his vicious beatings of hapless Africans. Witnesses said he seemed to enjoy using his chicote whip made from a hippo's hide. Twenty lashes scarred a victim for life. One hundred lashes meant death.

Living in Congo has not been easy. Today, the mad scramble for conflict minerals has replaced rubber. Congo's 27 trillion dollars in untapped natural resources make it one of the wealthiest countries in the world. (The uranium used in the atomic bomb dropped on Hiroshima was mined in

Congo.) Sadly, Congo's mineral wealth has been more of a curse than a blessing. Corrupt leaders exploit the populace. Congo's per-capita income is one of the lowest in the world.

Since 1960, Congo has endured endless civil wars. The Great African War, started in 1998, has claimed five million Africans, making it the second deadliest human conflict in history. Presently, 1200 people die each day from endemic violence.

Before the American puppet, Congolese President Joseph Mobutu was driven from office; he built a 158,000-square-foot opulent palace decorated with priceless treasures from around the world. Mobuto ordered the construction of a 10,000-foot runway to accommodate a supersonic jetliner. Mrs. Mobuto chartered the Concord for her shopping sprees in Paris. His people starved.

After a brief stop in Zimbabwe, Congo Affair starts in a fishing village located on a nameless tributary. The Congo River, oozing out of Africa's rectum, is 5000 kilometers of raging incivilities. The Bantu named the river Nazdi, the water that swallows all rivers. It resembles a black snake slithering through an uncharted wilderness. The discharge is so massive; freshwater sustained early seafarers 500 kilometers into the Atlantic Ocean.

The human race evolved from Africa. Did the severity of the African environment ensure our success as a species, or has our existence been a brief interlude on the fast-track to extinction? Like us, Africans are beleaguered by tribalism and the utter disregard for nature.

Will the destruction of Africa be the final chapter of human evolution?

# Author's note

Much of *Congo Affair* is factual. The plot and the characters are fictional. It takes place in a part of the world where extreme violence is extremely common. In 1994, the Rwandan genocidal massacre killed 800,000 people in 100 days.

Today, Africans face an uncertain future. Africa's vast natural resources are being squandered. Many Africans teeter on the edge of starvation. The standard of living for the average African is the same as it was in 1960. African politicians make the infamous Roman Emperor, Caligula, look like Mother Teresa. Africa needs more leaders like Nelson Mandela.

My first of 20 trips to Africa was 1968. At that time, 500,000 rhinos roamed the African plains. Today, poaching has reduced the rhino population to less than 25,000.

*James Gardner*

# The Lion Killer

## The Book That Started It All

Rigby Croxford, a white African and retired Selous Scout, is forced into action when a tourist disappears in the Bwindi forest. The father of the missing man seems concerned, but Croxford's gut tells him different: the father is hiding something. Danger follows Croxford as his search takes him from the Unites States to Zimbabwe and into Sudan.

Croxford experiences hard truths: Life is disposable. The land is beautiful. The search is fatal.

Gardner weaves a sweeping tale that exposes both Africa's brutality and her beauty in the first book of his Dark Continent Chronicles series. Have a look into the first pages of the book that started it all.

# Bwindi, Uganda
## Africa

**A blowly** clung to the underside of a leaf on a red-hot poker tree. The weaverbird perching on one of the tree's orange flowers, cocked its head to identify the insect. The bird tried to dislodge the insect by pecking, but the blowfly held fast.

It was time for the blowfly to seek out the carrion that would sustain her maggots. If the female started its search too early, it would have to fly through hungry jungle birds. If the fly waited for darkness, it risked being eaten by white-bellied bats. The weaverbird gave up on the blowfly, hopped off the flower, and onto an adjacent twig where it caught a purple butterfly in its beak. After smacking the butterfly on the twig, the bird swallowed it and flew away.

A gentle wind from the Congolese mountains carried a captivating stench. Sensory cells on the blowfly's antennae detected decaying flesh. The blowflies spiraled up through the canopy of mahogany and ironwood trees. The insects' hum hushed the rainforest. The sound spooked a colobus monkey; she tucked her baby to her belly and climbed higher in an ebony tree. A bongo antelope stopped browsing to investigate. The only sound was a chucking waterfall. Below the swarming insects, pink orchids, and yellow-flowered creepers suffocated thorny fruit trees and fig palms. Flocks of brown honeyguides and yellow-throated bee-eaters took to the air. For the birds, the smell of death meant a meal of blowflies.

Some flowers secrete a scent of rotting carrion to attract insects for pollination. This time the blowflies would not be fooled into pollinating. Nor would they stop to feed on chimpanzee and mountain gorilla dung piles. The flies swarmed over the top of the crab-wood trees and stands of bamboo. Red-breasted starlings and wattle-eyes picked them off by the thousands, but their numbers were overwhelming.

# THE LION KILLER

The insects followed the scent to a jungle clearing where eight gas bloated human corpses baked under a malicious sun. The female blowfly landed on a man's eyeball, crawled across his face, and disappeared into his ear. After depositing her eggs, the insect exited the man's ear canal and landed on the woman's face lying next to him.

A man wearing a white smock leaned down and pulled back a tarpaulin covering a woman's body. Her pink toenails indicated a recent pedicure. Her trimmed pubic hair was fringed by razor stubble. He uncovered the rest of her body. The nipple of her left breast was missing; it showed evidence of a human bite. The bullet that ended her life had entered her left temple, damaging the optic nerve, leaving one eye open and one closed. The man trapped the blowfly in a test-tube as the insect crawled out of the woman's nose. He corked the glass tube, labeled "Calliphoridae—from female cadaver number 5."

Graham Connelly jumped out of his mud-spattered Land Cruiser and ran into the undergrowth, where he vomited. He emerged from the bushes, looking sheepish.

Ian Laycock handed him a surgeon's mask soaked in camphor. "I say, old boy, not feeling well today, are we?"

"What the hell's going on here? Why haven't these bodies been taken someplace where they can be cooled down?" Graham asked, wiping his mouth.

"Don't blame me. The Ugandan military has jurisdiction, which means nobody's in control. This will crimp Uganda's eco-tourism. Here's a list of the dead." Ian handed the list to Graham. "We're having trouble identifying the bodies. I've rounded up the victims' passports, but we can't match them. The hyenas have been busy. Why do they always chew off their faces? It looks like the women were raped. Bloody savages. Here's my report. Any questions before I head back to Kampala?" Laycock asked, handing him the report.

"Who's the nerd collecting the bugs?" Graham asked, blowing into his cupped hand.

"Dr. Malcolm Rutherford, a forensic entomologist from Nairobi. Very well informed, our doctor. Did you know these bug doctors can identify cadavers' DNA taken from the digestive tracks of maggots? You're not going to be sick again, are you?" Laycock asked, grinning.

Laycock retrieved a pinch of ostrich biltong from the breast pocket of his khaki jacket and stuffed the dried meat into his mouth. He chewed and rolled it from one cheek to the other, and then gulped down the gristle like a pill. He walked over, twisted a thorn off of an acacia bush, and used it to pick his teeth.

"Jesus, bon appétit. How can you eat?" Graham asked, nodding at the bodies. "I wonder if there's anything in this world that could ruin your appetite. Give me your report. There's nothing I can do here.  Embassy Security Chief was supposed to be an adventure. I never thought it would be like this."

"My friend, you missed Rwanda," Ian began. "This is a garden party compared to what the Hutus did to the Tutsi population. Eight-hundred-thousand Affies killed in one-hundred days. The bodies were so thick on the roads that we had to drive over them. They made the most dreadful, popping noises. And let's not forget what's going on in Darfur. That's what I call proper family planning."

"Ian, you're an outstanding humanitarian, a real credit to our Queen. What about the missing American?"

"Nothing as of yet," Laycock answered. "The dead ones include six Americans and two Brits. A French woman, the safari guide, and his Ugandan tracker are being worked after at the clinic in Kasese. Afro's name is Peter Gono. He took one hell of a beating, but it looks like he'll make it."

"We need to make sure the proper authorities notify the families before the BBC gets on to this. The American woman who survived, what's become of her?"

"She's been taken to the American Embassy in Kampala. They tell me she's related to some VIP in the States."

"You're sure her husband is missing?"

"Quite, but what do I know? I work for British intelligence."

"British intelligence! There's a lovely oxymoron." Graham smiled disingenuously.

When Laycock spoke, it was around another mouthful of biltong.

"Very funny. You should try your comedy on the telly. See you back in Kampala. Don't lose the report–it's my only copy. Are we still on for Sunday?"

"Wouldn't want a minor international tragedy to interrupt our golf match, now would we? See you on the first tee at nine bells. I need two more shots," Connelly insisted.

"You're a thief. I'll give you the strokes, but you're buying lunch."

"Done. See you Sunday."

Laycock didn't answer. Instead, he raised his hand in acceptance and waved goodbye.

Connelly studied his friend in the rearview mirror. Ian Laycock had worked in Africa for almost thirty years. The military coups, the famines, and the genocidal lunacy had changed him. Britain's influence on the continent had dwindled to little more than pomp and ceremony, which meant Africa, had become a cemetery for Foreign Service careers.

Connelly found his friend's disparaging remarks about Africans odd. He was living with a Ugandan woman. Laycock's wife, like many European women, rejected Africa. She returned to England, and as her visits became less frequent, her husband took a black mistress. When his wife stopped visiting altogether, Laycock's arrangement became permanent. It was a common but frowned-upon indiscretion by many expatriates.

Connelly drove down the mountain road away from the carnage. Halfway down, he passed a line of military vehicles heading in the opposite direction. Christ, now you show up, he thought. Closing the window didn't lessen the smell. He pulled over and picked up Laycock's report.

### Bwindi Massacre

This is the eyewitness account of safari guide Robert Neff as collaborated by his Ugandan tracker, Peter Gono. Both men are fluent in Swahili, as were the perpetrators.

The following is a list of the deceased and my interpretation as to how they died. It should be noted that the bodies were attacked so brutally that any speculation as to the medical cause of death is suspect. Dr. Malcolm Rutherford was on the scene, and accordingly, his report should be available within a few days.

### Victims:
British subjects: William Smyth and Barbara Smyth.
American citizens: Roland Collins. Debbie Collins. James Cole. Jeffery Cole. Ralph Courtney. Margaret Courtney.

A French woman, Marie Camondona, was released, as were the safari guide, Robert Neff, and the Ugandan, Peter Gono.

Two Americans escaped—last names: Turner. Mr. Authur Turner is still unaccounted for as of 2100 hours, 15 September. After being treated at the medical clinic in Kasese, Mrs.

Turner was taken to the American Embassy in Kampala, where she remains in seclusion. The American ambassador has blocked attempts to question Mrs. Turner. It is my understanding that a private aircraft has been sent to Uganda to ferry Mrs. Turner back to the United States.

On the morning of the Bwindi Incident, safari guide Neff reported hearing small-arms fire coming from the direction of one of the outer camp chalets. He believed the shots were being fired by the Ugandan military involved in an anti-poaching operation. Within minutes, the camp was surrounded. Ten men armed with AK-47s and machetes swarmed into the camp.

Intelligence indicates they are part of the Interahamwe, an extremist group partially responsible for the 1994 ethnic genocide that slaughtered eight hundred thousand. A top Interahamwe commander operating inside of the Democratic Republic of the Congo has taken credit for the "Bwindi massacre."

His faction, the RPF (Rwandan Patriotic Front), claims the attack was in retaliation for the United Nation's Security Council's recognition of the present Rwandan government. The rebels led their victims on a twenty-kilometer grueling march that was intended to take them into the Congo. Because they were unfamiliar with the terrain, they forcibly used a local Ugandan camp tracker, Peter Gono, to guide them. Gono, disregarding his own safety, led them in a circle hoping to be intercepted by a Ugandan military patrol. The rebel leader, who is still unidentified, became suspicious and had Gono beaten until he confessed his deception. Neff stated, "That's when the discipline within the group started to breakdown."

According to Peter Gono, the Courtneys, who were in their late fifties, became fatigued and refused to go on. Mrs. Courtney was raped by four of the rebels.

Both Courtneys were executed by head-shots. The Collin's woman and Barbara Smyth were also raped and brutally killed in front of their respective husbands, who were also killed. During the confusion, Arthur Turner and his wife slipped away into the heavy underbrush. They floated down a river emptying into Lake Albert. Mrs. Turner was found wandering by a Ugandan military patrol. She was incoherent and was taken to a local clinic. Mr. Turner was not found. In my opinion, his survival is doubtful.

It is also my opinion that the rebels have escaped back into the Congo. They are now under the full protection of the Congolese president.

The Ugandan military has assembled an incursion force of approximately six hundred soldiers. Intelligence sources believe they are headed north to the Kivu provinces of the DRC. With as many as 25,000 Rwandan rebels operating in that region, it is doubtful that any of the perpetrators will ever be brought to justice. A more detailed report will be available in forty-eight hours.

Laycock

Graham Connelly rolled up the report and used it to swat a blowfly on his windshield.

# Spanish Cay, Bahama Islands
## One year later

Rigby Croxford treaded water thirty feet above a coral ledge where the Nassau grouper he'd speared had wedged itself into a crevice. A cloud of blood seeped from the ledge. When he heard the grouper's distress grunts, he lifted his diving mask and looked for his wife. He scanned the beach until he found her. Good, you're safe, he thought. He filled his lungs, turned upside down, and started for the bottom. He grabbed a purple sea fan and pulled himself under the ledge. The mixture of blood and stirred-up sand ruined his visibility. When he stretched his arm into the crevice, the grouper grunted. He squeezed his gloved hand into the fish's mouth and latched on to its lower lip. The grouper struggled, but Rigby slipped his other hand under its gill plate and started for the surface. When he popped up, he saw the dinghy bobbing on the horizon.

The damn wind must have blown it, he thought. He swam slowly at first but realized he wasn't gaining on the skiff. A movement caught his attention. It was a large black-tipped shark circling beneath him. He picked up his pace but dragging the fish hampered him. I've got to quit smoking, he thought. It was only a few yards to the skiff. The black-tip reversed its direction and swam at him. At the last second, he flung the grouper up into the skiff and spun around, but the shark was gone.

"I worked too hard to give it up to the likes of you," he thought.

The Croxfords were citizens of Zimbabwe. Rigby's ancestors had immigrated to Africa from Britain in the early nineteen hundreds. His wife, Helen, was born in Connecticut. When Helen's brother offered to let them use his yacht, they turned him down. When he mailed them airline tickets, they buried their pride and accepted.

Helen was a doctor. She felt guilty about leaving her patients, but she needed a break from African politics. Despite worldwide condemnation, their president, Robert Mugabe, continued his confiscation of the white-owned farms. It was only a matter of time before Mugabe tried to seize their farm. Helen knew her husband would not go quietly.

Earlier that day, they anchored in a lagoon on the leeward side of Spanish Cay. Their captain, Bonefish Foley, secured the boat's stern to a coconut tree and then set the yacht's anchor under a brain-coral dome. The old Hatteras lay captive to her moorings in the crystalline waters of Turtle Bay.

Captain Foley scanned the horizon. When he saw Rigby pop to the surface and fling the grouper in the skiff, he relaxed. The weather had treated them fairly, and with only a few minor mechanical problems, the cruise was running as smoothly as an island schooner sailing downwind. In two weeks, thought Captain Foley, the Croxfords, will go back to Africa, and I can go back home to Bimini. He picked up his knife and continued skinning a conch.

Something caught the corner of his eye. It was a yacht clearing the outer reef passage. The sun reflected off the yacht's bridge windows. Squinting, Foley watched men scurrying about on deck. The Bahamian looked at the shoreline to check the tide. Oh Lord, he thought, its high tide. Damn, Mr. Rigby's gonna be pitching a fit.

I gotta find us another island.

A crew member standing on the bowsprit directed the captain with hand gestures to help him avoid the coral-heads. The captain pivoted the yacht into the wind. The sound of the rattling anchor chain carried across the lagoon. Sulfur-smelling exhaust smoke covered Turtle Bay. The crew went to work, putting the inflatable tender and wave-runners over the side. When the yacht swung into the wind, her name and homeport came into view: *The Liti-Gator,* Palm Beach, Florida.

Foley heard the whine of an outboard engine. Damn, Mr. Rigby's gonna be raisin' some hell, he uttered to himself. Foley watched the skiff idle towards him.

"Goddamn it, Foley, there are hundreds of islands in the Bahamas," Rigby yelled. "Why does this son-of-a-bitch have to pick our island? He could see we were already anchored up. Inconsiderate bastard." He stuck his thumb in one of the grouper's eye sockets and his pointing finger in the other. He hoisted the fish up and waded ashore.

Rigby's wife, Helen, left the shade of a coconut tree and walked down the beach to inspect the fish. She closed her book and sighed.

"Check out the name. The Liti-Gator! Give me a break! As if we don't have enough lawyers."

"Yaaa, vell, I guess I must find us another island," said Foley. Like all Bahamians, he reversed V and W in his speech. "I don't expect people should be so unruly." He shook his head.

Helen pushed her sunglasses up, securing them in her hair. She grinned at her husband before speaking. "Are you sure you don't feel emasculated by this man's yacht?"

"At least my middle-aged wife looks decent in a swimming costume."

"Did you just say 'decent'?" Helen kicked sand at her husband.

Rigby grabbed his wife and pulled her into the water. She screamed, handed her book to Foley, and tried to push her husband's head under.

They held hands watching Foley filet the grouper. "It's not the end of the world," said Rigby. "Tomorrow, we'll pull anchor and find ourselves another lagoon. Whoever he is, he just violated a rule of common decency, that's all I'm saying." Rigby took a few steps closer to Foley.

"Anyway, we've got more important issues," he continued, putting his hand on Foley's shoulder. "I believe it's time for our daily spear-fishing competition."

"Not today, Mr. Rigby, I've got work that needs doin'," Foley said, picking up the fish. "Besides, there are too many sharks around 'des island. You go ahead."

"Suit yourself. Helen, what about you?" She ignored him and walked up the beach. Guess I'm on my own, Rigby thought.

Foley helped him push the dinghy into deeper water. Rigby hopped in, and Foley threw him the anchor line. Before he could start the engine, one of the *Liti-Gator's* wave-runners idled up behind him. The young Bahamian sitting on the wave-runner was as black as an eight ball.

Rigby started to voice his displeasure, but something stopped him.

"Ahoy, Captain. Say, my boss sent me to find some lobsters. Vould you know vhere I could find 'dem?" the young man

# THE LION KILLER

inquired. "My name's Kewin," he said, extending his hand. "Mr. Rigby has been findin' some nice lobsters on dem coral-heads," Foley indicated, pointing.

"Be careful. I've seen sharks," added Rigby.

Kevin looked fearful. "My boss will fire me if I don't bring back some lobsters. Could you take me with you?" he asked.

"I could use some company. Jump in. Captain Foley chickened out of our daily spear-fishing contest. I'm Rigby Croxford. This is Bonefish Foley, who happens to be the second-best spear fisherman in the Bahamas. I hate to blow my horn, but you're about to witness something special—a great diver in action. Isn't that right, Foley?"

"Mr. Rigby, you're a special one, all right. Lord, you can tell some big fibs," said Foley.

"Thanks," said Kevin. He shook each man's hand with the customary Bahamian limp handshake.

Rigby ran his skiff offshore. When he located a coral-head, he turned the helm over to Kevin and leaned over the gunwale to look through a glass-bottom bucket.

"Do you see lobster?" Kevin asked.

"As Foley would say, 'Dey is as thick as grains of san' on the beach.'"

"You sound like an Englishman," commented Kevin. "I'm from Zimbabwe. You could say, I'm an African."

"You're an African?" Kevin scratched his head.

"I'll explain later. Hand me those gloves."

Rigby pulled his diving mask over his face, grabbed his Hawaiian sling, and fell over the side of the Whaler. He turned upside down and disappeared. When he resurfaced, he had three lobsters skewered on his spear. On his last dive, he speared a hog snapper. They headed back to the lagoon. As they nudged up on the beach, Helen walked down to greet them.

"Any luck? I wish you wouldn't dive alone."

"I wasn't diving alone. Kevin was with me," Rigby said, holding up the spiny lobsters.

"Kevin, I'm Helen Croxford."

"It's nice to meet you. Say, I almost forgot. My boss wants both of you to have dinner with him tonight."

"Tell your boss we appreciate his hospitality, but we've already got something planned," Rigby answered.

Kevin looked disappointed and said, "Now I know he'll fire me."

"Young man," said Helen, "You can tell your boss we'd love to join him for dinner. The head chef and bottle washer needs a break. Besides, I'm dying to see his yacht."

"You take the lobster," Rigby demanded.

"Are you sure?"

"Of course, I'm sure. Now that my admiral has spoken, what time do you want us? What's your boss's name?"

"Cocktails are at seven. His name is Mr. Maxwell Turner."

Using binoculars, Rigby watched a seaplane land southeast of the entrance to the lagoon. Three passengers departed the plane and boarded a skiff. The launch deposited them at the Liti-Gator's stern. A man wearing a blue blazer and white pants met them as they disembarked. He offered his hand to the woman struggling for balance.

"How was the flight?" Max Turner asked.

"It was breathtaking," replied the woman.

"Molly, dear, why don't you go below," said Max. "It'll give you a chance to freshen up before dinner. I need to borrow your husband. Tucker, let's go topside. You can fill me in on our friend." Max motioned to a steward. "Make Mr. Dodge a scotch and soda." Max waited for Tucker Dodge to light his pipe and take the first sip.

"What did you find out?" Turner asked.

"Let's start with Croxford's brother-in-law. He's the one with the deep pockets. Croxford transferred the title to his Zimbabwean farm to him for the time being, Mugabe has been reluctant to confiscate the foreign-owned farms. Max, this could pose a problem. Money may not motivate this guy."

"You feel Croxford's my best shot at rescuing Arthur? Assuming he's still alive."

"Croxford's a legend in southern Africa. He was a decorated Selous Scout in the Rhodesian Bush War. A Selous Scout is like a Navy Seal on steroids. He fought as a mercenary in the Congo and Angola. And he's hunted in the Central African Republic and Sudan. If your son's alive, Croxford's the man to bring him out," answered Tucker.

"That's what you said about the last guy. After I paid him, I never heard a word," Max said, looking through a porthole at the setting sun. Turner stuck his nose in the wine glass and sniffed before tasting it. He placed his glass on the bar and turned to Dodge.

"Well, if Croxford's our man, you let me worry about hiring him. No man likes another man paying his way. I need to put this nightmare behind me." He patted Dodge on the back. "Thanks, Tucker. Nice job. Let's go below. Our guests should be arriving. I'm curious to meet Croxford."

The *Liti-Gator* looked like a lit-up New York skyscraper floating on its side. Her underwater lights illuminated the lagoon. Turner met the Croxfords at the top of the stairs on the fantail.

Maxwell Turner had spent a lifetime trying to enhance his masculinity. He was five foot six. His posture indicated he was trying to elongate himself. A facelift gave his eyes that slanted Hollywood actor look. He wore an expensive toupee, but the salt spray made it look like something women wrapped around their shoulders in the thirties. Turner was one hundred and seventy pounds of solid muscle. He shaved his arms to enhance the rippled effect. When he shook your hand, you could feel the calluses of a weightlifter. When he spoke, his accent sounded generic, but his tone was like the rhythmic notes of a bass saxophone.

"Good evening," Max said, extending his hand. "Croxfords, meet the Dodges. This is Tucker, or Tucky, and his better half, Molly.

What can I have my steward get you to drink?" Turner latched on to Helen's hand and refused to let go. It was his way of testing the waters. Rigby was oblivious to Max's flirtation. Helen pulled away gracefully

The group gave drink orders to an Asian-looking steward. Max ushered them into a salon that would have made a Saudi prince jealous. Fearful of soiling the expensive upholstery, Rigby sat on the edge of his chair.

"Before I forget, the lobster hors d'oeuvres are courtesy of Mr. Croxford. I'm afraid I had to give up diving. It's my ears." Max pointed at his ear painfully.

Something made Rigby think that he had fabricated the excuse.

"I can't tell you how happy this makes me. I mean accepting my invitation. Right upfront, I want to apologize for barging in on your lagoon. Now, where do you folks call home?"

"We live in Africa. Although Helen's a Yank by birth," answered Rigby. "Helen guessed you were a solicitor."

"She's right. What's your business in Africa, Rigby?"

"I'm a farmer and a professional hunter."

"Mrs. Croxford, what did you do before this fortunate man shanghaied you to the Dark Continent?"

"I'm a doctor."

"And where did you go to medical school?"

"Yale."

"Do you have any children?"

"One daughter. She's also a doctor."

"My God, beauty, and intelligence. As I said, Mr. Croxford, you're a lucky man. I'm afraid my academic credentials aren't as impressive."

Helen blushed as Max's visual frisk lingered on her a second too long. Turner walked over and stood next to the spiral stairway to the bridge.

"If you're interested, I'll give you the grand tour after dinner," he said, indicating he was speaking about his yacht with an expansive wave.

"We look forward to it," Helen said, hooking her arm through her husband's elbow.

Turner always reverted to using his wealth to attract women and belittle men. Rigby and his wife's display of affection for each other irritated him. He attempted to hide his annoyance, but couldn't.

"Of course, it's just another boat. You people look like real boaters. I wish I had the time."

"It's not our boat. It's on loan from her brother," Rigby said, acknowledging his wife.

"Max, you seem to be doing okay," Helen added, offering an olive branch to lessen the awkwardness.

"I'm doing all right. One step ahead of my creditors, as they say. Helen, I'm curious about your brother's boat. Those classic fifty-threes are hard to come by nowadays. Do you think he might have an interest in selling the old girl?" It was apparent his interest was disingenuous. Before Helen could answer, he turned away. "Excuse me. Yes, Bob." Turner turned to receive a message from a large bald man. Bob had a twisted nose. The folds of accordion skin on the back of his neck gave him the look of a Shar-Pei dog. His piggish eyes were not as repulsive as the way he enunciated his words with his lips extended like a goldfish. The steward handed a wine list to Rigby.

"Folks, I need to take an overseas call. Why don't you choose your wine? I won't be a minute. You all can get acquainted."

Rigby waited until Max disappeared into the wheelhouse. "Christ, a wine list. I reckon we need to improve the service on our classic boat." He used the wine list to block the sound. "What's with Bob? His head looks like a penis."

"Do you have to be so gross?" Helen whispered to Rigby, trying not to smile. "Give me that wine list. You don't know anything about wine."

"The amount of wine I've consumed makes me an expert. Although I must admit, Zimbabwean wine is probably better suited as a cleaning agent."

Helen was nervous about exposing her husband to the Dodges. She had gone to college with men like Tucker Dodge. He's probably a stockbroker, or maybe a mergers-and-acquisitions lawyer on Wall Street, she thought. He had undoubtedly graduated from a fancy prep school and would have followed in his father's footsteps by attending Yale or Harvard. His enunciation was too punctilious not to be Ivy League. His wife came from a wealthy family, Helen figured. People like the Dodges don't get married; they merge. She was Connecticut frumpy with thick ankles and heavy arms. She wore her hair in a bun. Her chinless face had no attractive features. Helen sized her up and realized that the Dodges' marriage wasn't a merger; it was an acquisition. Mrs. Dodge is the one with the dough, she concluded.

Molly rummaged through her Chanel handbag. When she located the cigarette-holder, she handed it to her husband without looking at him. He secured the cigarette, lit the end, and handed it back to her. She accepted it without thanking him.

*I knew it*, Helen thought, congratulating herself.

Helen looked at Rigby, with warm contentment. *God, I'm glad I married you*, she thought. She glanced at Tucker and then at his wife. Helen, you're too damn cynical. At least give these people a chance, she continued thinking. What she heard next would confirm her first impression.

"It must be exciting living in Africa," Molly directed at Helen.

"Yes, we like it."

"A couple of years ago, we went on a photographic safari in Kenya. We loved it. Didn't we, dear?" Tucker said, looking at his wife for confirmation. She nodded her approval.

"It was marvelous," Molly added.

"Mr. Croxford, I understand you're a professional hunter.

I've never liked hunting. The cruelty seems so senseless," Tucker said.

"I'm only working as a professional hunter until I can get back into farming."

"Mr. Croxford, what's your take on Mugabe reclaiming the white-owned farms and giving them back to the rightful owners?" Tucker inquired, sucking on his cigar until it ignited. He blew out the match and held up his empty glass, asking for a refill.

"Rhodesia was the breadbasket of Africa. Now the people are starving."

"You don't look like you're starving," Tucker stated.

"Actually, we were starving. That's why we've come to the Bahamas. It's a brilliant spot to fatten up," Rigby said with a forced smile.

Tucker continued. "And you feel no guilt for what the white man's done to Africans."

"Africa's complicated. You must live there to understand it."

"Come now, Croxford, I find that hard to believe."

Rigby's brow wrinkled. He looked squarely at Tucker. "Ducky, I have no regrets about trying to maintain order in Africa. I lost a lot of my best mates in something called the Rhodesian Bush War. I fought next to some courageous men—it might interest you to know, many of them were black. I'm sorry, but I'm not interested in your opinions." His acid tone had them squirming.

"The name's Tucker. Look, I apologize if I've said something to offend you. I'm just trying to understand your thinking." He turned away from Rigby's glare and stood up. "Wonder what's keeping Max," he mumbled, trying to quicken the clock-ticking silence.

Turner looked over the shoulder of his secretary. He read the following email to himself:

> To: Maxwell Turner
> From: Rutherford, London School of Medicine— Forensic Science Department.
>
> RE: Post-mortem pathology
>
> Dear Mr. Turner:
>
> DNA samples taken from human remains retrieved from the stomach of a crocodile killed on Lake Albert, Uganda, inconclusive because of the high level of corrosive digestive acids. More tests are required. Sorry to put you through this ordeal.
>
> Kindest regards,
> Dr. Malcolm Rutherford

"Is everyone getting to know each other?" Turner asked, walking back into the salon. "If you folks will follow me, I think they're ready to serve us dinner."

## OTHER TITLES BY THIS AUTHOR:

The Lion Killer

The Zambezi Vendetta

The Honey Guide

The Last Rhino

**available on amazon**

PENNINGTON PUBLISHERS

# THE LION KILLER

## DARK CONTINENT CHRONICLES BOOK I

*"I highly recommend The Lion Killer
I have seldom come across such
fine descriptive writing in a thriller."*
**James Patterson, America's Best-Selling Author**

*"Few really good books come out of Africa, but James
Gardner's The Lion Killer is one of them. His powerful
writing illuminates The Dark Continent."*
**Nelson DeMille, New York Times Best-Selling Author**

# JAMES GARDNER

PENNINGTON PUBLISHERS

# THE ZAMBEZI VENDETTA

## DARK CONTINENT CHRONICLES BOOK II

"*His powerful writing illuminates The Dark Continent.*"

—Nelson DeMille, New York Times Best-Selling Author

# JAMES GARDNER

PENNINGTON PUBLISHERS

# THE HONEY GUIDE

> "His powerful writing illuminates
> The Dark Continent"
>
> —Nelson DeMille, New York Times Best-Selling Author

## DARK CONTINENT CHRONICLES BOOK III

> "James Gardner takes you on a thrill ride through so many
> terrifying places and events in darkest Africa you have to pull
> the covers over your head to finish it."
>
> —Dan Jenkins, Novelist, Journalist

# JAMES GARDNER

PENNINGTON PUBLISHERS

# THE LAST RHINO

"His powerful writing illuminates The Dark Continent"

—Nelson DeMille, New York Times Best-Selling Author

## DARK CONTINENT CHRONICLES BOOK IV

" *A fascinating piece of writing...full of twists and unforgettable characters.* "

—Ann Bocock, host of PBS show *Between the Covers*

# JAMES GARDNER